Siren Song

Rebecca McKinney

BLACK
CAT
BOOKS

Rebecca McKinney is a writer, therapist and community development practitioner, based near Edinburgh. Her previous novels, as RL McKinney, include *The Angel in the Stone* (Sandstone Press, 2017), and *Blast Radius* (Sandstone Press, 2015). *Siren Song* is her first foray into the world of crime fiction.

Cover design, editing and formatting by letsgetbooked.com

Print ISBN: 978-1-5272-6616-2
eBook ISBN: 978-1-5272-6561-5

PROLOGUE

Before dawn, in the coldest hour of the morning, two men launched their inflatable dinghy out of a remote, rocky cove. There was no village here, no fishing boat, only a rutted dirt track and a stony, inhospitable beach. The two men breathed hot vapours into the air and rowed for an hour without speaking, pulling hard against the tide, keeping their strokes as smooth and quiet as possible. If either of them had qualms about the nature of their task, they harboured them in solitude.

Far from shore, they started the outboard motor. The lights of the land faded and a swell began to rise around them. Half an hour later, they cut the motor, searched the night for other boats and listened hard for any signs that they were not alone. They saw only faint starlight reflecting from the rolling hills of water and heard only the slap of waves against the boat.

Their inert passenger lay in the bottom of the boat, clothed in an anonymous grey tracksuit. The two men manhandled the body overboard and watched it slip into a trough between waves. There were so many bodies drifting about in this sea now, one more made no odds. The whole Mediterranean had become a mass grave, a purgatory for thousands of nameless, unidentifiable refugees. This one wasn't nameless or a refugee, but who would know the difference? The hair had been cut off and the water would disfigure the features and discolour the skin. Possibly the fish or the birds would feast on the flesh before it became too putrid.

The younger of the two men wasn't religious but he prayed for the body to float out to sea and for the soul to float up to heaven, and he prayed that this evil business would not blow back at him later. When he'd finished praying, he spat into the water and picked up his oars. The body rose high on the shoulder of a wave and sank again. Within a couple of minutes, it was gone.

ONE

By the time Harrison Jones got to Sandy Bell's Bar, he realised he didn't want to be there. He was tired and crowds could be overwhelming. More than once, he had stumbled out of a busy pub with other peoples' emotions threatening to split his head wide open. Nevertheless, he had promised to meet his friends, and at the time it had seemed preferable to another long evening by himself.

Harrison was, as his grandmother used to say, sensitive in a very particular way. It ran in the family, she told him before she died, although that didn't make the condition any easier to bear. It was worse when he spent too much time on his own. He was less able to close out other people's thoughts, other people's conflicts, other people's pain. People who didn't have to live with it described it as a gift, but most of the time Harrison wished he could switch it off. His inner life was complicated enough without the constant interference from other people, most of whom were strangers.

Before going inside, he closed his eyes, breathed in and out deeply and brought himself as firmly as he could into the physical present. He turned his face up into the rain.

It had taken him a long time to learn how to close it all out, and his techniques weren't always fool proof. Background music helped, especially the wordless, repetitive jigs and reels on offer in Bell's. He pushed into the warm, steamy pub, swept his hair back from his face, took off his glasses, dried them on his jumper and put them back on again. They steamed up immediately so he repeated the performance, wishing he could trade his sixth sense for better eyesight.

Louis Isaac and Karl Sigmundsson were ensconced at the window table to the right of the bar, locked into another round of one ongoing debate or another. They were part of a group of academics Harrison sometimes drank with: Louis a politics researcher from New York and Karl a sociologist from Iceland. Their minds were so preoccupied by theory that their company didn't trouble him. The less personal stuff the better, as far as he was concerned. They didn't know about his gift, of course. Very few people in his university circle did.

Harrison Jones moved in two worlds and liked to keep them separate.

He bought himself a pint of Belhaven Best, sidled between the damp bodies that filled the narrow room, and eased onto the bench beside Karl.

'I'm glad to see you escaped from the circle of hell that is marking,' Karl said.

'A temporary furlough only. I've ten or fifteen left to get through tomorrow.'

They murmured their commiserations and returned to their argument. Harrison's mind wandered, from semi-literate undergraduate ramblings to missing people. One missing person in particular. It had been thirty years now. Thirty years of nothing but speculation and heartbreak.

'What do you think, Harri?'

He forced himself back to the present. The bar was filled with a sociable racket, voices raised in debate, the fiddle and whistle just audible beyond it.

He shook his head. 'Sorry, what?'

'I was just saying,' Karl repeated, 'that what we are witnessing in the Scottish independence movement is materially different from the rise of populism in England and Trump's America. It is the rebirth of a progressive civic identity that is not based on exclusionary ideology ... '

'You can't call any form of nationalism progressive,' Louis countered. 'A rhetoric that places the concept of nation at the heart of the discourse is by definition exclusionary.'

'Perhaps, in that case, we must label the Scottish independence movement as something other than nationalism.'

Louis spread his hands wide. 'What should we call it, then? Let's ask the only Scot at the table. Harrison, wade in here anytime, buddy. What do you say?'

The only Scot at the table had heard enough academic jargon for one day. 'Fuck Trump and fuck the Tories, that's what I say.'

Karl laughed heartily. Louis tried to press him for a more satisfactory response.

To avoid speaking, Harrison downed the remainder of his pint. 'You know what? I'm shattered. Think I'll head off.'

'You just got here,' Karl protested.

'Aye, sorry.' He slid toward the edge of the bench. 'Not in the mood for setting the world to rights just now. I'll leave you guys to it.'

They whispered behind his back as he departed, but he was used to that. An Arctic wind had blown away the mist and brought the keen smell of winter. Stars were showing now through the thinning cloud. He was tired but not yet ready to go home to wallow in his thoughts. He turned left and headed up George IV Bridge.

There were still a few heavily-swaddled tourists in the vicinity of the Royal Mile but otherwise, the streets were quiet enough to stride out. Harrison hadn't quite made his father's height, but he had long legs and a stride that always had to be a little clipped when the streets were busy. Now he was able to move along at his natural pace, covering ground fast enough that he couldn't pick up the vibrations.

He walked down the Mound, along Princes Street and turned up North Bridge. Midway along the bridge, he saw a girl facing out over the wall, staring down at the glass roof panels of Waverley Station below. Her feelings radiated from her like shockwaves: failure, guilt and profound loneliness. They hit him square in the chest from twenty feet away. She was thinking about jumping. He could read it clear as a searchlight flashing out into the dark. Harrison slowed his pace and approached her cautiously.

She raised her eyes and stared out over the city, pretending to take in the view.

He came alongside her, allowing an arm's length between them, and said softly, 'This isn't what you want to do.'

She stared at him, mouth half-open. 'What did you just say?'

He jutted his chin toward the glass panels. 'It would be a pretty spectacular way to go, right enough, but you don't really want to. You just want help.'

'How the fuck do you know what I want?' Her accent was Irish. Northern. Hard-edged.

'Because you'd have gone by now if you wanted to. What's your name?'

She raised her eyebrows and didn't tell him her name.

'I'm Harrison Jones.'

'Harrison Jones?' she giggled. At least he'd managed to distract her. 'A heroic type, right? Should I call you Indiana?'

'You know you're not the first person who's ever asked me that. Can I take you somewhere? Do you want to go somewhere and talk?'

'Congratulations, that's the best chat-up line I've ever heard.' Her voice dripped suspicion but her mind was relieved.

'Thank you, but I'm not trying to chat you up. Do you think you need to go to the hospital?'

'Eh ... no. I don't think so.'

'So, you'll be okay?'

'Well, seeing as you're so concerned, I promise you I won't jump tonight.' Beneath her bluster, he picked up humiliation and shame about her melodramatic impulses. Behind that, an echo of violence committed in the past, in another place. This girl had a history.

'Okay then.' He pointed his finger at her. 'Stay alive.'

He left her standing there and walked home.

When he got back to his flat, he stood in the kitchen for a few minutes, waiting for the crowd inside his head to disperse. He needed to sleep, but more than that he needed guidance. At the end of the hall, there was a small, spare room where he kept his *Salvia divinorum* plants. Their leaves were his ticket to worlds beyond his own.

To make the journey, he plucked leaves from one of his Salvia plants and chewed them while he lit candles and let the room fill with incense. He sat cross-legged on the rug, closed his eyes and imagined himself walking a familiar path through a forest. After a while, he saw light through the trees and followed it out into the high, bare Andean plateau. He felt the unfiltered sun across his face and breathed the dusty, bone-dry air. From the shadows at the edge of his vision, people stepped into view. They were quiet and hesitant, waiting for him to make his choice.

He chose Tomas. Except the Tomas in this particular world came in the body of a condor: black and magnificent, with a snow-white ruff around his neck. He stood seven feet tall and spoke with the voice of a thunderstorm.

Harrison and Tomas walked around the edge of a shallow salt lake. As they walked, the condor changed back into the man that Harrison had known and loved: a black-haired, coiled spring of muscle and idealism. Salt crystals bloomed pink and orange under their feet. 'Rosa and the kids are okay. I spoke to her last week.'

Tomas nodded. 'I know. But you are not, I think.'

'It's thirty years today since my dad left.'

'The blink of an eye,' said Tomas.

'A lifetime for me.'

'You must learn to stop questioning and accept.'

'Accept what?'

Tomas just kept walking. Harrison waited impatiently for a couple of minutes.

'Tomas?'

Tomas stood still and looked into the sky. 'Accept that some answers will only come to you when you are ready to receive them. Your life will change soon. You will find someone.'

'Who?'

Tomas only smiled. 'You have already found someone.'

'Who have I found, Tomas?'

Tomas stepped away from Harrison. His fingers became long, black feathers and the great condor spread his wings wide and lifted off the ground. Harrison watched him soar toward the sun and disappear into the blinding light.

Then came the feeling of falling from a height, jolting back onto the rug in the spare room in his flat, returning to the ordinary world. For a few seconds, he lay with his eyes closed and the memory of the Andean sun still blazing on his skin. He took a deep breath and opened his eyes. The effect of the Salvia leaves had mostly passed, leaving only the familiar sense of dissociation that always hung around for a while afterwards.

His belly rumbled and he picked himself up off the floor. The flat was cold, and the thump of two sets of little feet on the floorboards upstairs only succeeded in making him feel lonelier. He checked his phone, found a missed call from an unknown number, and switched the phone onto silent. Then he toasted stale bread, ate it with cheese and Spanish ham and still felt empty. Digging into the cupboard, he had to shove aside the jars and packets that Lara had left when she moved out: organic muesli, seeds, almond-butter, and a collection of other expensive and tasteless vegan ingredients. She had tried her well-intentioned best to convert him, but in the end, broke up with him over his insistence upon eating things with faces. To him, it felt petty but she said it was a dealbreaker. Harrison thought it was a handy excuse. He was the real problem. How he was. How he was always going to be.

That was three months ago and her food was still here, going off. He couldn't bring himself to throw it away. Lara might still change her mind.

Lara wasn't going to change her mind. She had taken up with Jonathan Weaver, one of Harrison's colleagues in the anthropology department. Jonathan wasn't a vegan either. If anything, he was even more bloodthirsty than Harrison was. Well, good luck to them. Lara was never going to be the love of his life. It was just nice to have someone around the house, and he was, by necessity, selective about who he could let in.

He replayed Tomas's words. You have already found someone.

It wasn't like Tomas to be so cryptic. Harrison had found a lot of people, but none of them had changed his life in any meaningful way. Then the girl from North Bridge came into his mind. Was it her? It had been a passing encounter, albeit an unusual one, and he had assumed he would never see her again. Now he wondered if he might.

TWO

Lucy Merriweather lay on the bed and waited. There was a life outside of this room, but it was so far away from her now that it had become meaningless. The future was something other people could imagine, even hope for, but now she knew hope was the worst kind of torture there was. So, she waited, and she remembered. At least nobody could take her memories from her. Memories of the summer just past replayed in high definition detail.

The first time she entered Kostas's house, on a hillside south of Athens, she knew she had found her place.

She stood in front of the window. Kostas had personally shown her to a large bedroom with white plastered walls, a terracotta-tiled floor and an uninterrupted view down to the sea. Pink evening sunlight flooded in, warming her skin. From elsewhere in the house, she could hear laughter and the sounds of people arriving for the party. Nerves fluttered in her tummy as she glanced at her guitar case on the bed. This wasn't like any gig she'd played before. These people were here specially to hear her sing. There were people here who could make her or break her.

She hoped Tim was making himself presentable in the smaller bedroom next door. It was strange that Kostas had given them separate rooms, but now that she thought about it, she appreciated having the space to herself. She and Tim had shared the intense comradeship of travelling for six months, time enough for her to learn about his dark turns. Perhaps she would get away with sleeping in this big bed on her own tonight.

Tim didn't want to come here at all. They had argued about it, and as usual, when he didn't get his way, he became sullen and resentful. He couldn't understand why she would want to renew her acquaintance with her father's business associate, when she wouldn't speak to her father. He hadn't liked Kostas the first time they'd met, in Edinburgh, and didn't like him now.

It was easy to see why. Kostas was handsome, rich and cheerful. Tim was not. She had loved Tim for his political fire and commitment, but over these past few months, he had proven himself to be less inspiring in other departments. His depressive earnestness was beginning to bore her. So were his habits. He was blowing too much of what little money they earned on hash. Kostas made her laugh. More than that, he made her feel like she was glowing from the inside out.

She towelled her wet hair, worked a brush through it and left it to dry in its natural ringlets, then looked at herself naked in the mirror. Sometimes when she was able to step out of her mind and look at herself objectively, she saw beauty. Her body was still sleek and toned, although she was twenty now and not as willowy as she had once been. The pregnancy had changed her too, even though she had only allowed it to go a few months. Something about her body had been changed by it, although she knew she was the only one who could see it. She let her long, pale hair fall around her breasts and looked at herself from every angle: shy, seductive, rebellious, strong. No matter which of these she presented, there would always be men who wanted her.

She had power over them and she had learned how to use it early. If Lucy thought about it too much, she could shame herself, so she didn't allow herself to think. Lucy had ambitions and she was beginning to understand what she would have to do to reach them.

In Edinburgh, she performed in jeans and boots, but this was not Edinburgh. She sang softly to warm up her voice as she applied her makeup: just a dusting of bronzer on her cheeks, a little mascara and lip gloss. Kostas had let it slip more than once that he preferred the beauty of nature's creations to that which came from a jar. She put on a gauzy black sundress with a halter neck and a skirt that fell to mid-thigh. With the light behind her, it was just transparent enough to show the silhouette of her figure. She put on sandals that laced halfway up her shins and made her feel like a mythical heroine. A goddess, even. Her hair provided all the gold she needed. She tied the sides up into a messy knot and left the rest to flow down her back.

When Lucy was ready, she took her guitar from its case, opened the bedroom door and bumped straight into Kostas.

'Oh!' she said, stepping backwards. 'Sorry, I'm just coming. Am I late?'

'Of course not,' he said. His smile threatened to send her into meltdown. 'My God.' He lifted her hand and looked her over. 'You look ...' He paused and shook his head, then kissed her hand. 'Exquisite.'

Just then, Tim opened his door. There was no need for him to voice his anger. His face said it all.

'Ah,' Kostas said, patting his shoulder. 'There you are. It is time for the show, my friends.' He held onto Lucy's hand as he accompanied her down the tiled corridor. Two steps behind them,

Tim stared at the floor and retreated into one of his moody silences.

THREE

'I thought about killing myself on Tuesday night,' Amy Bell told her therapist.

Caroline's expression didn't change much. It never did.

Once a week for a year now, Amy had tucked herself into the huge, squashy chair in Caroline's office and dragged one sordid fact of her life after another out into the open. It was helping, but she still couldn't tell anyone about seeing Caroline. Where she came from, talking was considered a betrayal, or worse. People didn't go to therapy where she came from.

The statement hung over both of them for a few seconds, until Caroline said, 'Do you want to tell me about that?'

'We had a DOA at work. This poor guy ... social worker came to his house and found him unconscious on the living room floor. There was no food in the house. Nothing. Turns out his benefits had been sanctioned because he missed a Job Centre appointment and he probably hadn't eaten for a week. He had a heart attack. He was so far gone by the time we got there, cardiac arrest en route, dead. One missed appointment and they cut off his money? What kind of country does that to its own people?'

'I don't know,' Caroline said. Most of the time, Caroline didn't try to answer Amy's rhetorical questions, but this one must have touched her. 'I don't know what kind of country does that.'

Amy's voice rose slightly. 'A cesspit of a country where nobody gives a shit, that's what kind. Is that what we're supposed to be loyal to?' She paused, challenging Caroline to a response. When Caroline offered her usual intent but neutral gaze, Amy blew out frustration and continued.

'Anyway, after my shift I got off the bus on the bridges and decided to walk the rest of the way home. Just needed to clear my head, you know? I started thinking about how I didn't want to go home alone to a cold flat, and this ... thing came over me. Have you ever been in a boat, out at sea or on a loch and the water's calm, and then a squall comes up out of nowhere? And it practically picks you up and throws you down somewhere else.'

Caroline continued looking at her. It was like talking to a mannequin sometimes, but that was okay. A mannequin would never judge her.

'That's what it felt like. Like something was carrying me away and I didn't have any control over it. I stood there on North Bridge, staring down over the station and I could feel myself climbing over that wall and letting myself go. And I wanted to.'

'You wanted to?' Caroline asked, forcing Amy to clarify her intentions.

'I thought I did.' Amy tried to remember the feeling that had gripped her that night. It was less a desire than an idea that if she tried, she might just be able to fly away. And if she fell, then it would all be over in a couple of seconds.

'You wanted to die?'

'Yes. Well ... no, not die exactly. But leave. I wanted to leave here, and at that moment it seemed like the only option.'

'It seemed like death was the only place open to you?'

Amy nodded. 'Exactly. Like it was the only place left.'

'The only place left ...'

'That we haven't destroyed.'

'When you say we ...'

'Humans.'

Caroline let this hang for a few seconds, taking in its full weight. 'That must have been a very dark, frightening moment for you.'

'I was more angry than scared. I'm not scared of dying.'

'But you didn't jump.' A hint of a smile.

Amy shook her head slowly.

'Can you say why?'

Amy took a deep breath and looked out at rosy winter sunlight. She watched it illuminate the yellow grass on the crags for a few seconds. Each long blade cast its own dancing shadow. 'A man came up to me. This weird tall guy with a beard and one of those accents that you can't place anywhere. He walked up to me and said, "This isn't what you want to do." How the hell did he know what was going through my head?'

'Some people are naturally empathic. He saw that you were hurting.'

'Strangers don't do stuff like that.'

'Some do.'

'It was more than empathy. It was like he opened me up and looked inside. I can't explain it, but it was a unique feeling. Almost physical, like ... he was pulling a big long splinter out of me.'

'Relief?'

'Yeah ... maybe.'

'What did you do after that?'

'I went home and went to bed. I slept for ten hours.'

Caroline smiled, but she tilted her head slightly to the side and narrowed her eyes a little.

For the first time in a year, Amy caught a glimpse of disbelief. It was okay, because Amy still didn't quite believe it either.

When her session finished, she ran from Caroline's office, into Holyrood Park and along the road that skirted the base of the Crags. She ran hard, blowing past dog walkers and old women with shopping trolleys. The cold North Sea wind blew into her face. Easter Road was greasy and littered with the evidence of Scotland's poor eating habits. When she'd first come to Edinburgh, she'd heard that Leith was both sunny and trendy, but this part of it was neither. Between the high tenements and the towering grey and green stands of the stadium, the light rarely hit the pavement. This time of year, it felt like a deep wet canyon. Her dad would have died of an apoplexy if he'd known she lived here, spitting distance from the Hibernian ground. Enemy territory, he'd have said, and he'd have meant it.

But what her dad didn't know couldn't kill him a second time, and there were some old battle-lines that deserved to be buried along with him.

She lingered in the shower, letting the hot water wash away the poison that always came to the surface when she had a therapy session. When she got out, she smeared moisturising cream over herself, pretending in the steamy safety of her bathroom that she was a woman who had time to care about her skin. It felt pointless, although the sweet almond fragrance of the cream was soothing. The whole beauty regime thing had passed her by, and sometimes she wondered if she'd missed out on the gene that made women care about being feminine. Was it even a gene? Amy didn't know. She'd grown up in a household with three brothers, so maybe it was just the logical outcome of her upbringing. The only time in her life she had ever bothered with makeup was when she and Ricky went out on the town together, but there was no need for it now.

She spent an hour or so cleaning the flat, a weekend ritual that helped her reclaim some sense of control of the world, or at least her tiny place in it. The best thing about living alone in a two-room flat, or three if she counted the bathroom, was that cleaning never took very long. The worst thing was that once she'd cleaned, she felt like she was living in an Ikea display: cheerful on the surface, expendable beneath. Just like the rest of her life.

The man from North Bridge, Harrison Jones, kept materialising in her thoughts just the way he'd materialised out of the night to stop her from doing whatever she had been thinking about doing.

He'd turned it into more of a drama than it was. She'd only been standing there, feeling sorry for herself. She hadn't really wanted to jump.

Or had she?

She tried to remember exactly what it felt like when he spoke to her. It was the strangest sensation she'd ever experienced, like something less than tangible but still real being drawn from her body. Like she'd had an alien inside her, or a ghost.

He knew what he was doing to her, she was convinced of that. But what had he done? And who the hell was he? She made herself tea and sat in front of her laptop. She typed *Harrison Jones, Edinburgh* into Google and rubbed her hands on her dressing gown, torn between curiosity and trepidation. The first link that came up was for the university website. She took a deep breath, clicked on it and there he was. She hadn't paid particular attention to his appearance when she met him, but this was unmistakeably him, although younger and without a beard. He had brown hair, a serious expression behind a pair of geeky dark-framed glasses, and wore a tweed blazer over a black t-shirt. From his staff profile, she read that Doctor Harrison McKenzie Jones was a lecturer in social anthropology: *PhD Cambridge, 2009, specialism: belief, ritual, shamanic practice and healing, Latin America.* Below that, there was a list of publications, including two books with incomprehensible academic titles.

So the man was a boffin of some obscure religious shit. How did somebody get into doing that for a living, and what good was it to man or beast?

Cambridge. He had to be pretty damn toffee-nosed. But also pretty damn brainy. She'd accused him of chatting her up. Embarrassing.

The other web links were mostly academic: papers he'd given at conferences and that kind of thing. There were some entries from students on a website called Review My Lecturer. These were varied and entertaining. *A step up from the usual decaying fossils that teach in this place. Definitely on the spectrum. Oh my God, he's so sexy I could listen to him talk all day. Don't try to tell him any lies about why you need an extension on your essay, he sees right through you. A total mind-fuck.*

Scrolling down, she clicked on a link for a forum dedicated to tracking down people who had gone missing. A person called Jo had written, 'Please, I am desperate to find my brother. He vanished fifteen years ago and the police won't help. All trails have gone cold. What can I do now?'

Another person had responded, 'Get in touch with a man called Harrison Jones in Edinburgh. He'll help you when nobody else can. PM me your details and I'll give you his number.'

He'll help you when nobody else can. The line hit her, made her heart pound and her breath come up short. That was exactly what he did for her.

But how?

This might not even be the same man.

But it had to be. There couldn't be more than one person called Harrison Jones in this city.

FOUR

'You could, for example, interpret the Holy Communion as ritualised cannibalism.'

There were some nervous titters from the undergraduates around the seminar table, and a couple of sharp breaths. Fifteen young faces stared at Harrison, waiting for an explanation. He always secretly enjoyed shocking the middle-class Church of England types.

'This is my body; this is my blood?'

'It's just a metaphor,' one of the girls said.

'Some would say that the Eucharist actually transforms into the body and the blood of Christ. A believer is consuming Christ's flesh and blood in order to take the Holy Spirit—his power—into their own body.'

'But you can't make that comparison,' the girl pressed, sounding horrified.

'Why not?'

She couldn't answer this.

Harrison smiled and felt his phone vibrate in his pocket.

'Think about it. Okay guys, that's it for today. See you next week.' He pulled the phone out. It was an unknown number, so he didn't answer. A moment later, a voicemail message pinged in and a flush of anxiety ran through him.

The students filtered away, half of them still sniggering at his concluding remarks and the others already making their evening plans. He flipped his notebook shut and listened to the voicemail while making his way back along to his office. Having the phone stuck to his ear spared him from having to make conversation with the group of colleagues and postgrads who were having lunch in the department lounge.

He hurried past them and took in the details. The caller was female, English-sounding, with elongated vowels and fully enunciated consonants.

'Hello, Doctor Jones. My name is Elizabeth Merriweather and I would like to speak to you about locating someone. I would appreciate it if you could ring me back at your earliest convenience. Thank you.'

She sounded like the wife of a philandering politician. He decided to turn down the request, whatever it may be, and wished there was some way of purging his details from the internet.

In his office, he stood beside the window for a couple of minutes, watching students fighting the wind that tunnelled between the buildings of

George Square. It was early afternoon and already the light had taken on the dusky tint of evening. A familiar hollowness gnawed at his gut. It started the same time every year and continued throughout the festive season. If he had a choice, he would hibernate from early December until the end of January, when the light began to change and the first snowdrops came out. Failing that, he'd have to figure out how best to survive the Christmas holidays. Always the same dilemma: suffer it with his mother, impose upon the hospitality of friends, or flee to some lonely, amnesiac sanctuary in the sun.

He was just about to return Elizabeth Merriweather's call when there came three sharp knocks on his office door. 'Yes,' he said loudly.

The door creaked open slowly and a face peeked in. 'Um ... hello, Dr Jones.'

Why were these students always so damn meek? 'In you come,' he said forcefully, before looking up at her properly. He recognised the vibrations she cast toward him before he recognised her face. It was the girl he'd talked down from North Bridge two nights ago.

Girl was the wrong word. He could see that now in the light. She was a young woman, in her late twenties perhaps, with sandy hair in a tight ponytail, jeans and a dark blue hooded sweatshirt. She wasn't wearing makeup but had a lot of natural colour in her cheeks, and looked like someone who spent a lot of time exercising. She was calmer and less open to him this time. For the time being, at least, the crisis seemed to have passed.

'Hello again,' he said, although it felt like an inadequate greeting.

'Do you have a minute?' she asked.

'As you've taken the trouble to track me down, I suppose I do. Do I get to know your name today?'

'Oh ... yeah ... sure. I'm Amy. Amy Bell.'

'It's nice to meet you officially, Amy Bell.' Harrison didn't offer to shake her hand, but he motioned toward the spare chair. 'Have a seat if you like.'

She sat very upright, knees together, palms flat on her thighs. He caught a flash of her in combat uniform: vest, helmet, badge showing the rod of Asclepius. It might not be an explanation of the suicidal tendencies, but it suggested plenty.

'What can I do for you? Are you alright?'

'I'm fine, thanks. I hope you don't mind that I looked you up.'

'No, I don't mind.'

'You don't seem very surprised.'

'I'm not,' he said and, catching her curious expression, added, 'I'm the only Harrison Jones in Edinburgh, so that makes me easy to find.'

‘Oh, well ...’ She picked at a torn cuticle. ‘I just ... wanted to say thank you for stopping the other night. As you can see, I kept my promise. It was a stupid moment, after a particularly hard day. I wouldn’t have done it, but it’s nice to know that somebody cared. I’ve been thinking about it ever since.’

‘I’m glad to know I helped.’

‘The thing is, I can’t figure out how you knew what I was thinking. Not that many people jump off North Bridge, even if the Samaritans have put stickers all over it.’

‘It’s kind of a specialism of mine.’

‘What is?’

‘Knowing what people are thinking.’

‘Are you a psychologist as well as an anthropologist?’ She turned her eyes to the books and objects on the shelves behind him. Titles about spirituality, witchcraft, shamanism, ritual, healing practices: subjects that would seem dark and occult to her.

‘No. Would you like some coffee or tea? Or a whisky? I keep some for emergencies.’

‘Oh … no, thank you.’

‘Are you a student here?’

‘No. I’m a paramedic ...’ she trailed off and looked down at her hands.

His mind silently completed the sentence for her. ‘That must be a tough job.’

'Sometimes.' She paused and waited for him to respond. When he didn't, she continued, 'This might sound strange but when you spoke to me the other night it was like ... you did something. You took something out of me, something sick and crazy. You just took it away. I don't even know what it was.'

'A bad spirit, maybe.'

'Really?'

He shrugged awkwardly and offered her a smile, though inside he felt pretty crumbly. Her presence was almost overwhelming in this little room. 'I've seen a few strange things in my time. There's a lot out there that western science can't explain.'

She was staring at him like a cat watching a bird, coiled to pounce.

'Anyway, I really am glad I helped you. I hadn't forgotten about you. I'd been wondering how you were.'

She ignored this. 'But how do you explain it? Please, just tell me what you did.'

Clearly, she wasn't going to be content with a vague non-answer, and she wasn't going to leave until he offered her something more. Her blue eyes drilled into him, predatory, demanding the satisfaction of knowledge.

'I was being kind. It's a rare commodity these days.'

‘That may be true, but it was more than that.’

It was only fair. She never had the choice to hold back from him.

‘Fine. I’ll tell you, but you won’t believe me.’

‘Try me.’

‘I’m a psychic. More specifically, I’m a telepath.’

‘A what? That’s an actual thing?’ She stared at him; mouth half-open. An incredulous cough of laughter came out. ‘You really think you can read minds?’

‘It’s more skimming than reading, but yeah. I can prove it to you if you like, but I’d rather not. I don’t always find it very pleasant.’

‘You don’t find what very pleasant.’

Harrison sighed. ‘I’m like ... a radio receiver for other people’s emotions. That’s the only way I know how to explain it. I can tune into feelings, experiences, sometimes thoughts. Not always, and not for all people. You were wide open the other night because you were asking for help. Most of the time it’s not as easy.’

‘How do you do it?’

‘It just happens. I don’t know how or why.’

‘You’re right, I don’t believe you.’

‘You don’t have to, but you wanted an explanation and it’s the only one I’ve got.’

She stood up abruptly. 'I think I better go. I appreciate what you did for me; that's all I wanted to say. I'm not after having my cards read.'

'I don't read cards, so it's just as well.'

'Just as well,' she repeated, shaking her head slowly. 'I don't know who the hell you are, Indiana, but you're completely strange.'

'It's an occupational hazard. And my friends call me Harri, with an i.'

'Right, I'll remember that just in case you happen to be passing the next time I take a notion to jump off a bridge.'

'Amy, you asked and I told you.'

She got up. 'I'd better go. This is too weird. Thanks anyway.'

'Amy ...'

She stuck her hand up in front of her. 'Bye.' She backed out of the room, as if she was afraid of turning her back on him, and then pulled the door hard shut.

So you *are* the one, he thought. He sat for a minute, tilting back in his desk chair. Dusk was falling quickly in the shadowed square. He shouldn't have told her. He shouldn't have allowed himself to read her past. No wonder she thought he was strange. If that was the worst name she had for him, he'd got off lightly.

Maybe he'd been trying to impress her. He got the distinct impression that Amy Bell wasn't easily impressed.

The conversation had shaken him. She had given off such a hot, intense energy, as if something inside her had been forged in fire and had never cooled. Then, maybe it had. From the briefest glimpse he'd caught of her past, he knew she'd been in the army. She'd been at war. He'd witnessed enough bloodshed to know it stayed with you. It claimed part of you, maybe forever.

She was intelligent. Curious. Full of questions she had never been allowed to ask. And there was something else about her: something familiar.

He met other people like himself sometimes, but not often. Some made a career of it, others a religion. The others he encountered pretended not to recognise what they shared. Most psychics he met spent their lives denying what they were or trying to rationalise it away.

He took off his glasses, let the world go soft around the edges, then locked the office door. Turning off the light, he sat on the floor, his back against the lumpy wall of books behind his desk chair. In lotus position, he closed his eyes and tried not to be conscious of anything except the rhythm of his own breath. For a couple of minutes, he could hear the noises of the department outside his door: footsteps going up and down the stairwell, bursts of laughter, muted voices next door in Jane Parson's office, the clunking of hot water going through the pipes. Then it faded and his body swayed with his heartbeat. His heartbeat became a drum and he stepped in time with its beat into another place.

A steep-sided river canyon, thick with verdant jungle, a torrent of white water crashing through it, a rope bridge swinging over the water. He is standing on one side of the rope bridge, hands gripping the wet cables, his body gripped with terror. He's never been in this place before, but has a sense that somebody is waiting for him on the other side of the bridge, just out of sight. Somebody he hasn't seen in a long time. He glances over his shoulder and Tomas is behind him. 'Come with me, Tomas,' he says.

His mobile phone rang again and his eyes popped open. Heart clattering, the river still raging in his ears, he scrambled off the floor and grabbed the phone.

'Hello?'

'Is that Harrison Jones?'

'Yes, speaking.'

'Dr Jones, this is Elizabeth Merriweather. I left a message for you earlier.'

He wiped beads of sweat off his forehead and put his glasses back on. 'Yes, I got your message. I was teaching.'

‘I’m sorry to disturb you. I was given your name by a friend of a friend. I’m told you can be of assistance in tracking down missing persons.’

‘I do offer certain services in appropriate cases, if and when the police have exhausted their channels, however, I…’

‘The police are not involved.’

‘I see.’

‘It’s a sensitive situation. I’m not comfortable discussing it without having met you. Would you be willing to come to my house? I’m in North Berwick. I’ll pay you for your time and travel costs, of course.’

‘Mrs Merriweather, I’m afraid I’m not taking new work right now.’

‘You have to,’ she blurted, and he could feel her distress through the phone. ‘I have nowhere else to turn. I’m afraid I’ll never see her again.’

‘I could give you the names of some other people I know.’

‘But I want you for your particular skills. My daughter is … fragile.’

‘It’s your daughter that’s missing?’ He didn’t know why this caught him off guard.

‘Yes, it’s my daughter.’ Her voice cracked, very faintly.

‘I suppose I could come and meet you,’ he said, cursing his lack of resolve. His life would be so much easier if he ever learned to say no.

‘Thank you,’ she breathed. ‘Truly, thank you.’

‘I don’t teach tomorrow morning, so I can take a wee drive down then.’

‘Tomorrow would be fine. Ten o’clock, if that’s not too early for you. Twenty Abbotsford Road.’

Harrison jotted down the address. ‘Right. I’ll see you tomorrow morning, then.’

‘Thank you, that’s very kind. Dr Jones, is there anything I should prepare for your coming? Do you require any special ... equipment, or anything?’

‘It can be helpful if you have something that belongs to the missing person.’

‘My daughter’s room is exactly as she left it when she moved out two years ago. You’ll have your pick of things she left here.’

‘Fine,’ he sighed, feeling the beginnings of a headache. Always the first sign of overload. He put the phone down, turned on the computer and closed his eyes while it was whirring to life. It was pitch dark outside by the time he woke up.

FIVE

Amy left George Square and walked quickly in the direction of Nicholson Street, embarrassed by her behaviour in Harrison Jones's office, and by her abrupt departure from it. For the second time in their brief acquaintance, he had created a feeling in her that she couldn't describe, even if she wanted to. He had seen right into her. It was startling, but it wasn't invasive. It felt like being examined by a trusted doctor. Like he could heal her, no matter how badly hurt she was.

He had said something about a bad spirit. Was that what it was? Did he think she was possessed by something evil?

If he did, she thought, he would be right.

Ever since Afghanistan, she had felt like she had been carrying something dark and alien around inside her body. Some parasitic demon bred of war. You could see it moving like a shadow through the ruined villages there, through the burnt fields and cratered mountainsides. You could see it behind the eyes of the locals. It had burrowed itself so deeply into her brain that she thought it would now be impossible to remove it without also removing part of herself.

Sometimes it made work unbearable. It had taken her years to learn to defend herself against the things she saw in the course of any given nightshift. You couldn't afford empathy when you came face to face with a bloodied or potentially dying person. You had to avoid looking into their eyes, but sometimes it happened. You lingered just long enough to glimpse one outcome or the other. And you would know, with absolute certainty, that what you saw was true.

To kill time before going home, Amy went into a charity shop and browsed through racks of other people's discarded clothing. She tried on a black parka, which was heavier and longer than the sporty waterproof jackets she habitually preferred. It had a thick fleece lining and a voluminous hood that fell down low over her eyes. The coat felt like padded armour, as if it had been designed to keep out more than the Edinburgh winter. Amy handed over the cash for it and wore it out of the shop, pulling the hood against the drizzle.

The hood closed out so much of the street noise that she could almost hear Harrison Jones speaking to her. His voice was clear and soft, and his accent was mostly Scottish but had undertones of other places. Every so often, something almost

Irish crept in. He had been interested in her, but not in a predatory way. He didn't look at her and see a piece of meat, the way so many men did. First impressions mattered to Amy. She had always been able to pick up other people's intentions quickly, sometimes even before they had a chance to speak. She could smell a bastard a mile away. In her unit, they had called her the Sniffer Dog.

So, you are the one, his voice whispered. It had sounded so clearly in her ears, even though he hadn't actually said it. One what? He had known she would turn up, and he seemed to think that her appearance was a confirmation of something. It ought to terrify her, but the impression that came off Harrison Jones was of kindness, first and foremost. Beneath that, a kind of scientific curiosity. At least he would be open to what she might tell him, unlike most people she met. There was always a point in conversation beyond which Amy knew not to venture. Not with anyone. Not even Caroline.

Harrison's ready description of himself as a telepath should have been ridiculous, but wasn't. Her hasty retreat was part of the act she felt she should play. As she dodged her way along the busy pavement, she found herself wanting to believe him.

She remembered the frustration of not being believed. It was like the gathering pressure of air pushed through a tunnel by an oncoming train. He would be used to that; he knew she wouldn't believe him, even if she should. She should have stayed and heard him out.

She made her way home and prepared a meal for herself: chicken breast with a little pasta and salad. She ate in front of the television like she always did, because eating alone in silence filled her with despair. Often, her nights were preceded by the kind of fluttering anxiety that made her sweat and killed her appetite, but tonight felt different. She felt stronger than she had for a long time.

Harrison Jones had done something to her.

What had he done?

Whatever it was, she almost liked it. Washing the dishes, she looked out at the tenement windows across the green and tried to remember what it felt like. But it was like a dream and she couldn't get close. What was it, exactly?

Who are you, she asked the empty kitchen. What are you?

SIX

Abbotsford Road stretched west from the wealthy, pretty seaside town of North Berwick, running along the edge of the golf course that separated the houses from the long stretch of yellow beach. Harrison drove slowly through thick haar, looking for number twenty. He found it through a pair of sandstone pillars: a Victorian Gothic pile at the end of a long gravel drive. The gardens were trim and bedded down for winter: weed-free borders, wet lawn, pruned hedges. A stand of Scots pines stood at the back of the house, tall and ghostly through the fog.

He pulled up beside a silver Mercedes, cut the engine and got out into the cold, salty mist. His middle-aged blue Golf looked like a poor relation beside the Merc, and he hoped this Mrs Merriweather wouldn't think that he looked the same.

Amy Bell had been on his mind as he'd driven down the coast road this morning. It was a shame that he had come on too strong and frightened her off. He should have taken her phone number or email. He should have offered to meet her again, to explain more. The trouble was, the more Harrison tried to explain, the less believable he sounded.

Too late now. If she wanted to, she could come back.

Over the crunch of his shoes on the gravel, he could hear the sea turning onto the sand and the cawing of rooks in the pines. The damp chill penetrated his layers of wool and settled in his bones.

Harrison stepped up six wide stone steps to the front door and placed his hand on the bell. He paused to take in the sadness of the house, with its turrets and chimneys and many tall skinny windows, those wraithlike trees at the back, the rooks that gathered in their branches. It felt like the house was sucking all the oxygen from the air.

He rang the bell. A dog answered with several deep, proclaiming barks. It took a minute, perhaps more, for the door to swing open.

'Mrs Merriweather?'

'Yes. Hello, Dr Jones.' Elizabeth Merriweather subjected him to an unsubtle visual inspection before saying, 'Come in, please.'

She was a striking woman in a long grey tunic and a dark red pashmina. She was tall and slim, with silver-blonde hair swept back into a bun, probably no older than her mid-fifties. By her voice, he'd assumed her to be older.

Behind her, a copper Rhodesian Ridgeback stood growling. She glanced at the dog. 'Simba, hush. Don't worry about him, he's a big baby. It's a pleasure to meet you.' She offered her hand.

As soon as Harrison touched her skin, he was hit by another volley of emotion. It was more than sadness; it was anguish. And guilt: intense, gnawing guilt that squeezed at his chest.

He tried not to flinch, but she must have caught something in his eyes because she asked, 'Is everything alright?'

Harrison rubbed his hands on his damp coat, trying to hide his suspicion. 'Yes, fine.'

'Let me take your coat.'

He slipped it off and wished he hadn't. It was barely warmer in the tiled lobby than it was outside. 'Thanks.'

She hung it on a stand. 'Well then, come with me.'

The dog strutted beside her, parading his balls the way a soldier parades a rifle, glancing over his shoulder at Harrison and issuing a low rumble. Like most posh people Harrison had met, Mrs Merriweather was unapologetic about her inhospitable dog.

The walls of the lobby were hung with gold-framed portraits and landscapes, some of them very old. The furniture was antique. He knew without having to ask that this house had been in her family for several generations.

'We'll sit in the study, it's the warmest. I have coffee made, if you'd like some, or tea ...'

'Coffee's perfect, thanks.'

'Milk and sugar?'

'Black, please.'

She showed him into one of the smaller rooms that looked out to the back of the house. There was a piano, two armchairs and a green leather sofa. Bookshelves lined one of the walls, stocked mainly with leather-bound collections: the kind of books that people bought because they looked good on the shelf, not because they wanted to read them. He assessed her for a couple of seconds and changed his mind. She had read them all. She read to escape from her life.

The shelves also held photographs, small paintings and drawings in mismatched frames, vases, handmade clay birds and horses. These were the kinds of mementoes that would tell him what he needed to know.

A fire flickered in the wood-burner, putting out a welcome radiant heat. Harrison stood in front of it for a moment, trying to dispel the chill that had settled into his bones.

‘It’s raw today,’ she said. ‘Please make yourself comfortable. I’ll be back in just a moment. Simba, come.’

Harrison stayed by the fire. When she went out of the room again, he looked at the photographs on the shelves. There were pictures of three different dogs, one of a younger Elizabeth Merriweather riding dressage on a shiny chestnut horse, and one of a pretty young girl with a spectacular mane of pale blonde curls. He stared at her. Thirteen or fourteen, probably, on the verge of womanhood but lying like a kid on her stomach on a daisy-speckled lawn, propped on her elbows with her bare brown legs stretched behind her. This was the girl, without a doubt: the missing daughter.

Harrison brushed his fingers along the silver frame. It whispered her name to him: Lucy.

Lucy Merriweather.

He touched the frame again and got something else: anger. Elizabeth’s anger. Lucy’s anger. Furious but indistinct words fired back and forth like artillery. It felt like touching an electric fence.

Harrison snatched his hand away and sat down. Simba came back into the room, claws clicking on the floorboards, nose working. He woofed softly, sniffed at Harrison’s fingers, licked them, then gave another resonant bark.

'It's alright, lion-dog,' Harrison said. 'I know it's your house. I'm not going to hurt you.' He patted the dog's back. Simba allowed himself to be rubbed, but he felt stiff, as though at any moment he might change his mind and take Harrison's hand off.

It was a relief when Elizabeth came in with the coffee and a plate of shortbread biscuits on a tray. 'Oh, you've made a new friend,' she said, and Harrison wasn't sure if she was speaking to him or the dog.

'I'm not sure about friend.'

'Slip him a biscuit and he'll love you for life.'

'Ah, right.'

'There you are. I hope you like it strong.' She lifted a mug of black coffee from the tray and presented it to him.

'Thank you.' He took a polite sample sip. It was strong enough to strip paint. 'This'll wake me up.'

'I need about three cups of that to get me going in the morning,' she said, taking her mug and sitting opposite him. 'I'm so depressed, it takes all my effort to even get dressed these days.'

He wasn't sure what she wanted him to say about this, so he gave her an uncomfortable smile. 'What can I do for you, Mrs Merriweather?'

'Please, call me Elizabeth. May I call you Harrison?'

‘Of course.’

‘Let me guess. Your mother was a fan of Harrison Ford.’

He sighed. There were times when he seriously considered changing his name. ‘It was my grandmother’s maiden name. So … I’m sure you’re aware of the nature of my services, or you wouldn’t have called.’

‘Yes. You came highly recommended by Georgia Tait, who is an acquaintance through a good friend. You found her long-lost twin brother.’

‘I remember. That was a happy outcome.’

‘Well, I’m hoping for the same, obviously, although ...’ Her voice trailed away. ‘I can’t tell you how grateful I am that you’ve taken the time to see me today.’

Instinct told him not to let her get too friendly. ‘How long has Lucy been missing?’

‘How did you know her name?’

Harrison forced himself to swallow the gullet-burning coffee and put down his mug.

Elizabeth gave a nervous laugh. ‘Oh. I’m sorry. You’re at it already. I did call you for your abilities.’

‘Most of the time, things just come. I try to respect people’s privacy as far as I can.’

‘I dare say I’ll have to bring the old family skeletons out to show once more. Have you had this gift all your life?’

'Yes,' he lied. 'It runs in the family.'

'Fascinating. I'm an avid believer in the paranormal, which is why I called you. I'm confident you'll be just the person to find Lucy. Can I ask you about your methods? How do you do it?'

'It's like picking up vibrations in the air. It's a sixth sense I have, if you want to call it that. In the majority of cases, I can't read minds. I feel emotions and occasionally individual thoughts, but only if they're strong ones. And I can't see the future, so I'm afraid I can't guarantee the outcome of a case any better than a mainstream investigator would.'

'Can you tell if a person is ...'

He waited, allowing her time to say the words.

' ... still alive, or ...'

'Most of the time I can, once I get close enough. Do you have reason to believe Lucy might be dead?'

'No,' she said with some force, trying to reassure herself. 'In fact, I'm not even sure she's missing. Or rather, Lucy is missing to me but as far as she's concerned, she may be exactly where she wants to be.'

'So, you'd say her disappearance was voluntary?'

'Oh yes, absolutely. This is why the police won't look for her. In their view, Lucy has purposefully separated herself from her family and everyone she knows. That may be unfortunate, but it isn't criminal.'

Harrison suspected she was lying about the police, but he couldn't tell what the truth was. He stood up, walked back to the shelves and forced himself to touch the silver frame again. A burst of fury, bordering on hatred, shot through him so powerfully that he wanted to throw the photograph across the room. He caught his breath. This may have been Lucy's home, but it was no place of safety.

'You only have to touch things,' she said, watching him from behind. 'That is truly remarkable.'

And bloody sore, he wanted to add. His hand burned, although he knew without looking that there wasn't a mark on it. He waggled his fingers back to life and sat down again. 'I'm getting her, loud and clear.'

'And? Is she alive?'

He turned back to face her. 'I wouldn't like to make any assurances at this point.'

'Oh.' Her hopeful expression faded and she swallowed heavily. 'I see.'

'Before we go any further, Elizabeth, I have to ask whether Lucy might be…' he hesitated, wondering whether it was wise to ask this so soon.

'Might be what?'

'Whether she might be better off if I didn't go looking for her.'

Her mouth gaped slightly, then a sheen of tears formed over her eyes and spilt down her cheeks. 'Oh, damn it, I wasn't going to do this.' She covered her face with a tissue and blew her nose. 'I'm so sorry.'

'It's okay. Take your time.' Harrison sat on the leather chair across from her and waited for her to pull herself together.

She wiped her eyes and stuffed the tissue back inside the sleeve of her jumper. 'I'm alright. Go ahead.'

'Are you sure?'

'Yes.' Her expression became remote and stony, and suddenly she reminded Harrison of his own mother. It was the same look his mother gave him whenever he mentioned Dad. 'Ask what you like.'

'Why did she leave?' he asked gently.

Elizabeth placed her hands on either side of Simba's broad head and seemed to talk more to the dog than to Harrison. 'My husband was abusive, to both of us.'

'I see.' Harrison allowed his tone to soften, just a little. It was the truth, he knew, albeit incomplete. 'I'm sorry.'

She indicated for him to continue, although kept her eyes firmly on her dog.

‘Where is he now?’

‘Quentin and I are separated. He lives in Edinburgh, with whatever young thing he’s currently fucking. Pardon my language.’

Harrison said nothing. The woman was a tormented knot. Despite the abuse, she was still jealous. It was surprisingly common.

‘To answer your earlier question, she may feel she’s better off away from here. But she’s my daughter. Do you have children, Harrison?’

‘No,’ he said bluntly, hoping she couldn’t read into this single syllable. There would have been a child by now, maybe two, if he and Sophie had managed to keep things together. But it was almost six years since she had handed the engagement ring back to him, so it was a moot point.

‘Then you can’t understand what this feels like, psychic or not.’ Elizabeth got up from her seat and crossed to the window. The dull winter light robbed her of what little colour she had left. She gathered the pashmina up around her neck and looked out at the mist. ‘I suppose I’d better explain. There are certain details that I would prefer to keep between us.’

‘Everything you say is strictly confidential unless I think there’s a life in danger. We don’t have to do this right now, Elizabeth. If you want to have a think about it for a few days, I can send you over my terms and rates.'

'I don't care what it costs me. I can tell you're a trustworthy man. Please, just help me find my daughter.'

'If you're sure.' Harrison sat back and waited for the story.

SEVEN

Lucy knew she would never be truly free, but at least she had been able to pretend for a while. There was liberation in moving through foreign cities, a stranger in a crowd of strangers, carrying only her rucksack and her guitar. The shadows that had followed her for as long as she could remember stayed away as long as she kept moving. Her past life belonged to somebody else.

Kostas was the only point of continuity with that old life. It was a dangerous connection, but for him, she was willing to risk it.

'I've had enough of this place,' Tim said, sucking on a bottle of beer and kicking his feet out in front of him. They were in a small bar in the Plaka district of Athens, which Lucy liked for its authentic feel, even though most of the patrons were tourists. A din of languages washed around them like warm, muddy water.

'You want to go somewhere else?'

'Not the bar. I mean this city.' He shrugged. 'It's getting old.'

‘What’s getting old?’

‘Travelling. Living out of a bag. Foreigners. Fucking Greek plumbing.’

‘We’re the foreigners here.’

Tim grunted. His eyelids were heavy and reddish, and Lucy couldn’t decide if he looked stoned or ill, or both. She was losing tolerance for him, and the volume of substances he was putting into his body.

‘Well, I’m fed up with it. I think I might go home,’ he said.

‘We can’t go home. There’s so much to do here.’ Their volunteer work in the co-operative generally consisted of making food and handing out parcels of donated clothing. The older volunteers generally dominated the more interesting tasks, like teaching and supporting refugee families with the relentless paperwork they needed to move on from their temporary prison. There were volunteers from all over the world, mainly middle-aged and older women, Christians and hippies trying to appease their First World guilt.

Most of the time, Lucy found the work boring. But still, it felt more worthwhile than sleeping and smoking all day in their grungy rented room, which was what Tim would most likely be doing if she didn’t force him up and out each day.

He made a dismissive face. 'What's the point?'

'We're helping.'

'You think so, do you?'

'Oh, here we go.'

'No, listen to me. We're not helping these people. Not really. Not in any way that's going to make any difference. You think you have the first clue about what these people have been through? You want to know what they see? They see a naive, rich brat who has nothing better to be doing with her time than handing out sandwiches. You're pissing in the wind, Lucy.'

'You're the one who got me into this!'

'Yeah, so you keep saying. I've done my bit.' Tim shoved his hands into his pockets and slid down in his chair. 'It doesn't change anything. You help one refugee; another one turns up tomorrow. What's the point?'

'What about the gigs?'

Tim laughed. 'Gigs. That's a farce and all. You think Kostas gives a toss about your talent? You're a piece of tail to him, that's all.'

Lucy wanted to slap him. 'Oh my God, you're such an arse. He's a married man.'

Tim arched one eyebrow and made a patronising expression. 'As if that ever stopped anybody with a dick. Where is this mythical wife? Don't you think there's a reason she's never there?

Anyway, I don't care anymore. You're welcome to him.'

'I'm not sleeping with him.'

'You will, though.'

'Piss off, Tim.' She turned her shoulder toward him and watched the lively group at the next table, silently willing them to invite her over.

'That's exactly what I'm going to do.' Tim started to rise from his chair.

She turned around again, and could tell that this time he meant it. For the first time, she feared he might actually do it. 'You can't just…leave me.'

He sat down again. 'Then come home with me.'

'I don't want to.' She felt that old, trapped desperation again, that sense of a figure looming up behind her. 'I can't. I'm not going back.'

'What…not ever?'

'Not if I can help it. I am never going back there, and I swear to God, Tim, if you tell my parents or anyone else where I am, I will personally hunt you down.'

'You're such a drama queen. Just go and make it up with them. Think of the money.'

'The money?' Rage kindled inside her. He had pretended to believe all those things she told him about her family, but he never did. He was just like everyone else. 'Why? Do you think there's something in this for you?'

Tim didn't answer.

'Fuck you, Tim.'

'Fine.' He stood up so abruptly he almost knocked over his chair. 'I'll see you later.'

Lucy watched him go. Slowly, she swallowed the rest of her beer, torn between disappointment and a growing spark of excitement. This wasn't the first time Tim had threatened to leave, but now he looked serious about it. Facing the prospect now, she wondered why it had filled her with such panic before. She used to feel safe with him, but not anymore.

With Tim gone, she would be on her own for the first time in her life. She let her eyes move around the room, scanning the crowd of beautiful young men and women. They were all laughing and debating and telling stories. She wanted to be among them, but nobody paid her any attention, and she wondered why. Sometimes she wondered if the taint of her past life had left a mark on her.

After a while, she got bored and walked out into the busy street. The night was warm and filled with the smells of grilled meats, garlic and women's perfume. Curling tendrils of music emanated from some club. She drifted through the neighbourhood feeling ghostly, like she wasn't really here at all.

Back in their rented room, Tim was in his underpants, snoring on the bed. The room smelled of cigarettes and bad plumbing. She could hardly bear the thought of getting in beside him, so she sat on the wooden chair by the window and stared out at the rooftops, crisscrossed by wires and washing lines.

'I want you to go home, Tim,' she said.

He sat up. 'What?'

'I said I want you to leave.'

'I'm not going without you.'

'Yes, you are. I don't want to be with you anymore.'

'You want me to disappear so you can go running to Kostas.'

'It's nothing to do with Kostas.'

'Yeah.' He laughed. 'You're such a tart.'

'And you're disgusting. I can't even look at you.'

'Whatever.' He lay down again and faced the wall. 'Say what you like.'

'I'm not sleeping beside you.'

'Sleep on the floor, then. I hope you like cockroaches.'

'I want you to go.'

He didn't move.

'Tim.'

He continued to ignore her, so she took off a sandal and threw it at him. It bounced off his back, and he sat up abruptly. 'Lucy, what the fuck?' He chucked the sandal onto the floor.

'Would you just go!' She hurled the other one at him, harder this time.

'Jesus!' He blocked it. 'What's wrong with you? Bitch Season, much?'

'Shut up!' she shouted at him. 'Just shut up and get out of bed. Pack your stuff and get out!'

'Where the bloody hell am I meant to go at this time of the night?' Tim was laughing at her, still refusing to believe she meant it. His laughter was like a blowtorch under dry kindling.

She launched herself toward him and began to batter him with her hands. She slapped his bare chest and shoulders. He held his hands up to protect his face.

'Ow! For fuck's sake, Lucy, stop!'

But she didn't stop. She couldn't. She wanted to see blood. She wanted to batter him down to a spineless pulp. She hit him until her hands began to hurt.

Finally, he swung his hand and caught her hard across the cheek. It shocked more than hurt her. She fell back on the floor, curled up and started to cry.

'Fine,' he said, so quietly she could barely hear him. 'I'm going.'

She couldn't watch him as he pulled his clothes on, gathered his few belongings and stuffed them into the rucksack.

'Lucy.' He dumped his full rucksack by the door and knelt beside her. 'I'm sorry I hit you.'

'Just go.'

'Try to get some sleep. I'll call you in the morning.'

'Don't bother.'

He sat there watching her as she rested her forehead on her arms and stared at the floor. She squeezed her eyes shut and waited.

'I love you, Lucy.' He let another minute pass, then stood up and left without another word.

EIGHT

Amy liked being strong: strong enough to bench press fifty kilos, do twenty chin-ups and beat off more or less anyone who might try something on with her. Not that there was much need for fighting these days, but it had been bred into her by her father, her older brothers, even her mother. You had to fight for your place in the world, and sometimes for your life. When she joined the TA, the fitness and the war-play came easily. Real war turned out to be something else.

She jogged home from the gym, made her post-workout smoothie with chocolate, banana and peanut butter, then showered. The day was pretty grim. By two o'clock, what little light there had been earlier was already starting to fade. It had turned wet. She couldn't face the thought of town with its throngs of sweaty Christmas shoppers, and she had already been online to buy the few presents she would send to her family. At five, she was looking forward to settling in front of the telly when Lynn Strachan from work sent a text, saying,

Heading up town, curry, a bottle or three, dancing. You coming? Amy ignored it, but made the fatal error of leaving her phone switched on. Two minutes later, it rang. She ignored it, and it vibrated itself to the edge of the table. Lynn was not a woman to be ignored.

'You're coming out, Honey. You don't get to say no this time.'

'I'm already in my jammies.'

'That can be fixed. Get your lippy on and meet us at seven at All Bar One. If you don't turn up, me and Kate and Shona will come to your flat and drag you out by your hair.'

'I'd like to see you try.'

Lynn laughed: a squawk indicating that she'd already started drinking. 'Three nurses against you? You don't have a chance, doll. You promised the next night out, you'd come. Get dressed and get yourself in a taxi. We'll even pay it for you.'

Amy groaned. Lynn wasn't going to take no for an answer, and she had promised. She'd been promising for months. The girls were trying as hard as they could to gather Amy into their friendship, and Amy was trying as hard as she could to resist. She had no good reason, other than her obstinate commitment to self-sufficiency.

Is it self-sufficiency or isolation? She could almost hear Caroline asking. Amy wondered what was so wrong with isolation.

‘Okay,’ she relented. Her belly fluttered with worry that had no specific source. If she gave herself permission to listen to it, she would never go anywhere. Leaving the flat was the hardest part; it would be okay once she got out. ‘You win. I’ll meet you up there.’

‘Good girl.’

Five hours and as many glasses of white wine later, she was stumbling along Queen Street, clinging to Lynn’s arm to keep herself upright in the heels she’d never learned to walk in. The curry was sitting heavily in her belly and it wasn’t going to mix well with the wine, but she was also drunk enough not to care. Dinner had been filled with wild stories about things that happened in A&E, unwelcome advances from patients and sometimes doctors, and the endlessly creative means by which the citizens of Edinburgh found themselves blue-lighted to hospital. Amy’s sides hurt from laughing more than she was used to, and she wondered why she had been so resistant to coming out.

They made their wobbly way to a club called The Jam House, which was more adult and less studenty than the other Edinburgh clubs Amy had been to. It was filled with hen parties, office groups, clusters of mums set free for an evening, and heavy-set forty-something dad dancers. Amy had never been a clubber. The thumping music made her head hurt and there was always an underlying odour of sleaze. But the music here was good, a playlist of songs she knew and could sing along with, and it was nice to be in a place where she felt young. She had a vague notion that the ridiculous strappy sandals had torn her feet to shreds, but that would be tomorrow's problem.

It was after midnight when a hand landed on her shoulder. She spun around on the dance floor and found herself face to face with Ricky. He looked worse than he had the last time she'd seen him: thin and shadowed, fed on a diet of cigarettes and alcohol.

'Oh my God,' she spluttered. Her happy high collapsed and she was immediately filled with a familiar dread. This was not the kind of place he would normally frequent, and yet she had known. She had felt it. 'What are you doing here?'

'Same as you, eh. Trying to get a bag off.'

'I'm not,' she said automatically. She shouldn't have. He wanted her to feel guilty. He wanted her to have to defend herself. 'Not that it's any of your business if I am.'

This is why I don't go out, she reminded herself. It had been fifteen months since she'd asked him to move out, but only nine since he finally stopped calling her and banging on her door in the middle of the night.

'I don't care what you do anymore,' he said, but his tone was too casual to be believable.

She didn't know what to say to him and didn't want to encourage him to hang around. Edinburgh was a glorified village; they would have to expect to bump into each other from time to time.

She glanced back at Lynn and said loudly, 'Lynn, this is Ricky.'

'Oh aye.' Lynn stepped up beside Amy and sneered at him like he was a piece of rotten meat. 'I'm thinking the crowd in this place has gone a bit downhill, Amy. Bit low class, you know what I mean? I say we move on.'

'I couldn't agree more.' Amy gave Ricky one last glance. She'd had junkies in her ambulance who looked better than he did right now. 'We're off. Have fun with ...' she scanned around for any of his mates, 'whoever you're with.'

Turning her back on him, she allowed Lynn to pull her off the dance floor.

'Oh my God, thank you,' she breathed when they regrouped with Kate and Shona. 'He was the last person on earth I thought would turn up in here. It's so not his scene.'

'He looks like his scene should be down around the docks somewhere. What did you ever see in him, Amy?'

Amy shrugged. It would be impossible to explain in here. 'Ricky wasn't always that bad.' That was as forgiving as she could bring herself to be. 'Let's get out of here.'

Outside, revellers were out in the streets. People were shouting, laughing, singing, staggering through the winter night in their shirt-sleeves and short dresses. Behind the clouds, there was a full moon, and for some reason, that always made everything wilder. Amy let herself spare a single thought for her colleagues who had drawn the short straw tonight.

'Where to?' Shona asked. She was the youngest and freshest of them all. 'I'm not ready for home yet.'

'Girls, I'm done. I think I'll jump in a taxi,' Amy said. The encounter had defeated her.

'Oh no way, we're just getting started.'

'Don't let me stop you. I'm knackered.' Amy rummaged in her handbag for her purse while the others discussed options for continuing their night. She pulled out a twenty-pound note and tucked it into the pocket of her jeans, stowed her purse and looked for a taxi. Hackneys rumbled up and down the street but not a single one had a yellow light showing. She might have to walk some way before she found one.

'Thanks for asking me. It's been fun.'

'You coming to the Christmas night out?' Lynn asked.

Amy had been avoiding any and all mention of festive nights out.

‘Not sure yet. I’ll see you next week, girls.’ She headed off in the direction of home, striding as powerfully as she could in the hateful shoes.

She got as far as Leith Walk and still couldn’t find a taxi. The straps of her sandals cut across the top of each foot, sending searing pain up her legs. But she was halfway home and there didn’t seem much point in spending money on a fare now.

It was only when she turned into a quieter side-street and left the city centre crowds behind that she realised she was being followed. The footsteps came from rubber-soled shoes and were very slightly syncopated: he walked with a limp. He also breathed heavily and coughed softly every thirty seconds or so. Amy didn’t have to turn around to know it was Ricky.

She forced herself to keep walking without changing her pace. She wouldn’t be able to outrun him in these shoes, even with his bad leg, so she needed to get near enough to home before she confronted him. Because she had to confront him. This could not be allowed to happen again.

He followed her all the way to Easter Road, falling back a little as she turned right onto Albion Road. She ducked into the shadow of a recessed doorway and waited for him to round the corner. When he did, she stepped straight into his path, grabbed him by the collar of his jacket and kneed him as hard as she could in the groin. He grunted and doubled over, cursing and struggling for breath.

'You fucking bitch,' he blurted.

Amy kicked his injured leg with a spiky heel and he crumpled like a play-acting footballer, clutching his knee. She gave him a shove, placed her foot on his gut, leaned over him and spoke softly. 'You stay the fuck away from me, Ricky. If I see you in my street again, I'll see to it you can't walk away.' A final kick for emphasis.

'Awright, darling?' asked a passing drunk. 'You needing ma help?'

'No, I don't need your help, thank you.' Amy left Ricky lying there and jogged home, slammed the stair door behind her and ran up the stairs. She pulled off the heels and examined the raw patches and blisters. She rubbed on some Savlon, thinking as she did so that the original designer of stiletto heels must have been a sexual predator. Ten minutes passed and she had almost started to wonder if Ricky had crawled away back to whatever rock he'd been hiding under these past nine months. She made a cup of tea and the tightness in her chest began to ease.

Then, inevitably, the buzzer. Two, three, four times, echoing angrily up the stairwell. The banging on the door. The shouts from outside. 'Amy! Open the door, Amy, you fucking Irish whore. You're mine, bitch. You're mine.'

She had to ignore him. Letting him see her or hear her would only fuel his fire. She could hear footsteps in the other flats, the noises of neighbours waking up and opening their windows. Paul in the flat below hers shouted down, 'Get to fuck, Ricky, or I'll call the polis.'

Amy phoned the police herself, then sat down on the kitchen floor with the light off and waited. Eventually, it went quiet downstairs. Outside it started to sleet, and Ricky must have sidled away to nurse his wounds. By the time the patrol car came around, he would have been long gone.

She crawled into bed in her tracksuit, afraid to get undressed, and lay still, listening to the night. With every little creak or thump from the old pipework, she flinched and felt adrenaline shoot down her legs. Caroline had explained it all to her: the flood of cortisol to the brain, the overwhelming need to protect herself, the fight or flight mechanism, the chronic stress of managing her body's responses to threats real and perceived.

Ricky was a very real threat.

She dug in the storage box under her bed, pulled out her brother Ian's old flick knife and lay down with it under her pillow.

NINE

Harrison woke with a prickle of nervous energy running down his spine, as if there had been a lightning strike and spare electricity was still fizzing around the room. The dream had left an impression of the colour green. Intense, cavernous greenery. He imagined that it had been that mountainous jungle again, the place with the river and the rope bridge, but he couldn't summon any more detail than that. A hazy memory of his father's face hung in his mind: his father's face as it had been thirty years ago, not as it would be now. Was his dad out there, in that jungle? And was that jungle actually a place in this world, or was Alastair Jones trying to communicate with him from some verdant green afterlife the way Tomas did from his Andean mountainside?

And if so, why? Why now, after all this time?

'Just tell me the fucking truth,' he said aloud into his empty bedroom. Sometimes the grief was as raw as it had ever been. He lay like that for a while, starving for answers that never came, then forced himself out of bed.

It was Saturday morning and the flat was cold. He wanted to pull the duvet over his head and go back to sleep, but his mind was too noisy. He'd been working too many hours, counselling angst-ridden undergraduates, marking and trying to make progress on a paper that apparently didn't want to be written.

He shouldn't have taken the Merriweather case. The detective work had been a clever way of funding himself through his PhD. He'd always intended to give it up once he secured a full-time academic position, but somehow new clients kept finding their way to him and he could never bring himself to say no.

Right now, coming up for Christmas, what he really needed was a holiday. Somewhere warm and far away from other people.

But the case intrigued him. They all did. The patchy stories, with their blurry details and blacked-out sections. The quiet mysteries. Something big had been blacked-out of Elizabeth Merriweather's story, a deliberate omission yawning in front of him. He could sense that, whatever it was, she held it back out of fear and shame. And underpinning that, guilt, which compelled her to try to hide something from a man she knew she couldn't hide anything from.

Harrison was fairly sure she'd brought him in because she wanted the thing to be found out. People often did, despite the repercussions.

It was a distraction from his own life, and it depressed him how badly he needed that.

He turned the heat up, made coffee and watched the news. It was even more surreal than anything that came at him out of the spirit world: Brexit negotiations stalled in quicksand, families torn apart on the US-Mexico border, environmental meltdown. He turned off the television. These days he missed Tomas more than ever. He wished he could ask Tomas what he thought of the world's darkening trajectory, wished he could absorb some of the optimism that Tomas carried until his dying day. *Things will get better, compadre. They will, because we will make them. This too shall pass.*

This too shall pass.

But when?

Tomas had faith, Harrison less so.

He went into the spare room, picked a few Salvia leaves and wrapped a wool rug around his shoulders. Normally he didn't make a habit of journeying in the morning because it had the potential to turn the rest of the day on its head. But right now, he just wanted to see Tomas, seven-foot condor or not.

Images began to come very quickly, but they weren't of the place he was expecting. Even before his consciousness altered fully, he was aware that he was being taken somewhere different this time. Yet it was somewhere familiar and not so very far from home. He was in Edinburgh, walking down Easter Road, turning along Albion Road toward the towering stands of the Hibs ground, stopping outside a dirty sandstone tenement. A skinny man with short black hair was shouting up at a window on the second floor. Harrison became that man for a moment. He looked down at his body and saw that his chest was a ragged, empty cavity. His heart was dying in a jar inside that window, and he couldn't reach it.

This wasn't the person he was looking for. Harrison stripped off the black-haired man's body, left it like a suit crumpled on the pavement, and went upstairs. Someone was calling out to him, willing him to come. She was hiding inside the flat, afraid to leave or look out the window. Lucy, he thought: hiding in plain view, only a few miles from home.

He knew he was wrong as soon as he stepped inside the flat. The girl sitting on the floor beside the bed wasn't Lucy Merriweather; it was Amy Bell.

Please come, she said.

He opened his eyes and was back in his flat, but the Salvia was still working through his system. For a few minutes, he could still almost see her, sitting on the floor of her bedroom. Her fear smelled like an old, dusty wool coat. This wasn't a one-off incident, and the black-haired man wasn't a stranger.

Harrison wondered about going down there. In normal circumstances, it was too early in the morning to turn up unannounced at the home of a person he'd only met once—or twice, if the bridge incident counted—especially when she hadn't even given him the address. But these weren't normal circumstances.

Or, possibly, they were. Maybe this was Amy Bell's normal. She had called for help before and he'd come, and now she was asking again. She was asking him to prove himself, or maybe she was trying to prove herself.

He got dressed and headed out, taking the car even though he probably should have given the Salvia longer to wear off. He could only hope the streets didn't deliver any detours into the Andes or the as-yet inexplicable jungle, but as he drove, Edinburgh remained its colourless November self. It was just getting light and the streets were quiet as people nursed their Saturday morning hangovers.

A few minutes later, he turned along Albion Road and drove straight past a tenement that looked exactly as it had in the vision. He parked out of sight around a corner and walked back, watching out for the man he'd seen. He allowed himself to be open to the energies of the street, letting the inside of his head receive the hum of dozens of poorly tuned voices. He picked up arguments, sex, muffled dreams and money worries, but nothing sinister. The man had vanished, if he'd ever been here at all. It was possible that he was only a projection of Amy's mind: a memory or a nightmare.

He paused outside a door with peeling black paint and looked at the names beside the buzzers. There it was, second floor flat 2: Bell. A shiver ran up his neck. Sometimes his abilities spooked him, even after all these years. Harrison took a deep breath and pressed the button.

'Who is it?' came Amy Bell's abrupt voice.

'Harri Jones.' He hoped shortening his name would make him sound more like a friend.

'Shit,' she said. 'You came.' There was a long pause, and then the door buzzed open. Harrison climbed steps that were worn and indented by a hundred years of weary feet. Amy was waiting at her door, dressed and not at all surprised to see him.

‘So, it’s really true, then, Indiana.’ She stood aside to let him in. Her flat was small and immaculate. She needed order and predictability; things had to be in their place.

‘I’m afraid it is.’

‘Do I even want to know how you found out where I live?’

‘I saw it in a vision.’

‘A vision.’

‘Yeah.’

‘Right.’ She fixed him with a stare, cynical but not entirely disbelieving.

‘Did you ...’ He wasn’t sure of the right word. ‘Did you call me?’

‘Maybe I did.’ She lifted her hands from her sides. ‘Lucky you, you don’t even have to wait for a girl to give you her number.’

‘Is this okay? Me turning up here? It seemed like you were scared of somebody and I didn’t know what else to do.’

‘So, you came.’ She seemed to laugh at herself. ‘You must think I’m pretty helpless.’

‘I’m reasonably sure you’re not helpless, but are you alright?’

‘Yeah, I’m alright. Do you do this often?’

‘Not very often. Sorry, I know it’s a wee bit weird.’

‘A wee bit.’ Amy chuckled at him. She slipped her feet into a pair of sheepskin boots that were lying beside the door and took her coat and scarf down from a hook. 'Can we go somewhere? I want to get out of here.'

'Where?'

'I don't care. Just ... somewhere else.'

He had planned to spend a couple of hours on the Merriweather case and then settle down to some writing, but he had a feeling that Amy Bell would have found a way to overwrite his plans, no matter what he tried to do today. There was a connection between them. She could communicate with him remotely and he could hear her more clearly than almost anyone he'd ever met. That had only ever happened with other psychics.

The question was, did she know? He suspected she did, and that was why she had sought him out.

'Okay. Come on.'

She followed him downstairs and along the road, hurrying to keep up with his long stride. 'Where we going?'

'I parked a bit away, just in case your man turned up again.'

'My man? You saw him?'

'Yeah, I saw him. Who is he?'

'Ricky. He isn't my man anymore. Do you always walk so fast? We're not all six-foot-five.'

'Six-two.' He cut his stride. 'Sorry. So, Ricky's your ex ...'

‘Ex-fiancé. I had to take out a restraining order against him last year.’

‘Not a guy to take no for an answer, I gather.’

‘I’d rather not talk about him right now. Where are we going?’

‘I thought we could go back to mine. You look like you could do with a good breakfast, and we can talk there. No-one will bother us.’

‘You live alone?’

‘Yeah.’

‘No wife or kids or ...’

‘No.’

‘Right ... sorry. I didn’t mean to ...’

He pressed the button on his key and stopped outside the car. ‘It’s fine. Hop in. If you’d rather go somewhere more public, just tell me.’

‘No, yours is fine. Like you say, I'm not helpless.’ She slid into the passenger seat and buckled herself in. When he got in beside her and shut the door, she said, ‘You were right. I did call you. I wanted you to come. I don’t know why you instead of someone else. I don’t have very many people in Edinburgh that I trust, and I ...’ She stared out at the street and shook her head. ‘I don’t know.’

‘How did you do it?’

‘He followed me home from a club last night. Ricky. And he stood out there for ages, banging the door and bawling my name. I was so scared and upset that I just curled up in a little ball in my bedroom and thought very hard. And somehow, a few hours later, you turned up. How would you explain that, Indiana?'

'Just call me Harri, please.'

'You're not answering my question.'

'How would I explain the fact that you called me from across town, without the benefit of modern technology? I don't know, Amy. I think it's possible that you're a little bit like me.'

She glanced at him as he turned left onto Easter Road and headed uphill. 'Damn it. I knew you were going to say that.'

TEN

Elizabeth Merriweather stepped into Brown's of George Street and unwrapped herself with as much authority as she could muster, draping her black wool coat over her arm and announcing herself to the hostess. She was shown to a booth, where she sat and waited for Quentin. He had asked for this meeting, and she knew he would be late. That was always his way: to set the terms and control the interaction from start to finish. The City had taught him well.

The restaurant was full of noisy groups: friends, couples with young children, generations of extended families. She wondered what people thought when they saw her sitting on her own. Maybe they didn't think anything. Most likely nobody even noticed her at all. If they did, they would pity her in the worst way. Young women dining on their own were mysterious and attractive. Older women were just sad.

Elizabeth fended off the over-eager waiter and glanced at her watch. She would give Quentin ten more minutes. She tapped her red-lacquered nails on the table and waited.

He arrived, flushed and windblown, just as she was putting her coat on to leave. The sight of him filled her with dread. Her body had learned to submit to him, even when her head wanted to run.

'So sorry, phone call came in just as I was getting in the car. Had to deal with it.' He pecked her cheek without intimacy and she flinched away from the damp touch of his lips. 'I appreciate you coming into town. I've got a hell of a lot on this weekend.'

At close proximity, Quentin was sweaty and bloated. He was ill or drinking too much, or both. His mortality was showing, and this gave her confidence. 'Whereas I have nothing better to do than drive all the way up from North Berwick, only to be kept waiting for twenty minutes.'

'It couldn't be helped. Don't be spiteful, Lizzie, it doesn't make this horrid business any easier.'

She hated how small he made her feel. 'What did you want to discuss, Quentin?'

The waiter chose that moment to pounce. Quentin ordered himself smoked salmon on toast with scrambled egg. Elizabeth asked for a Bloody Mary.

'Aren't you eating, Lizzie?'

‘I’ve lost my appetite,’ she said curtly. ‘Don’t let me stop you.’

He laughed heartily. ‘You never have. So, it’s time we made this official. I’ve spoken to my lawyer about getting divorce proceedings underway.’

Elizabeth didn’t know what to say. They had been separated for more than two years but he had steadfastly refused to discuss divorce. There were always other women so it had suited him perfectly well to move out, but he hadn’t wanted to let her go either.

‘Have you found some other poor fool who wants to marry you, Quentin? Is that it?’

‘Of course I haven’t. Let’s just say I’ve seen the error of my ways and realised it’s time to cut you free. You’re quite right, it’s time to close the door on this chapter.’

‘Fine,’ she said, although without the relief she needed. There had to be some motive. ‘Well thank goodness you’ve seen sense.’

‘I’d like to get the house on the market.’

And there it was.

Elizabeth drew in a breath and raised her chin defiantly. ‘The house can’t be sold, Quentin. It belonged to my parents.’

‘And now it belongs to me.’

‘It belongs to both of us. It’s been in my family for a century. It’s Lucy’s home.’

'Lucy's not coming back to it, you know that.'

She leaned towards him. 'I don't know that, and I'm not leaving it.'

'You'll have to, I'm afraid. I need to free up the capital.'

'Free up the capital? My God, Quentin, have you lost any shred of decency you might once have had?' She fought to keep her volume under control. 'You don't need the money.'

He slumped back in the wooden booth and Elizabeth caught a flash of worry on his face. The little twitch in his cheek gave away his anxiety. 'This Brexit fiasco has royally buggered things.'

'Your financial difficulties are not my problem.'

'They are if you want to be kept in the luxury you're used to.'

'I will happily embrace poverty to be free of you.'

'That crumbling old pile of stones will get cold very quickly.'

She leaned closer to him again, hissing through gritted teeth, 'Don't you dare try to threaten me. As far as I'm concerned, you abnegated your duty to Lucy and me, and so have no further claim over us or our property. I will instruct my solicitor accordingly. In fact, you should count yourself lucky I don't press charges against you.'

'Press charges?' He snorted. 'For what?'

'For what?' She raised a single eyebrow. 'You know very well what for.'

Quentin gripped her wrist and breathed fumes in her face. 'You know damn well your little accusations will never stick. Do you really want a long, expensive fight, Elizabeth?'

'No, but I'm prepared to give you one. While I'm here, Quentin, I might as well tell you, I've hired someone to help me track down Lucy.'

'You've hired someone? Who?'

'A private investigator.'

He laughed again. 'Oh, good Lord, Lizzie. Some hopeless waster who couldn't cut it as a cop?'

'Not at all. He's rather special, so I'm led to believe. I'm quite confident that he'll find her.'

'Unlikely. But if he does, what then? That girl never wants to set eyes on you again. We both heard her say it. You really think she's going to come home willingly?'

Elizabeth smiled coldly. 'We'll see about that. And when she does, she may just be ready to tell her story. Perhaps we both will. What do you think about that?'

'What story would that be?' Quentin asked, as if he had already forgotten what they'd just spoken about. He smiled mildly at her, his puffy face smug and unconcerned. He was a master at baiting others into action and shrugging off all responsibility.

Elizabeth paused, astonished. What story? Memories ripped through her, but Quentin made her question them. She hated him for it. 'The things you made her do.'

Quentin examined his clean, pink fingertips. 'Nobody ever made that girl do anything in her life. You raised a spoiled, wilful brat. If the fact that she turned into a filthy little slut bothers you, Lizzy, maybe you should take a hard look at yourself sometime.'

'Don't you dare…' she whispered, with such a fury burning in her that she felt like she might explode. Her hands wanted to go for his eyes. She clenched them under the table. This was not the place for a scene. 'Whatever I had to lose is gone, Quentin. I'm not afraid of you anymore. You have a choice. I will divorce you quietly on the condition that you leave me with the house. If you don't ...' She lifted her fingers from the table, indicating that the ball was now in his court.

Quentin had his poker face back on and there would be no further discussion with him.

She slid out from the booth and slipped her coat on just as the waiter arrived with their drinks. 'I'm so sorry, I can't stay,' she said sweetly.

Walking away from Quentin was a skill she should have learned a long time ago. 'Just put the drink on my ex-husband's bill, if you don't mind.'

ELEVEN

Harrison lived in one of the leafier streets of the Grange, on the ground floor of a subdivided Victorian house. Amy followed him along a tiled hallway to a large kitchen that opened out into the enclosed garden. It was one of those middle-class places that always made you feel like you were stepping back in time: a fireplace, an oak table strewn with books and papers, a deep Belfast sink. There was a pleasant smell of wood smoke mixed with fresh coffee.

'Apologies, tidiness isn't my strong suit.'

'Don't worry. It's nice,' she said, trying to quell the nerves in her belly. Coming to his office had been safe enough, but stepping into his kitchen felt intrusive. She looked around at the ordinary details of his home life: laptop, dirty coffee cups beside the sink and laundry drying on the rack. The thing he'd said in the car was hanging between them, but she wasn't ready to go back to it. He'd tapped so quickly into something nobody else had ever accepted.

He took off his coat and draped it over a chair, gathered some of the loose papers into a stack and slipped them into a folder labelled Lucy Merriweather. Noticing that she hadn't taken off her coat, he asked, 'Is it cold in here?'

It was, but she said, 'It's fine.'

'I'll get this going.' He squatted in front of the fireplace. She watched him scrape last night's ash into a pile, add some old newspaper and kindling on top of it and light it with a single match. He added a couple of birch logs and waited for the flames to lick them before standing up again. 'Breakfast? On cold winter mornings like this, my dad used to make pancakes with blueberries and maple syrup.'

'You want to make me pancakes?' She held her hands towards the fire.

'I want to make myself pancakes, and since you're here I'll make you some. Unless you'd rather have something else.'

'Pancakes sound good.' She couldn't remember the last time anyone had made her breakfast, and the loneliness of her life bounced back on her hard. Four kids in a three-bedroom terraced house and she still grew up alone. How did that work?

'Coffee?'

'Yes please.'

'Have a seat, Amy.'

She sat at the table and watched him put the coffee on and get the pancake makings underway. He knew his way around a kitchen, even if he didn't seem to be good at making small talk. That made a change. All her life, she'd been surrounded by men who would dominate conversation from a chair without lifting a finger.

'Does your dad still make you pancakes?'

He scooped flour into the mixing cup and avoided eye contact. 'My dad left when I was ten, so no.'

'Oh. Sorry.'

'It's alright.' The tone was far too casual to be believable.

Another silence stretched out. A succession of questions followed but she held onto them.

He glanced up from his mixing, and although he didn't open his mouth, she heard him say, *Whatever you want to know, just ask.*

She lurched to her feet. 'What the fuck is going on? I can hear your voice in my head.'

'Can you?' Sounding more curious than surprised, he poured two cups of strong, black coffee and slid a small jug of milk over to her. 'Is that normal for you?'

'No!' Her hand shook as she poured milk into her cup, and she could feel the rush of adrenaline in her thighs. She took a sip and tried to calm herself. 'Nothing about this is normal.'

'When did it start for you?'

'I don't know. I don't even know what *it* is!'

'Describe it to me.'

'I'd call them premonitions, I guess. Sometimes I know things have happened or are going to happen. Sometimes I know somebody's going to call me right before they do. Sometimes I get a feeling and I know something bad is going to happen. Sometimes I have a dream. At work, I see the outcome of an emergency before it happens. Sometimes I try to warn people that something bad is going to happen to them, but they never listen to me.'

'And the bad things happen?'

'Yes.' She closed her eyes and fought the sudden urge to cry. 'So, you don't think I'm talking crazy superstitious bollocks, like everyone else?'

He shook his head and his eyes were so full of empathy that she wanted to crawl into his arms and curl onto his lap like a child.

'Am I psychic? Is that what you're telling me?'

'Yes. It's called precognition.'

'You do believe me, don't you?'

'I do, but you can understand why a lot of people might not. Most folk are afraid of things that threaten their realities. In our culture, we've mostly dismissed any possibility of the spirit as something separable from the body.'

'In English please, Professor.'

He smiled. 'When I was maybe twelve or thirteen, I read a book about shamanism. It was all about different shamanic practices across the world. Shamans are people who can travel out of their bodies, if you want to put it that way. They can travel into the future or the past, or into spirit worlds ... alternate universes, maybe. They can heal people. They can speak to the dead. They hear things from afar, they see things from afar. It was an eye-opener. It explained a lot about how I was.'

'And you've always been this way?'

'No.'

'So how did it happen for you?'

He looked out the window and seemed to be considering what to tell her. 'When I was a wee boy, my dad taught me to sail in this little wooden boat he'd made. When I was eight, I had a daft notion to take it out myself. A wind came up and needless to say, I got into trouble. The boat capsized and I was in the water for about three hours. It was April and the water was bloody cold.'

'God. You're lucky you didn't die.'

'Very. I was hypothermic and hallucinating by the time a local fisherman pulled me out. After that, I couldn't switch the hallucinations off. That was the start of ... everything.'

That little pause at the end made her wonder if there was more to the story than he was telling her. She had the feeling that none of her questions had simple answers.

'You must have studied this at uni. Can't you explain how this works?'

'That depends what kind of explanation you're looking for,' he said, putting down the mixing bowl and picking up his coffee. 'Most cultures across the world accept that there is some form of energy or life force that moves through all of us and connects us.'

'In a galaxy far far away, they call it The Force.'

'Aye, that's it, though I couldn't raise a spaceship out of a swamp if I tried.' He laughed, and she was grateful for his momentary lapse into a less schooled accent. 'These ideas underpin martial arts, yoga, reiki, and most indigenous healing practices. Even here, not so long ago, we had that connection with each other and with nature. We drew wisdom and truth from things we could feel but not touch. We understood that we were only small parts of something much, much bigger.'

'Right ...' she said slowly, waiting for this new idea to sink in. It was like an embryonic flame, which burned brightly when he was speaking but began to die away when he stopped.

'Doesn't that defy the laws of physics or something?'

'Not necessarily. Maybe it's all to do with quantum entanglement, or …'

'Sorry, quantum what?'

He took two red apples out of the fruit bowl and held one in each hand, spread apart. 'It's the idea that sub-atomic particles that seem to be unrelated, that might even be millions of miles apart, are linked and can act on each other in some way.' He turned the apples simultaneously. 'How do we explain that?'

Amy shook her head. 'I have no idea. Where does God figure in all this?'

'God is just another way of trying to explain the connection. Are you a believer in God?'

'No. Are you?'

'I'm spiritual in my own way, but not in a Christian sense. Maybe there's something supernatural out there, or maybe there's no such thing as supernatural, only the nature we don't yet understand.'

She butted in. 'Sorry for asking so many questions, but why you? Or me? How can I see into the future when other people can't?'

'You ask much better questions than any of my students.' He shrugged. 'In my case, I believe coming close to death opened my mind to something that most people don't tune into. In your case, you tell me. Maybe time isn't as linear as we like to think it is. Maybe there is some little part of you that can step off the straight line and move in different directions.'

'I don't understand that. How can time be a shape?'

'Ah!' He laughed. 'See, you do get it. We tend to treat time as a two-dimensional arrow, travelling in one direction only. That's because our culture tells us to see it that way. If we accept that it isn't a shape at all, if all times exist simultaneously, then our notions of past, present and future change quite profoundly.'

'So you know what you said to me in your office? That you could prove it to me but you don't find it that pleasant? Why is that?'

'Because if emotions are energy, then they each trigger their own reaction in me. It's a physical reaction, it hurts.'

'Always?'

'If a person is angry or frightened or sad ... yeah, it hurts.' He cut himself off abruptly and cleared his throat. 'Anyway, you're right, it's all too mind-bending for this hour on a Saturday morning. Pancakes. You mind throwing another log on there?'

The fire was well established now, so she placed a fat log on top of it. Harrison ladled circles of pancake batter onto the griddle. Her stomach growled as soon as the warm, buttery smell rose toward her. When the first two pancakes were ready, he put them onto a plate and passed them across to her, with a bottle of real maple syrup. 'Canadian comfort food.'

'So, you're Canadian? I keep thinking I hear little hints of Irish in there.'

He nodded, smiling. 'I thought my Newfie accent was long gone.'

'Newfie? Newfoundland? That's where you're from?'

'Originally. I was born there and we lived in St. John's until I was six. Then we moved to Scotland and stayed through the west, in Argyll. I've lived a lot of different places since then. Dad was Canadian, Mum's Scottish.'

'Your dad *was* Canadian? He's dead?'

He paused, the spatula hovering above the pan. 'We don't know.'

'Oh. Sorry.'

He acknowledged this with a token nod, then directed his attention back toward the pancakes.

Amy chewed slowly, keeping her questions to herself, not wanting to overstep the mark. 'This is good.'

'Thank you.' He ate the next two pancakes, standing up across from her while he cooked more.

'Can I ask something else?'

He glanced up from his food. 'What?'

'Do you tell people? The people you work with and ... you know, girlfriends?'

'Only when I'm sure I can trust them. Most of my colleagues at the university don't know, and I spend most of my time covering it up. It's not always the easiest thing to live with.'

'You make it sound like a disease.'

'I've sometimes thought about it that way.'

'Great.' All her life, she'd been separated from the people around her by an invisible barrier that she could never define and never break. There was a place in her, an inner sanctum that no other person could be allowed to enter. Perhaps now she had the beginnings of an explanation, although there was little comfort in it. It sounded like a life sentence.

Her eyes felt raw and swollen and, now that the keen edge of hunger had been dulled, she began to realise how tired she was. 'Do you have any good news this morning, Professor? I've had a really long night, and I'm a bit hungover.'

'The good news is you're not alone anymore.'

This brought on a whole new line of questions. What did he mean by that? What if he was getting the wrong idea? She began to feel slightly panicky. Not that he was bad looking. Far from it. But he had to be quite a lot older than she was, and he wasn't even close to being her type. A horrifying image of trying to make conversation as his date at some academic dinner party flashed inside her mind. That was definitely not going to be a premonition, she would make sure of that.

'Can we be straight about one thing? I'm not going to hop into bed with you just because we have some kind of freaky psychic thing going on.'

To her surprise, he laughed. 'That's a relief.'

'I don't know whether to thank you or be insulted.'

'Don't be insulted. I've just come out of my latest ill-fated relationship and I'm not looking for another one anytime soon.'

'You're pretty alone too, aren't you?'

He poured more coffee but didn't answer her question. He didn't need to.

She pushed her plate away. 'I'm stuffed. And I'm bloody knackered. I didn't sleep much at all last night.'

'Do you want me to take you home?'

'I can get the bus if ...' She didn't want to go home, but couldn't tell him that.

'There's a settee in my study,' he interrupted. 'It's pretty comfy for sleeping on.'

Gratitude made her eyelids even heavier. 'Thank you. If you have to go out anywhere, just go. Do whatever you need to do.'

'Come on,' he motioned for her to follow him. Across the hall, there was a book-filled study, with a desk and a worn-out brown sofa. 'I'll get you a quilt.'

He left her sitting there, embarrassed and chilled with exhaustion. This whole thing was ridiculous beyond belief. Sleep was all she needed. Two or three hours and she'd be herself again, and she could go home. Ricky wouldn't come back; she didn't know why she was so worried about him.

He came back again with a thick quilt and a pillow. 'Here you go. I'll be in the kitchen. I've got some work to do.'

She hugged the bedding against her chest and felt like an orphan. 'Thank you, Harri. This is all a bit strange, huh?'

'Like I said, strange is an occupational hazard.'

'I'll be out of your way soon.'

'You're not in my way, Amy,' he said quietly, and pulled the door closed behind him.

TWELVE

The fact that Amy Bell was sleeping in his study was enough to distract Harrison from settling down to any meaningful work. He hoped she was sleeping and not prowling around his study, digging into the details of his life. She could be, he supposed. Not that he had much left to hide from her except credit card numbers. He'd spent so many years disguising himself, like the phantom of the bloody opera, and it was a relief to take the mask off.

He touched the back of the chair she'd sat on at breakfast and closed his eyes. A gnawing sensation gripped his stomach. Her need for knowledge had compelled her to seek him out, but he hoped he hadn't overwhelmed her. He'd prattled so much this morning and hadn't left her much time to talk. The teacher in him loved an audience.

She had left an echo of memory in the room. From it, he could picture a quiet girl with a scatter of freckles across her nose and a thousand-yard stare. A curious, introspective child who tended wounded birds, picked scabs to watch how the blood ran and clotted, and who had seen violence at an early age. She carried the sound of breaking glass in her ears, as though it was the first thing she could remember hearing. There was a deep rift right inside her.

He crept around as quietly as possible, folding his dry laundry so he wouldn't have to catch her eyes drifting up to his boxer shorts on the pulley, and washing up the breakfast dishes. When the kitchen was clean, he opened the file he'd made up for Lucy Merriweather and forced himself to concentrate. He mapped out what he knew of Lucy's story, or at least Elizabeth's version of it.

Lucy was a healthy, vibrant young girl who was good at everything she did: she loved to ride, loved to dance, loved to travel, loved to help people. Most of all she loved to sing, and she had the kind of angelic high, pure voice that made grown men weep. She had close friends and was always popular. When Elizabeth and Quentin argued, Lucy retreated to her treehouse at the far end of the garden, and Elizabeth believed she had been spared from the bloodiest details.

Things began to change when Lucy came to the end of primary school. She wanted to go to North Berwick High School with most of her friends, but Quentin insisted on sending her up to

Loretto. That was when all of the troubles started. In hindsight, Elizabeth wished she'd fought Lucy's corner on the school front, but she'd had her own snobberies. After all, if they weren't going to buy their daughter a fine education, what was the point of Quentin working so many hours and being away so often?

Lucy started getting into trouble. At thirteen, she was coming home drunk. At fourteen she was sexually active. At seventeen, just before she was due to sit her exams, she told her mother she was pregnant. In the face of relentless questioning, she steadfastly refused to name the father. Elizabeth rushed her in and they dealt with the pregnancy early, before anyone else found out about it. Needless to say, the exam results were not what they should have been.

All the while, Elizabeth and Quentin's relationship was disintegrating. Quentin hit out, with his tongue and sometimes with his hands. He slapped Elizabeth, bruised her arms, put his fingers around her neck and threatened to crush the life from her. He stopped bothering to hide the fact that he saw other women and Elizabeth stopped pretending to care.

Lucy stopped hiding her disgust with both of her parents. She raged against them, told them she hated them, called them names that Elizabeth couldn't bring herself to repeat. Instead of going to university, Lucy took a low paid job with a charity, working on the streets among homeless people and drug addicts. She busked on the Royal Mile for spare change and tried to get gigs in small bars and clubs around town. The last time Elizabeth saw Lucy, she was living in a shabby communal house in Portobello with a dozen other people, men and women, not all of them young or reputable. She had moved on from there about eighteen months ago and from there the trail had gone cold. It was a starting point, at least.

There were holes in the story – big ones – for example, the nature of Quentin's abuse of Lucy and why Elizabeth had never done anything about it. She made out that it had all started when Lucy began to rebel in secondary school, but Harrison had the feeling that it went back a lot further. Lucy hadn't been the happy child her mother made her out to be, although she might have learned to pretend.

He changed clothes and went for a run, headphones in to keep the rest of the world out. Running was barely tolerable when he was in his twenties and hadn't got any more enjoyable, but the toll of a sedentary job was worse. He'd watched too many of his colleagues in the department become pallid, with bad backs and creaky hips. Through running, and allowing himself to be thrown around by younger, meaner guys at the martial arts gym twice a week, he was determined to avoid the slide into middle-aged complacency as long as possible.

He pushed himself twice around the Meadows at as fast a pace as he could sustain. When he got home, he found Amy awake and sitting at the kitchen table. She was skimming the pages of *Spirits of the Mountain*, the book he had written about Tomas and the other miners in Potosí.

'Good sleep?'

She gave him a sheepish smile and closed the book. 'Yes, thank you. You've been running?'

'For my sins.'

'I love running.'

'I hate it. You like the book?'

Instead of answering, she asked, 'Do you use all those big words deliberately so the people you write about can't understand what you're saying about them?'

He laughed softly. It was the question every anthropologist dreaded most.

'I think we write that way to make ourselves sound clever to other academics, and that's it. Anyway, it doesn't matter. Most of the people in that book speak Quechua or Aymara. Not all of them can read. My friend Tomas spoke four languages fluently, including English. He'd have understood the book.'

'He's dead?'

Harrison paused and decided not to explain the ongoing connection. It would only make him sound crazier than he already did. 'Yeah.'

'I saw the pictures of you with him. What happened to him?'

'Mining accident.'

Amy winced. 'Can I ask you another question?'

'Sure.'

'Who is Lucy Merriweather?'

'Ah ...'

'You left the papers sitting there. I didn't mean to snoop.'

Harrison filled a pint glass of water and gulped it down. 'I do some detective work on the side. I find people.'

'You find people? What, like, missing people? The same way you found me?'

'Yeah, more or less.'

'So, you're a psychic detective?' She sounded genuinely impressed for the first time. 'That's pretty cool, Indiana.'

Harrison sighed. 'Do you have to call me that?'

'You're stuck with it now. How come you do that? Don't tell me you need the money.'

'I started it because I needed the money. Now I do it mostly for the pleasure of seeing people reunited. I don't take that many cases on, and I keep saying I'm going to stop. I'm starting to think I should have turned this one down.'

'How come?'

'My clients' details are confidential. I shouldn't be discussing this with you.'

'Don't worry, I'm not going to tell anybody. Is Lucy Merriweather the missing person?'

'Yes. How much did you read?'

'Nothing. Just the name.'

'It's probably best if we leave it at that.'

'Who is she?'

'Just a girl.' He didn't want to talk about Lucy Merriweather, but Amy was probing him so deeply it felt like she could see straight into his head. She had opened him up and was pulling out pieces of knowledge, like toys out of a box. It was uncomfortable. This was what it was like for Lara, he realised. And Sophie before her. This was what happened to anyone who got too close to him.

'Nobody's *just a girl*,' Amy said. 'Something bad's happened to her, hasn't it?'

He pushed damp hair back from his forehead. 'I think so. I think something very bad has happened to her.'

'How do you know that?'

'I can feel it.'

'Maybe I could help you look for her.'

'I don't know if that's a good idea.'

'Why not? You can teach me how to use this ... thing ... I have, rather than just being battered around by it all the time.'

He slouched down on the chair across from her, conscious of his sweaty shirt and moist hair. His glasses were smudged and sticky, so he took them off. Without them, one Amy became two. Sometimes he wondered whether his vision was really that bad or his brain perceived a different reality. Maybe the glasses were tricking him into seeing a clarity that wasn't there.

'Give me your hand.'

'Why?'

Harrison reached across the table. 'Just give me your hand.'

She hesitated for a moment, then laid her hand over his. He squeezed it gently and closed his eyes. Sounds filled his ears: gunfire, artillery, the shouts of men. She was on her knees in the dust, leaning over a soldier, pressing her hands down over a bloody hole in his abdomen.

He opened his eyes and slipped his hand away. Then, purely on impulse, he said, 'Okay.'

'Okay what?'

'Okay, you can help me look for Lucy Merriweather. But just to warn you, not everybody is alive when I find them.'

'I understand,' she said. 'So how does it work? What do we do?'

He stood up. ‘We need to go see some people in Portobello. Let me get a shower.’

The Portobello house was big and old, but shabby. There were half a dozen bicycles stacked against the wall, recycling bins overflowing with bottles under the front windows, weeds coming through the steps. Green mould crept around splintering sash window frames.

‘What do you want me to do?’ Amy asked when Harrison rang the bell.

‘Just take it in. See what you can pick up. We’re not the police, we’re not here to interrogate anybody, but listen to your instincts.’

She nodded silently as the door creaked open and they were faced by a young woman with yellow dreadlocks and rings in her nose.

‘Hi,’ she said.

‘Hi.’ Harrison mimicked her tone. She was young and lacked any obvious natural suspicion. He opted for a direct approach. ‘I’m hoping you can help me. We’re trying to find a girl who used to live here. Lucy Merriweather? Do you know her?’

‘Yeah, but I haven’t seen her for like a year and a half or something,’ she said openly. Her accent was English and slightly dopy. ‘Sorry, who are you anyway?’

‘I’m Harri Jones and this is Amy. We’ve been asked by Lucy’s family to see if we can find her. They haven’t had any contact with her for some time and they’re worried about her, obviously.’

‘What are you, like ... private investigators or something?’

‘That’s right.’

She gave a little snort of laughter. ‘Okay. Do you want to come in or anything? Joe’s here, he knows Lucy as well.’

‘Thanks. We won’t take much of your time.’

They followed her inside. The inside of the house matched the outside: strewn with empties and leftovers, infused with smells of old food and cannabis. Harrison picked up the wafty, paranoid vibrations of people who were permanently stoned. A door creaked open, and a couple of expressionless faces peered out and then disappeared. Harrison could also feel Amy bristling behind him.

The girl showed them into a lounge and indicated for them to sit on a sofa draped with faded Indian cotton throws. ‘I’ll get Joe.’

As soon as she left, Harrison stood up again and explored the room, running his hands over the dusty shelves and chairs, picking up old books and candle holders. He could tell that Lucy had been here, but not recently. A guitar leaning in a corner behind a lamp drew his attention. He picked it up and placed his fingers over the frets. The strings were dead with dust and old sweat. A woman's voice sang in his mind, fragile beauty layered over something hard and dark. Briefly, he saw her face, half-hidden behind a veil of pale gold hair. There were people watching her, mostly older men. They were transfixed by her voice but they wanted more than that. They wanted her body. They wanted her. They would put their hands deep into their pockets to have her. She was performing for them like a bear in a circus, and she wasn't happy about it. He took a deep breath.

'Are you okay?' Amy asked.

He'd almost forgotten she was there. 'This was hers.'

'You can tell that just from picking it up?'

'Yes. Here.' He handed her the guitar.

'What do you want me to do with it?'

'Just hold it. See what happens.'

She shook her head and gave him a doubtful look, but drew the guitar in close to her body and ran her fingers down the strings. It made a dull, dissonant chord. 'Am I supposed to feel something?'

'You might not. We're all different.'

'Bloody private investigators or something,' said the dreadlocked girl's voice in the hallway. She came back into the room, followed by a skinny man with a crew cut and Maori facial tattoos that he was too white to wear convincingly.

'How's it going?' he asked, rubbing his eyes. 'Brit says you're looking for Lucy Merriweather. Who sent you?' His accent was from the same part of the world as his body art.

'Her mother.'

'Yeah well, Lucy doesn't want anything to do with that bitch.'

'I'm aware of that. Can you tell me why?'

'I only know that her parents are the kind of self-absorbed capitalist pigs who are going to be first against the wall.'

Harrison scratched his beard. 'Nothing more ... specific than that?'

'Do you need a more specific reason to hate someone?'

Anger crawled up his neck. He'd indulged in plenty of revolutionary talk in his time, with university mates and especially with Tomas. But Tomas, who had more reason than most to want to line up capitalists against walls, never spoke of it. He spoke of education and healthcare and housing. He spoke of sharing, not killing. This guy on the other hand, was just an idle waster.

'Has anyone else come looking for her?'

'Only her old lady, mate. She came a few times, asking around.'

'The thing is ... Joe, is it? I think Lucy may be in some danger. We just want to make sure she's safe.'

'What kind of danger?'

'Let's just say she's a vulnerable young woman. So, you say she moved out of here about a year and a half ago?'

'Yeah, that's right.'

'And do you have any idea where she went?'

Joe shook his head. 'Nah, not a clue.'

At that point, Brit spoke up. 'She went off with some bloke. Tim, I think his name was.'

Joe raised his eyebrows, showed a flash of displeasure. 'Why are you telling them?'

'Tim?' Harrison pressed. 'Second name?'

Brit continued. 'No idea. He was from somewhere in the Midlands, a bit wet. If it's any use, he worked for some charity that helped refugees.'

'In Edinburgh?'

'Yeah, Craigmillar or Niddrie, one of those places. He was a singer as well. Nice enough guy. He wouldn't do anything bad to Lucy. He was properly in love with her.'

'You're sure about that?'

She shrugged. 'He could have been an arsehole, who knows, but he was alright when he was around. Lucy liked him enough to leave here for him.'

'Was she happy here?'

'Everyone's happy here,' said Joe. 'Are you like ... police or something?'

'Do I look like a cop?' Harrison asked.

'No, but she does.' He nodded at Amy.

Amy leaned forward and said in a husky Belfast drawl, 'I'm no cop.'

Joe relaxed again. 'I don't know any more. Lucy was never going to stay anywhere very long. A year and a half's a long time, she could be anywhere by now.'

'Okay.' Harrison stood up. 'Thanks for your help.'

'That's all you want to know?'

'If we have any other questions, we'll get in touch. Oh, this guitar belonged to Lucy, didn't it?'

'Might have.'

'Can we take it?'

'What for?'

'To give it back to her when we find it.'

'Help yourself,' said Brit. Her attention had already moved onto the tobacco pouch Joe had in the front pocket of his shirt.

'Let's go,' Harrison muttered. Holding the guitar by its neck, he strode quickly to the front door and jogged down the steps, trying to shake off the acrid haze of the house and its occupants. 'Bloody hippies.'

‘At least now you’re speaking my language.’ Amy hurried alongside him. ‘You look spooked, Indiana, what’s up?’

He stopped dead and faced her. ‘For Christ’s sake, Amy!’

‘What?’ She stood her ground; eyes alight with something he hadn’t seen in her before. She liked teasing him, and the more annoyed he got, the more she’d do it. Amy Bell wouldn’t be the first woman to tell him he took himself too seriously.

He willed himself to lighten up. It had been a lifelong effort. ‘Nothing. Let’s get a coffee.’

They put the guitar in the car and walked down to the promenade. Dogs and their walkers breathed clouds of steam into the still air, and a layer of smoke sat low over the horizon: a brownish streak fading to pink and then watery white. They bought drinks from a converted green Citroen van, and sat on the wall, holding the steaming paper cups under their chins.

Amy blew on hers, took a hesitant sip. ‘The café just along would have been warmer.’

‘Mmm,’ Harrison breathed. Hell was an overheated café full of highly-strung gluten-avoiders. Sometimes it was easier not to try to explain himself.

Amy swung her right leg over the wall and sat astride it, facing him with a catlike expression. 'Tell me what happened in there?'

'When I picked up the guitar, I saw Lucy. She was in a room somewhere, maybe a bar, and she was singing. She didn't want to be there.'

'What do you mean she didn't want to be there?'

'I mean ... she wasn't there by choice. Someone was making her perform for a bunch of men.'

'When you say you saw Lucy, was it in the past or something that's happening now?'

'The past. She had the guitar.'

'Maybe a different guitar?'

'I don't think so. Some objects are powerful.'

'Such as?'

'Anything, as long as it's important to somebody. We give objects power by investing emotion in them. Musical instruments almost always have stories to tell.'

'And you can pick this up just by touching something?'

'Yes.'

'Jesus, that's freaky shit. Okay, so ... what do you think it means?'

'It means she was in trouble before she left here.'

‘You think Joe Tattoo knows more than he’s telling us?’

‘He doesn’t know anything. He’s just a prick.’

‘What’ve you got against hippies?’

‘Self-centred, self-righteous, entitled layabouts. Don’t get me started.’

‘That’s awfully judgemental of you, Professor.’ She laughed at him as she shook the cooling foam around her cup. ‘I say we need to track down the boyfriend.’

Harrison nodded. ‘Tim, the wet Brummey.’

‘If he works for a refugee charity in Craigmillar, he shouldn’t be that hard to find. I’ll go online and do some checking around if you want.’

‘Okay. You might be a natural at this.’

‘That’s just logic, it’s not psychic. I didn’t pick up anything out of the ordinary in there.’

‘I know. Just because you have a capacity for it doesn’t mean you can switch it on anytime you like. You have to train yourself.’

‘Can you help me do that?’

‘You need to think seriously about whether you want me to.’

‘Harri, what did you see when you held my hand?’

He wondered how much to say. ‘I saw that other people’s lives are precious to you. Maybe even more precious to you than your own.’

She looked away and blew a curl of frozen breath into the air. 'Maybe that's why I want to do this. I don't like being at the mercy of some weird power I can't control. I want to be able to use it for something good.'

'The more you use it, the more at its mercy you'll become. You need to know that.' He felt a heavy weight, as if he was responsible for bringing her even more deeply into this murky world than she already was.

'I understand.'

'You think so?'

'I'm not an idiot, Harrison.' She paused momentarily, staring at her left foot. It hung a few inches above the pavement and she kicked her heel against the wall like a child. A lock of sandy hair blew across her face. She pushed it behind her ear and said, 'Listen. I saw my brother Ian die before it happened. I tried to warn him and my parents, but none of them believed me. Afterwards, they thought I had information from the other side and they blamed me.'

'By the other side, I assume you mean the nationalists.'

She nodded. 'Ian was involved in things he shouldn't have been involved in. Not serious paramilitary activity, but petty gang stuff, tit for tat nonsense. One night, coming up for the Twelfth, there were skirmishes running up and down the

Ormeau Road. Somebody had a knife ... that was it. It wasn't a pre-planned killing; it was just stupid lads who used politics and religion to try to justify scrapping on a Saturday night. He was only nineteen.'

'How old were you then?'

'Thirteen. I'd had a few…I don't know…flashes of things before, but nothing like that. My parents were more shocked by me than they were at losing Ian. I don't know what was worse, Dad thinking I was some kind of Real IRA double agent or the rest of them practically accusing me of witchcraft.'

Harrison could feel how raw that betrayal still was for her. 'Do you ever see your family now?'

'Mum started talking to me again after Dad died. We keep things as superficial as possible: the merits of *Strictly Come Dancing* over *Britain's Got Talent*, that kind of thing. One of my brothers calls me occasionally. The other one avoids me like the plague. I don't think they'll ever get their heads around it. It's fine, I've accepted that I can't change their minds. But if I can help you find this girl? Or if I can help keep someone safe? Maybe it's all worth it.'

'Maybe,' Harrison said.

'Is that why you still do this, when you don't need the money?'

'I guess it is.' He chucked his cup into a bin and stood up, pulling his collar up and sinking his hands into his pockets. 'I never thought I'd have a partner in this business.'

THIRTEEN

'Paul, do me a favour. Tell me if you see Ricky around here again.'

Paul McShane filled the doorway of his flat, holding a can of Tennants. Sunday afternoon was beer time at Paul's, and he didn't appear pleased to be interrupted. He was a die-hard Hibernian supporter with a habit of pumping iron to Irish rebel songs, a functioning alcoholic and a man who never laughed except at other people's expense. But for all that, he was a decent neighbour and he'd come to her assistance more than once before.

'I promise you, Amy, I'll do more than that if I see him here again. What happened to the restraining order?'

'You think Ricky ever gave a shite about that? He moved onto someone else, that's all. That seems to be finished now, unsurprisingly.'

'He was limping pretty bad the other night.'

'Aye, because I gave him a kicking with my stiletto heels on.'

‘That’s not like you.’

‘I’ve given a few kickings in my time.’

Paul coughed. ‘I meant the stilettos.’

‘No, you’re right about that. Not me.’

‘You want one of these, hen?’ He swilled his beer can and looked appreciatively at her bare, mud-splattered legs.

‘No thanks, Paul.’

Back in her own flat, the anxiety returned. Every half hour or so, she felt compelled to peer out the window and scan up and down the street. There was no visible sign of Ricky, but she could feel him. It was like the faint scream of a rocket, far off but still incoming. She’d been feeling it for months, shrugging it aside and trying to dismiss it as imagination. At her weekly sessions, Caroline suggested post-traumatic stress and recommended treatments. Amy resisted. She couldn’t tell Caroline that the things she saw coming were more than just projections of past experiences, bloody as they were. A single day with Harrison Jones had taught her more about herself than a year with Caroline.

She stretched, then immersed herself in the bath. By the time she got out, it was nearly dark, so she filled the flat with soft amber candlelight and focused on Lucy Merriweather. It was almost unbelievable that Harri could pick up the psychic scent of a girl he’d never met, just by touching her guitar. The man was like some kind of undercover superhero: a brainy Clark Kent without the muscles and the underpants over the trousers. Either that or he was the world's most convincing fraud. Part of her wanted to believe that, but the bigger part knew he was as genuine as they came.

Amy got nothing from the instrument except the smell of old smoke. Now she stared at the photograph of Lucy that Harri had given her, until the pretty young face dissolved into a fractured blur. She put her fingers on the picture, closed her eyes and tried to filter out the sounds of the building and the city outside. Nothing. She breathed deeply, listened to her breath, and sat until she slipped into a doze. Her head leaned forward and she began to dream.

She dreamt of a yacht, moored at the far end of a long, stone quay. It was the biggest and blingiest in a display of floating bling. The crowded streets of the town rose up a hill behind the harbour. They were Mediterranean in character: whitewashed walls, red-tiled roofs. In her dream, she was looking for a way onto the yacht at night: swimming through black water and climbing up a small ladder. As she slipped over the gunwale, an unseen man grabbed her. He clamped one hand over her mouth and nose, and wrenched her arms behind her back with the other. She struggled but there was no strength in her limbs.

She tried to scream but she was suffocating behind the man's massive hand. He got her down on her back, knelt on her chest and took his hand away from her mouth only to replace it with the barrel of a pistol.

The gun roared in her ears and her head snapped upright. Opening her eyes to flickering candlelight, she caught her breath and waited for the residual panic to subside. Nightmares were nothing new, but a yacht on the Med made a change from the usual Afghan dust. Who could tell where it came from? Some late-night Bond film she'd watched once, or old memories of her army training.

Anyway, it was only a dream.

Her belly rumbled. She wandered to the kitchen and stared in at the sparse contents of her fridge, frustrated with herself. What good was being psychic if the sight evaded you when you needed it?

She settled for cheese on toast. With the plate beside her computer, Amy started with the obvious: a social media search for Lucy Merriweather. It was possible Harri had already done that, but he hadn't mentioned it and he didn't seem like the natural social media type. Maybe it had so much psychic information gathered in one place that it would fry his nervous system, or maybe he just didn't need it. Jesus, you could blow

Mark Zuckerberg out of the water if you could only patent what Harrison Jones had.

Lucy had a profile on Facebook, but had security set to block access to everything but her picture. She had over a thousand friends, but Amy couldn't see the list.

How could someone with over a thousand friends just disappear?

She tried Instagram and Twitter next. Nothing. That in itself suggested that Lucy wanted to keep her whereabouts hidden.

She searched *refugee charity, Craigmillar* and found a listing for an organisation called Lothian Asylum Seeker and Refugee Network: LASAR-Net for short. The registered address was Niddrie Mains Road. She jotted this down and clicked through the website. It was only a small project, running on a shoestring budget with three part-time employees – none of them named Tim or Lucy – and a handful of volunteers. She read that their main business was befriending asylum seekers and refugees and helping them settle into life in Edinburgh.

She clicked back over a couple of years of postings on the website. There were pictures of group meals, celebrations, young people playing football, men and women sitting around a table practising their English. She skimmed over the pictures quickly, half wondering if any of the

Afghans she knew might by some fluke have ended up here. Often, she thought of the translators who had worked for them at Bastion, young Hassan and the others. They had made themselves pariahs in their communities and traded their futures for a few meagre pounds. If anyone deserved asylum, they did.

A photo caught her eye and she stopped clicking. People were sitting around cabaret-style tables in a community hall, and on the stage in front of them was none other than Lucy Merriweather. There was a man with long, mousy hair and a scrappy beard beside her. Their mouths were open and they were smiling at each other across their guitars.

'Hello Tim,' Amy said aloud to the empty kitchen.

She scrolled through the rest of the site but could find no other pictures of Tim or Lucy. But now she knew he was a musician and that they played together. She searched *Edinburgh musicians Tim Lucy* and scrolled past several listings for a singer called Tim Lucy, who appeared to be a regular in the Newcastle country music scene. Then, two pages of results later, she found an old posting for a spoken word night at Summerhall, with live original music from Lucy Merriweather and Tim Cartwright. Bingo.

Tim Cartwright, Summerhall went into the notebook.

She searched for *Tim Cartwright, Edinburgh singer/songwriter*. Half a dozen listings came up, none of them more recent than a year past June. It was as if he and Lucy had dropped off the face of the earth. The question was, why?

She swallowed the last cold crust of toast and picked up the telephone. It rang before she even touched the screen, and Harrison's name appeared.

'Okay, that's just creepy,' she said.

'What?'

'I was literally just about to ring you.'

'Sorry.'

'Listen, I've found out a thing or two. Our boy is called Tim Cartwright. I'll send you a link to his photo. The charity they were connected with is called LASAR-Net: Lothian Asylum Seeker and Refugee Network, but he doesn't appear to have been on the staff list there. Neither does Lucy. They've played a few gigs together around town, but nothing in the last eighteen months.'

'Brilliant, Amy. I might go over there after my seminar tomorrow morning. You want to come?'

'Sure. I'm not working until the evening.'

'Anyway, I just wanted to check you're okay.'

'Aye, I'm grand, Professor.'

'You know I'm not a professor, right?'

‘You know I’m only teasing you, right?’

‘All quiet on the Ricky front?’

‘No sightings, but I feel a disturbance in the Force.’

‘The Force ...’ he paused and she could tell he was holding back a comment. Maybe he was too cerebral for repeated Star Wars analogies, but the comparison comforted her. It suggested happy endings and triumphant music.

‘Are you worried? Do you want me to come over?’ he asked.

She tried to imagine Harrison Jones squaring off with Ricky. She couldn’t imagine him squaring off with anybody. ‘Thank you for offering, but it’s fine.’ She peered out the window at the damp empty street. ‘I can handle him.’

FOURTEEN

Professor Gordon Leigh-Davies was the head of the social anthropology department, and widely tipped to be the next Dean of Faculty. He was also inappropriately preoccupied by the feminine curves of more or less any woman who crossed his path. He especially liked them on the plump side, young and dark-skinned: more or less the polar opposite of his wife Gwyneth. Lately, the principal object of his desire was Aziza Maalouf, a twenty-four-year-old PhD student from Cairo.

Harrison found Monday morning postgraduate seminars torturous at the best of times, but the waves of lust emanating from Gordon while Aziza stumbled through the outline of her thesis-in-progress made this one unbearable. He'd arrived five minutes too late and all the seats in the room had been taken except the one beside Gordon. The seminar room was cramped and Gordon kept jabbing Harrison with his elbow and bumping him with his knee under the table. Every time they touched, Harrison received another flood of Gordon's hormonal imagination. The vibes he put out ought to be enough to merit jail time.

The contents of any man's mind could be pretty sordid. Gordon wasn't unique in this. It wasn't fair to demonise the man. Gordon didn't know, and couldn't help, that Harrison was reading him like a morning tabloid.

Harrison willed himself to concentrate on Aziza's talk. Like most PhD papers, it was heavy on theory and tangled in angst. Aziza had done some excellent research among women peace activists in Palestine, but the material almost disappeared amongst the jargon. Gordon and his cronies kept the seminar going far longer than it needed to, with questions, which weren't really questions at all, but cleverly-engineered displays of their own brilliance. Harrison glanced at his watch and turned his shoulder toward Gordon.

When the interminable session finally ended, Harrison attempted to make a clean getaway. He'd arranged to pick up Amy at one and it was now nearly half-past twelve. Gordon cobbled him.

'Harri, do you have a minute?'

'A quick one. I have an appointment.' He followed Gordon to his office and shut the door. Thankfully, now that there were no women in sight, Gordon's state of arousal had returned to acceptable levels: terror threat level reduced to moderate.

'What's up?'

'I'd like you to take over supervising Aziza, if you can possibly fit her in. I know you're busy.'

'How come?' The question was unnecessary for any reason except keeping up appearances.

'I believe she would benefit better from the wisdom of your particular approach and ... ehm ... youth, I suppose.'

'Youth?'

Gordon held out his hands. 'It's all relative, of course.'

'She came here specifically to study with you.' Silently he added, *You lecherous old bastard*, and hoped Gordon would pick it up.

'I've discussed this with her and she's amenable. I'll be open with you, Harri. She and I have some differences of opinion. I believe she's too close to her material. Too passionate, shall we say.'

Or not passionate enough. 'And that's a bad thing because ...'

'It compromises intellectual rigour. You know that.'

'It's a sin you've accused me of on many occasions. We're writing about living, breathing, struggling people.'

'In an attempt to elicit wider human truths.'

'I thought it was to recognise their lives, for their sakes.'

'And therein lies our problem. Maybe it's a generational thing.' Gordon gave one of his mild, patronising smiles. 'This is exactly why I thought of you for Aziza. I believe you'll give her the space and support she needs for writing up as quickly as possible.'

'So you can clear her out of here.'

'Let's be honest, she's never going to set the world alight.'

'Jesus, Gordon, could you be a bigger misogynist if you tried?'

Gordon laughed. 'Oh, Harrison. Aren't we all misogynists, if we're honest with ourselves?'

'Not all of us.'

'No, of course you're not. But you're the man for Aziza. You're the best teacher we have. The students love you.'

'Being loved by students isn't always seen as the mark of a successful academic.'

Gordon's chair creaked as he leaned back. In the cold fluorescent light, he looked florid and deeply frustrated. 'Harrison, forgive me for saying this, but sometimes I get the feeling you'd rather be doing other things. Travelling in other realms, shall we say?'

Harrison didn't try to deny this statement. 'Well I *was* hoping to get back to Bolivia next year.'

‘If you don’t take Aziza, she may be forced to find a place with another university. It wouldn’t be the best for our reputation, internationally.’

‘Rich parents might send their tuition cheques elsewhere.’

‘Harri ...’

‘Okay, Gordon. I’m sorry, that was uncalled for. I’ll take her on, it’s fine.’

‘You’re sure?’

‘Aye. There’s a good thesis in her, I’m confident of that.’

‘Good man.’

Harrison checked the time again. ‘I’m going to be late.’

‘Is it a medical appointment? Nothing of concern, I hope?’

‘Eh ... no. Nothing of concern.’

LASAR-Net occupied a tiny shop space in Niddrie, between a tanning salon and a boarded-up butcher shop. Graffiti adorned the cladding to the left of the door: *terrorist scum.*

‘Nice,’ Amy muttered, slamming the car door.

Harrison glanced at her. ‘How do you feel about asking the questions?’

‘Okay. Why?’

‘I think you’ll be better at it than me today. I just want to listen.’

‘I’m expecting a fifty per-cent cut, Professor,’ she said.

She was teasing again, but he wasn’t in the mood. He stepped away from her impatiently. ‘Amy, I fully intend to pay you for your contribution.’

‘Oh no, I’m not ... I wasn’t expecting you to. I’m just along for the ride out of curiosity.’

‘You’re doing a job; you deserve to be paid for it.’

‘We can discuss this later. Are we going in or not?’

The woman at the desk inside was looking out at them. She was plump, with purple hair piled in a tangled nest on top of her head and piercings in her nose, lip and eyebrow.

‘Yes, we’re going in. Take a direct approach, tell her who we are and trust yourself.’

Amy pushed the door open and smiled at the woman. ‘Hello.’

‘How can I help you?’ the woman asked. There was a silver stud in her tongue. To Harrison’s surprise, she was local and broad-spoken. He’d been expecting another posh dropout.

‘Is there a manager in today?’ Amy asked in return.

‘Aye, I’m Nessa Walker, I’m the manager.’

‘I’m Amy and this is Harrison. We’re hoping you can help us find a couple of people who used to work here. Possibly they were volunteers? Lucy Merriweather and Tim Cartwright.’

‘Lucy and Tim haven’t…’ she cut herself off, as if realising she’d given away too much already. ‘And who are you, like?’

‘We’re private investigators.’

‘Private investigators.’ She smothered a sceptical laugh. ‘Who hired you?’

‘Elizabeth Merriweather. Lucy’s mother.’

Nessa Walker’s pierced eyebrows arched and her smile faded. ‘Oh aye.’

‘I take it you know her.’

‘Only by reputation. You’d best sit down. You want a coffee? Tea?’

‘Tea would be grand, thanks.’

‘Aye, tea for me as well, ta.’ Harrison said, allowing himself to slide into a broader accent. He could tell already that Nessa would respond better to that version of him than she would to the university don. He spread his hands on her desk and images flickered past him, a film trailer of her life. University had been a childhood dream for her, but the reality had not worked out so well. It had taken her the better part of twenty years to fight back from the breakdown she’d had there.

Nessa reappeared with three mugs. ‘Here we are. Are they in trouble?’

Amy glanced at Harrison, wondering what to say.

'We hope not,' he said. 'Lucy's mum is pretty worried. Have you seen them recently?'

Nessa's expression turned to worry. 'No. What's going on?'

'That's what we're trying to find out,' Amy said.

'Right. Sorry.'

'It's alright,' Amy waved away her apology. 'How were they involved with the charity? Were they employees of yours?'

'No, they were volunteers. Tim Cartwright got involved first. He was young and a bit ...' she twiddled an eyebrow ring as she considered her wording, 'earnest, you know, but he was committed and he had good ideas. He was decent at raising money, which we needed badly.'

She stood up, took a leaflet out of a file box and handed it to Amy. 'That'll tell you all about us, if you want to know more.'

'Thanks.' Amy glanced at it and put it down. 'Go on. What did Tim do to raise funds?'

Nessa sipped her tea. 'He liked organising gigs and performance nights, and they always pulled in a few hundred. He was good at that. I mean, I know he was trying to get his musical career off the ground at the same time, like, but that was no skin off my nose.'

Harrison picked up a purple pen from the desk and rolled it between his hands, focusing in on the little vibrations and stirrings of memory it held. It spoke of unfulfilled intelligence, anger at the injustices of the world, deep personal commitment, and a profound fear of returning to her previous darkness. Nessa Walker was straight up and honest. It made a welcome change.

'How about Lucy?' Amy asked.

'Lucy did some volunteer work with us. She did the gigs with Tim. A bonny singer. I'm telling you, that girl could have been a superstar. But she was troubled, I always felt.'

'Troubled?' Amy reflected this and leaned forward slightly, seeking Nessa's gaze. 'How?'

She was good at this, Harrison observed silently. There was a reassuring but compelling tone in her voice that kept the distractible Nessa on topic.

Nessa's eyes flicked to Amy and then to Harrison. She seemed unsure of how much she should share. 'I don't know. I always knew there was some history there, like, but she never told me the full details. She could be in your face and totally clingy one minute, and the next minute flying into a rage over nothing. I always got the impression that she was pretty damaged. Poor attachments and all that.'

'Do you have any idea where she is now?'

'Last I knew, she was still in Greece.'

'Greece?' Amy glanced at Harrison, mirroring his annoyance.

'Aye. They went over together, the pair of them. That's a story itself. She was obsessed with Kostas Gianopoulos. Poor Tim, I knew she'd chuck him in the end.'

'Kostas ...'

'You've not heard of him? I'm surprised Mrs Merriweather didn't mention him. He's a friend of hers and Mr Merriweather's. So Lucy said, anyway. A businessman of some description. I met him last year when he was in town for a few weeks, negotiating some deal.'

'What kind of a businessman?' Harrison interrupted sharply.

Nessa sat up straighter in her chair, startled by his abrupt tone. 'I couldn't say for sure.'

'A dodgy one?' Amy pressed.

She shrugged and relaxed again. 'As far as I'm concerned, they're all dodgy, but maybe that's just me. He might be a property developer or something like that. I thought he had something to do with a chain of hotels, but I never asked for details.'

Nessa turned her eyes to Harrison. 'I don't know anything else about him. Lucy brought him to the office a few times. He was never anything but nice when he was here, like. Charming, handsome, and very generous with his money. He bought clothes for some of our clients, toys for the bairns, bags of food and all that.'

'Did that seem genuine to you?' Harrison asked.

Nessa's fat brows drew together. 'He came over as pretty genuine. Or he seemed it, but ...' She paused, blew across the surface of her tea. 'I have to say, I never trusted him. We're just a wee charity. I never understood why he was so interested in us, or why he wanted to help us.'

'How did he help you?'

She hesitated briefly, before saying, 'He gave us a big donation.'

'That was nice of him,' Harrison commented.

'Aye, it was, but…' She radiated guilt and uncertainty, like she was afraid of being discovered to have done something corrupt. 'Do you ever just get a feeling about someone?'

'All the time,' said Harrison. 'Tell me about that. What did you feel?'

'That he was after something in return.'

'From the charity? From Lucy? What?'

'I couldn't honestly say. Anyway, he went home and the next thing I know, Tim resigns from the board and tells us that he and Lucy are going travelling.'

'When was this?' Amy asked.

'A year ago, thereabouts.'

‘Lucy Merriweather’s mother doesn’t seem to know she left the country.’

‘No? Well, I’m not that surprised. Lucy was quite open about the fact that she hated everything her parents represented. She was adamant.’

‘And so off they went and you haven’t heard from them since?’

‘I got an email from Tim a while ago. September sometime. He sounded really down. He said he and Lucy had been volunteering with some kind of co-operative in Athens, helping refugees, but that Kostas Gianopoulos had invited them to his home to do a gig for his friends. I can just imagine Tim with all those rich buggers.’ She laughed softly, untied her hair and ran her fingers through it, so that it looked like a halo of aubergine-coloured candyfloss. Then she gathered it back into the band again.

‘Next thing he knew, they were going there every weekend, and Kostas was buying Lucy clothes and promising to launch her singing career. Tim thought Lucy was possibly sleeping with Kostas. He said it had all been just one big party and admitted that he’d been smoking a lot of hash and snorting lines. Lucy broke up with him, which I can’t say surprised me. Tim said he didn’t know what he was going to do, or where he was going to go, but he felt he had to leave Athens. He had wanted to come back home with Lucy, but not without her.' She held her hands open in a helpless gesture. 'And that was the last I heard.'

'So that was September,' Amy said, obviously trying to piece together a timeline. 'Tim and Lucy broke up, and she went off with this guy. Kostas …?'

'Gianopoulos. Aye. Poor Tim, he was pretty disgusted with the whole situation. I feel bad for him, eh. She broke his heart, like, properly.'

'Did you write back to him?'

'Aye. I said he'd always be welcome back here, but he never replied. I hope he hasn't gone off the deep end. He could be pretty depressive at times.'

'Do you think he might do himself damage?' Amy asked.

'It's a possibility.'

'Did he come back to Britain?'

'Not sure. Like I said, he never replied to me.'

'I don't suppose you know how to get in contact with his family, do you?'

'I don't know…he never mentioned them much.'

'He's from Birmingham, is that right?'

'Coventry.'

'Ah, right.' Amy wrote this down.

'That's all I know.'

'Nessa, you've been incredibly helpful,' Harrison said, indicating that the questioning had finished. 'Do you still have that email from Tim?'

'Aye …' she paused to think for a moment, holding her mug under her chin and looking at them through the thin shimmer of steam. 'I could print out a copy for you, I guess.'

'That would be great, thank you.'

She made a few clicks on her computer, and the printer behind her whirred to life. 'Here you go.' She handed over the sheet. 'It's not very ethical, giving you this, but…I am a wee bit worried if I'm honest. I don't know what it is about Kostas Gianopoulos, but I think he's dangerous.'

'You don't happen to have a phone number for Tim, do you?'

Nessa shook her head. 'The number I had for him isn't working anymore. I did try to ring him a few times. I've sent him messages on Facebook, but he hasn't replied to anything. If I had to guess, I'd say he's holed up somewhere, extremely depressed. I just hope it's nothing worse than that.'

Harrison handed across a card. 'If you hear anything or think of anything else, I'd appreciate it if you could let me know.'

'Aye, sure.'

'Thank you so much. We appreciate you taking the time to speak to us.'

‘No bother. Good luck, eh? I don’t think Lucy and Tim had any idea what they might have been getting themselves into. I’d hate to think something awful’s happened to either of them.’

‘We’ll find them, I promise,’ Amy said.

Harrison stood up, anger jolting through him like a shot of adrenaline. Of all the things she could have said, this was the worst. ‘Let’s go, Amy.’

‘What did I do?’ she asked as soon as they were back on the street. He was striding away from her, embarrassed by his display of irrational anger and afraid of hurting her with it.

‘Nothing. It’s fine, come on.’ He unlocked the car, slid in and pulled his door shut.

Amy got in beside him. ‘It doesn’t take a psychic to see you’re pissed off. Tell me what I did wrong.’

Harrison put the key into the ignition, started the engine and sat for a moment. Then he turned it off again and took a deep breath. She might have a natural instinct for this, but she had much to learn. ‘So this is the most important rule. Never promise anybody we’ll find a person. Never do that.’

‘Oh.’ She closed her eyes as the understanding came.

‘We might find her dead. We might not find her at all. This thing has all of a sudden got a lot bigger. She might be at the bottom of the Mediterranean for all we know.'

Amy tilted her head back and pressed her palms into her eyes. 'Surely not.'

'Are you predicting the future right now, Amy? I sincerely hope you are.'

She let out a wobbly breath. 'No.'

'No. Please just ... don't make promises we may not be able to keep.'

'I'm sorry.'

She touched the sleeve of his coat and he knew she was sorry for more than just the thing she'd said to Nessa. A bone-crushing weight pinned him to the seat. He closed his eyes and gripped the steering wheel. Sorrow was always the most painful emotion.

'Are you okay?'

'Yeah.' He couldn't begin to put it into words. He started the engine and drove back toward town. Amy sat silently beside him, and he could feel her humiliation. 'I shouldn't have snapped at you. You did well in there.'

She glanced at him. 'That's coming from personal experience, isn't it?'

'Yes, as a matter of fact, it is.'

Amy nodded. 'I'll know better the next time.' Silence fell between them and she faced away from him, watching the passing lights. After a time, she said, 'I'm working nights the rest of the week, so might be out of touch.'

Harrison thought it was probably best to have a break from each other. 'Okay.'

'What about this Kostas Gianopoulos, then? It sounds like she might be in Greece with him.'

'Sounds like it. He was a friend of her parents, and she's sleeping with him in Greece and they have no idea? What does that say to you?'

'That she likes older men and she's ashamed to tell her folks?'

'That's one interpretation.' Harrison could think of many others. He sighed and drummed his fingers on the wheel as the traffic around the Cameron Toll ground to a standstill. 'Greece. Great.'

'That might complicate things a wee bit.'

'Just a wee bit.'

FIFTEEN

The dress they laid out for her that night was black lace, figure-hugging and off the shoulders. Lucy tried it on and looked at herself in the mirror, holding her hair up off her neck. It was a perfect fit. They always were. She spread her hands over her belly, closed her eyes and thought about Kostas. For a few minutes, she pretended that she had Kostas's baby growing inside her. That would have changed everything.

Kaliope couldn't give him a baby, but Lucy could. She could have, if they'd had a little more time, and surely then he'd have let Kaliope go. Their marriage was a sham anyway. It was all about the money. Lucy knew what that looked like. She'd grown up with it.

Maybe it could still happen, if she could go back home with him.

Who was she kidding? It wasn't her home. It was Kaliope and Kostas's home. Still, Kostas said he would let Kaliope go for her. He promised, and she still believed him.

She'd have to finish here first, but Victor had asked her to extend her contract for another month. She had agreed because it was the easiest money she'd ever made. She sang for an hour every evening, and other than that, all she had to do was lie around in the sun, read books and drink wine. The sea was pure turquoise. This was more like an all-expenses-paid holiday.

If she was honest with herself, she was a bit bored. Apart from Agata, the older woman who looked after her, there wasn't anybody to talk to.

She wished she hadn't agreed to stay on here. Kostas consumed her. She entertained herself with memories of the life she had tasted. It had been a perfect life, even if it had only lasted a few months. When she and Tim first went with Kostas to his country villa, she thought they had arrived in heaven. She loved every aspect of the estate: the whitewashed walls, the arbours shaded by pale green vine leaves and magenta bougainvillaea, the blue-tiled swimming pool, the orange and lemon orchards, the olive groves stretching far across the undulating hillside, the scent of bay leaves, the view sweeping down over the sea.

The first night Kostas asked her and Tim to play, the reception was so enthusiastic that Lucy dared to believe that they might be on the brink of a breakthrough. Kostas knew many record producers, and not just Greek ones. He had contacts in London, New York, Austin, Los Angeles.

Kostas's people brought out wine, champagne, gin, whisky, ouzo and as much food as you could eat. When the company filtered down to those with the most commitment and endurance, he brought out proper Turkish hookahs and the best green she'd ever smoked. There was harder stuff on offer, whatever you wanted, but Lucy didn't bother with it. Kostas never partook, and she was high enough. In fact, she was flying.

Sometimes Tim went off somewhere and she wouldn't see him the rest of the night. His jealousy made him so downright mean that Lucy stopped caring what he swallowed or snorted or shot into his arm. If he wanted to waste himself, she was tempted to seize whatever opportunity she could for herself and leave him in the dust. She was the one with the voice. Guitarists were a dime a dozen.

Tim wasn't ignorant, even when he was wasted. He saw that she was falling for Kostas, as vehemently as she denied it.

Kostas was more than twice her age. He was also a married man, although Kaliope spent most of her time travelling and he indicated that they both preferred it that way. Lucy asked if there were any children. 'God has not seen fit to bless my wife with fertility,' Kostas said.

But God had most certainly blessed him in other ways. He could speak five languages fluently and argue a point so well you couldn't imagine disagreeing with him. He had the physique of a classical statue. His curling light brown hair was almost exactly the same colour as his skin, and his eyes were emerald green when the light hit them. When Kostas spoke to her, when he flashed a smile across a crowded room, it felt like the sun glowing right down inside the core of her body. By comparison, Tim was scruffy, inarticulate and embarrassingly English.

Weeks passed in a giddy whirl of voices and tastes and passions. At first, it was hard to believe that she had a place among these people, but the more she sang for them, the more confident she became. They gathered around her, gushed about her voice, took selfies with her, brought her flowers and gifts. She floated in a golden haze while Tim got more jealous and miserable by the day.

When Tim walked out, she called Kostas and asked him to come get her. He arrived in his big black Range Rover and took her home. They were alone together at his house for the first time, and he made love to her under the grape arbour.

There was a single knock on the door and Agata entered in her usual brusque fashion. 'He has asked to see you before you sing tonight. You must come.'

'I'm almost ready,' Lucy said, applying her lipstick. 'Do I look good?' She'd swallowed one of the pills that eased the nerves, and washed it down with wine. It had made her head giddy and her legs soft, but everything was easier that way: the singing, the broken conversation, and accepting the wandering hands of the old men.

'You are like the sunshine itself,' said Agata. 'He will be pleased.'

Agata led her upstairs to Victor's stateroom, where he welcomed her with kisses on each cheek. 'My dear. Please, sit.' He slid over a silver bowl containing caviar. 'I have something for you to taste.'

'I'm not a fan,' she said.

'Oh, I believe you'll like this,' he said, scooping the glistening black beads onto a spoon and bringing it toward her mouth. 'Try.'

When his voice took on a certain tone, you couldn't refuse him. She opened her mouth and accepted the spoonful, trying to let the gelatinous, salty mass slide down before she could taste it.

'Divine, isn't it?'

She pressed her fingers over her lips and nodded. 'The best I've ever had. Victor, my phone is out of credit, so I can't reach anyone. Is there any way for me to top it up?'

'Of course, we will do that for you. Remind me in the morning. Lucy, there is something I wish to discuss.' He paused and closed his eyes, as though a pain had crossed his chest. 'I am led to believe that you have, on occasion, been willing to perform in ways other than singing.'

'Oh, I ...' Her face grew hot. How could he have known about that? 'It was a long time ago, and I needed the money. I know it's a horrible thing to do.'

'Shh, my beauty,' he whispered. His fingertips brushed her cheek. 'Never be ashamed of what you are. You misunderstand me. I bring this up because tonight I have some very special friends coming and I would like their visit to be memorable. I would like to propose adding this extra service into your contract of employment, Lucy.'

'You want me to sleep with people?' She could hear herself saying the words, but the scene felt unreal, as if she was only acting in a play she'd been in before. The lines were so familiar, they had become part of her, and as hard as she might try, she would never forget them. But she had sworn never to act this role again.

She tried to shake some clarity back into her head. 'That's not what I signed up for.'

His hand closed around her wrist. 'Nevertheless, my dear, that is what you will do.'

SIXTEEN

Death didn't require war, terror or other sinister forces. Some people brought it on themselves without any help. An obese diabetic in a house full of beer cans and takeaway boxes. A teenage girl with a bottle of pills and a razor blade. A cyclist with no light and no helmet. Some nights were like that. Amy washed her hands for a final time, splashed water on her face and wondered what forces were responsible for deciding who made it and who didn't. You could blame yourself if you wanted to, but most things were out of your control. The damage was done before you got there. Heavy traffic delayed you a minute too long. A person's card had been drawn. Fate had fingered them. Maybe it was natural selection: the ill, the weak and the reckless were weeded out for the good of the species.

Except that couldn't be right. She didn't consider herself ill, weak or reckless. Yet, little over a week ago, she'd been standing on the bridge. She still didn't know what had taken her onto the bridge that night or where those desperate thoughts of surrender had come from. What Amy did know was that if she hadn't had those thoughts at that moment in time, she wouldn't have met Harrison Jones.

Maybe it was true that everything happened for a reason. That's what her mother always told her. Amy had always railed against her mother's fatalistic acceptance of everything bad. Ulster was the way it was for a reason. Her brother died for a reason. Yeah sure, Amy would shout back, but whose reason? Her mum said it was God's.

Amy couldn't believe in God, but now at least she could believe in herself. She could believe in the feelings that came into her, the feathery vibrations that tickled her skin and made her pulse race. And she could believe, with one hundred per-cent certainty, that Ricky would be waiting outside her door when she got home. She slowed her gait and curled her fingers.

Turning the corner, she released her fists. Ricky was sitting on the pavement with his back against the dirty tenement wall, huddled down there with the dog piss and old juice bottles, looking for all intents and purposes like a rough sleeper. It was still early morning, and people on their way to work veered around him, seeing him as little more than an obstruction in the road. He was half asleep and didn't notice Amy coming.

Whatever menace he had carried with him when he'd come here had leaked away into the gutter.

'What the fuck, Ricky?'

His eyes opened and he looked up blearily. He was shaking with the cold. 'Where've you been?'

'Work. Where do you think?'

He shrugged, like he had to ask the question but didn't care about the answer.

'You look like a homeless tramp.'

'Why do you have to be so nasty?'

'It's not nasty, it's just the truth, and you shouldn't be here. You aren't part of my life anymore, Ricky. I don't owe you anything.'

'You used to love me, doesn't that count for anything?'

'It might have, if you hadn't been an abusive, bullying bastard.'

'Abusive?' He managed a shuddering laugh. 'You're the one who practically kneecapped me the other day.'

'You were following me. That is not okay. Go and get up off your arse and quit being so pathetic. What is it you want, exactly?'

He struggled to his feet, face creased with pain, and stood there looking like a beaten dog. The seat of his jeans was soaking. 'I just want someone to treat me like a human being. I fought for this country, I almost lost my leg for this country and now it tosses me out like a piece of shite.'

Amy sighed. Just when you were working yourself up to turn your back on him, he came out with the sob story and made you feel sorry for him. Always his favourite trick.

'What's happened?'

'I've nae cash left. Nothing in the bank, and a few coppers in my pocket. They've sent me to the fucking food bank so I can eat, like. You telling me that's a decent way to treat someone who put his life on the line for this country?'

'It's not a decent way to treat anybody. What happened to your dole?'

'A job came up, some crappy thing in an office up the West End. I went to the interview and honest to God, the boy that interviewed me was a wee soft faggot in a suit and tie. He smelled of fucking ladies' perfume. I thought, there's no chance in hell I'm going to survive working for him, so I walked out on the interview. What does the arse do? He phones the Jobcentre and tells them. So that's me punished. Cut off. It's a fucking disgrace. I should be signed off. I'm disabled.'

'You could do an office job. You could do a lot of jobs. And the other weekend, you were out on the razzle. You apparently had plenty of money then.'

'Final blow out, eh? Before the starvation rations kicked in. I don't want an office job.' He shivered and rubbed his hands up the arms of his inadequate jacket. 'I'm bloody freezing, hen, can I just come up for a wee bit and get warm.'

'No, you can't.'

He took a step toward her and extended a hand. 'You're a cold-hearted bitch.'

Amy stepped out of his reach. 'Sure, I might be that, but just to prove to you that the entire world isn't out to get you, I'm going to buy you breakfast. Come on.'

'Nah.'

'Don't be an arse. Come before I change my mind.'

He followed her meekly to the café around the corner and consumed a fried breakfast like he'd been lost in the wilderness for a week. Amy drank tea and tried to remember the man she had once agreed to marry. It was hard to bring him back now; the spectre in front of her was barely recognisable as the same person. It was even harder to bring back any feeling for him except a kind of annoyed pity.

'You need to get help,' she said. 'You're not coping.'

Ricky jabbed a finger toward her. 'And whose fault is that?'

‘You tell me.’ He stuck the last bite of sausage into his mouth and glared at her.

‘Don’t you dare try to blame me for the state you’re in.’

‘Maybe we could ... you know ... try again.’

She dragged her hand down her face. ‘Oh Ricky, for Christ’s sake.’

‘I love you, Amy.’

‘Grow a pair and get over it.’

‘That’s nice. Really fucking pleasant, you, eh? What happened to Do No Harm, Doc? You mind that one?’ His volume rose and a couple of people turned their heads.

She let a moment pass before saying quietly, ‘I’ve met someone.’

This caused some guilt because it wasn’t like that with Harrison. It wasn’t going to be like that with Harrison either, but Ricky didn’t have to know that.

‘Oh aye, who?’

‘A nice person, that’s who.’

‘How long has this been going on? Did you not think to tell me?’

‘Long enough, and why should I have thought to tell you?’

‘Because you and me belong together.’

‘Get some help, Ricky.’ She took out her purse and dropped thirty pounds onto the table. ‘Keep the change. Buy yourself some rations.’

‘I don’t want your charity, Amy.’

‘Then you shouldn’t have come begging. See you later.’

‘Can I have your new number?’

‘No.’ She left him sitting there and went home to get changed.

To avoid another potential encounter with Ricky, she changed the route of her run. She wound her way around the back of the stadium, through the housing estates and eventually to Portobello. Amy pushed herself faster as she ran along the promenade, trying not to let anything enter her mind except the music from her headphones. Toward the far end, she dropped to a walk, her lungs squeezing like bellows, and cut down onto the beach. It was a decent morning, pink clouds stretching across a pale blue sky, and milder than usual for the time of year. The water looked like an undulating aluminium surface.

She walked down to the tideline, picked up a stone and threw it into the water, watching the ripples spreading out in rings. The waves carried a melody, with what almost sounded like a human voice: a girl singing, from very far away. She closed her eyes and listened.

Lucy Merriweather only wanted to get away. All her life she’d been controlled by other people, used for her voice and her face by those whose duty it was to keep her safe. Her parents looked at her and saw pound signs. And so, she fled, but she couldn't get away. The further she tried to run, the more entangled she became.

Amy opened her eyes again. It felt like someone had breathed words in her ear or told her a story when she was half asleep and barely conscious of hearing it. She possessed a new titbit of knowledge, one that was potentially vital to the case, but she had no idea if it was true. It could be clairvoyance, or it could be imagination. Where did you draw the line between one and the other? Even after everything Harrison had shown her, she wasn't ready to trust herself.

But Harrison trusted her, and this was the job. She called him.

'Amy. You alright?'

'Can you talk?'

'I'm heading off to teach in five minutes. Something up?'

'I wanted to ask what you think about Lucy's parents. There's more to them, I'm pretty sure. They're in this up to their necks.'

'How do you know?'

'I just feel it.'

'So do I, but how do you feel it. Describe that.'

She looked up at the sky. 'I'm out for a run. I'm standing here on Portobello beach, where we know she used to come, and something just crossed my mind. Like part of a story. A feeling of oppression, or ... exploitation, maybe? And it was definitely Lucy. I could see her. It's almost like I was her for a second or two.'

'Right. Good. That's good. Well done, Amy.'

She laughed. 'I haven't done anything. Where does this come from?'

'That's the million-dollar question, isn't it? Let's just go with it for now.'

'Anyway, I want to know what she was running away from. I'm going to do some more digging around online. See what kind of background information we can pull out.'

'Don't you ever sleep?'

'Not as much as I should. I'll let you know what I find out.'

SEVENTEEN

When Elizabeth Merriweather opened her front door, an icy draught hit her in the face. Wind howled through the house and a door in another room banged shut. She froze mid-step and her pulse began to quicken.

'Simba,' she called. He was always at the front door when she came home, a whirling dervish of paws, tail and tongue, practically knocking her over. She'd been away for several hours; he should be desperate to greet her and get outside.

'Simba!'

Nothing, except the banging door and the cold air. Elizabeth scrabbled to remember whether she had been out the back this morning. Might she have left the French doors open? It was possible, but she had no memory of it. She'd been with her solicitor all morning and then with her friend Anna for lunch. She had been very naughty to drive home after three glasses of wine, and now she regretted it. Her judgement was impaired. She couldn't think clearly.

She kept her coat on and walked slowly toward the kitchen. The French doors were wide open, creaking on their hinges, the vertical blinds clattering.

'Stupid girl,' she muttered, dropping her handbag on the island. The dog could be anywhere by now. If he was still on the grounds, he would have come running when he heard the car. She'd have to go out looking for him.

'Simba!' she called out across the back lawn. She stepped outside onto the path and scanned both directions. At first, she saw no sign of him, but then something caught the corner of her eye. Just around the corner of the house, lying on the path, the tip of a tail.

'Are you playing silly beggars, daft dog?' she asked him, although she knew he wasn't. It was like the time Lucy fell off her pony and didn't get up, after so many falls where she dusted herself off and climbed back in the saddle.

This wasn't like that at all, it was worse. Simba was dead. His eyes were open and his long tongue was lolling, foam drying in a crust around his lips. Elizabeth screamed.

EIGHTEEN

The first three chapters of Aziza's thesis sat in front of him. The prose was so dense, Harrison was surprised that the half-inch stack of paper didn't crush the desk beneath it. There was no real line of thought, or perhaps there were dozens of lines, all haring off in different directions and petering out. Here and there, she had dropped in passages of elegant, vivid description of the women she had known, their hardships and their rare triumphs, but these were too short, and almost hidden in the academic bullshit.

She sat opposite him; emanating a slavish desire to please. To be fair to Gordon, Aziza was, without doubt, exquisite to look at: long black hair tied up high, kohl-rimmed eyes, a figure of rolling hills and valleys.

Harrison took off his glasses. It felt less dangerous to look at her this way. 'So, I've read it.'

'All of it?' She sounded surprised.

'All of it.'

'Thank you. I am grateful that you took me in, Dr Jones. I have let Professor Leigh-Davies down, I think.'

'Aziza, you haven't let him down. He just felt that your work is more compatible with my approach, and ...' he floundered. A momentary fear of drowning.

'Coming to Edinburgh University is a very high honour for me. If I had to leave, it would be the most awful thing for me.'

'You don't have to leave.'

This merited a flickering smile and a briefly bowed head. Through the blur, he could see the sunlight glinting off her hair.

'There's some good material here.' He took a deep breath. 'However, I'm going to be honest, these chapters need some work.'

'Yes, of course, I know ... I'm trying so hard.'

She was ashamed of herself for not getting it right on the first go, but behind that, he sensed a deeper fear. She had some form of threat hanging over her. It felt ominous, possibly deadly. He studied her for a moment, wondering how to reassure her.

'Maybe you're trying too hard. There's so much theory, it's losing its meaning.'

'So, you want me to rewrite this?' She was ready to cry now. 'These chapters have taken me six months.'

Writing up could take her years at this rate. What was Gordon trying to do to him?

'I'd like to ask you to go away and write me a one-page summary of what the thesis is about. Don't cite any references, don't refer to anyone else's work, just tell me in your own words. Keep it simple.'

'One page?'

'Just one. Remember you're writing about real people with real lives. Keep that in mind at all times, and you'll stay right.'

'Thank you, Dr Jones. I will bring that to you tomorrow.'

'Next week is soon enough. Don't rush it.' Supervision once a week would be more than enough. Given the chance, he thought she might be banging down his door every day.

She lingered for a moment, gripping her notebook across her chest. 'I would like to tell you something. I fought with my father to be allowed to come here. He paid so much money for my education all my life, and then he wanted to arrange a husband for me. An old man, almost as old as my father himself, a businessman he knows. We made a deal. If I receive my PhD, I will be free to marry whom I choose. If not, I will marry who my father picks. In my country, when you are a beautiful daughter of a wealthy man, you are a tool for his business and that's all. Here, it's better. Here, they respect you for your mind.'

'I wish that was always the case, Aziza. Thank you for telling me that.' He was surprised that she had. 'You're not leaving Edinburgh without your PhD.'

She touched the corners of her eyes with her fingertips and drew away tears of relief. 'Thank you.'

When she had gone, he stared out the window for a couple of minutes. Her words repeated in a loop. *In my country, when you are a beautiful daughter of a wealthy man, you are a tool for his business and that's all.*

Not just in her country. He thought of Lucy Merriweather. Another beautiful daughter of a wealthy man. The vision of Lucy singing for all those old men.

Possibilities began to play out in his mind and he began to wonder if this should be a police matter after all. It was time to speak to Elizabeth again.

The phone rang. It was as if she'd known. 'Elizabeth,' he answered. 'Are you alright?'

She was practically sobbing down the phone. 'Somebody has poisoned my dog.'

‘Thank you for coming so quickly,’ she said, standing aside to let him in. Her face was milk-white, her eyes red-rimmed and swollen.

He allowed himself a single second to be relieved that Simba was no longer there to greet him, before shaking her hand. He could feel she was heartbroken, but there was something else in her too. Fear, and something darker and more opaque. ‘I’m so sorry.’

‘Thank you, again.’

The aftershock of malice stirred the air. It raised the hair on the back of his neck and stirred adrenaline in his legs. ‘Have you phoned the police?’

‘I don’t think they’ll concern themselves with a dog, do you?’

He suspected she knew exactly who was responsible for this, and that she didn’t want the police involved. ‘Somebody broke into your house. They deliberately fed him poisoned meat.’

‘Yes.’ She led him to the kitchen and motioned for him to take a seat. ‘It could be my neighbours over the back. They’ve hated Simba since I got him. Complaining endlessly about him barking, suggesting he frightens their children. They threatened to report him to the council as a dangerous dog if I didn’t muzzle him when we were out walking. Absolutely ridiculous. He’s never bitten anyone.’

‘Is that honestly what you think?’

She turned away from him without answering.

‘An attempted burglary?’ he offered, in the hope of drawing something else out of her.

‘They haven’t stolen anything, as far as I can see.’

‘Maybe they wanted Simba out of the way before they come back and take what they like.’

‘I haven’t much worth stealing, really.’

Harrison allowed this to go without comment. He had always hated the false modesty of the British elite. As far as he was concerned, it was an embarrassing attempt to cover up the inequalities of the class system.

She brought out a bottle of Glenlivet. ‘Can I tempt you?’

‘No, thank you.’

He wondered what made her offer him alcohol, when she knew he had to drive back up to town. Maybe she thought it would muffle his senses. Maybe she didn’t want him picking up too much. If so, she was too late. He could almost see them, the shadowy figures of two men, one prying open the French doors and the other standing in wait for Simba, a packet of raw mince at the ready. They knew the dog, they knew the house, and they knew Elizabeth’s movements.

She smiled weakly and brought out a single crystal tumbler, dropped three ice cubes into it and poured the whisky over them, almost to the top. Her hand trembled a little, making the ice tinkle against the glass. 'My nerves are shot.'

'No wonder.' Harrison crossed the room and placed his hands on the buckled section of the doorframe. 'They used a crowbar. You'll have to replace these doors.'

'Yes, I know. I have a man coming soon.'

'You may want to consider installing an alarm system.'

'Quentin always wanted one, and I accused him of being paranoid.'

He opened the door, scanned the garden and followed the path along to where the dog still lay. She'd covered him with a wool blanket, as though to keep him warm. Harrison moved the blanket aside and touched the fur between the dog's ears. There was spittle around Simba's lips, some of it bloody. Poor beast. Whatever had done the work, it had been painful and not particularly quick.

Elizabeth lingered back and watched him, gathering her wrap closer around her chin. 'Who could do that to a helpless animal?'

Helpless wasn't the word Harrison would have used, but still a living creature that didn't deserve such an inhumane fate. He closed his eyes and let an image come. The two men were young and dressed as tradesmen. Another emotion stirred the air around the dog. It might have been regret, or even shame. He pulled the blanket back over Simba's head and stood up. 'The men who did this weren't out to get your dog, they're out to get you. They're trying to frighten you.'

'How do you know that?'

Either she doubted him or she was trying to put him off the scent. 'Elizabeth, you hired a psychic detective. If you don't want me to use my skills, then we can settle the account right now.'

'I hired you to find my daughter.'

'Which I am trying to do. These two things are connected, as I'm sure you already know. You know fine well who's behind this.'

'Of course I don't. What on earth gives you that idea?'

'The fact that you called me here today and not the police?'

She didn't reply to this.

He sighed and stepped around her, back into the warmth of the kitchen, sat down on the stool and waited for her to close the doors. 'Does Quentin have any reason to want to intimidate you?'

She stared at him with feigned incredulity, so conditioned to defending her husband that she couldn't acknowledge the blatant evidence against him. 'Are you suggesting Quentin did this?'

'He didn't do it personally, but he paid somebody else to. You've already told me the man was abusive, there's no need to protect him.'

'He might have slapped me a few times, but he loves dogs. He would never deliberately hurt Simba.'

'You haven't answered my question.'

'Quentin always wants to intimidate people. That's how he's made his money. Bribery and intimidation. He now wants a divorce and wants me to put the house on the market to free up the capital. It must mean he's in some kind of financial difficulty. He won't hesitate to bully me until I agree, but he wouldn't do this. Will you please tell me what this possibly has to do with Lucy?'

'I feel it. I can't see the details yet.'

'Oh, for heaven's sake.' She gave a nervous, intentionally dismissive sort of laugh. 'Are you any further forward in locating her?'

'I think so. I'm fairly confident that she's not in Edinburgh.'

'Oh good, so you've established that there is one city in the world where she isn't.' Elizabeth stood impatiently and stared away from him, arms crossed and hands running along her upper arms. 'Just tell me where she is.'

'I can't. I'm getting closer, but I don't know exactly.'

‘When will you know?’ Her voice assumed an imperious tone.

‘Maybe when you start giving me the information I need.’

‘Like what?’

‘Like, for example, why Lucy ran away? Why she really ran away. You made her sing for people, didn’t you? People he wanted to influence?’

Elizabeth sat and rested her elbows on the marble worktop, hands together in a praying gesture. ‘At first, we merely encouraged her to sing for guests, some of whom were Quentin’s business contacts. Her voice was so enchanting, Quentin thought it softened men up and made negotiations easier. I have to admit, I saw it work many times. I thought it was a good idea ... at first.’

‘But Lucy didn’t want to do it.’

‘She didn’t mind when she was younger. She was a bit of a show-off that way, you know? But later, it changed. Quentin made her do it even when she refused, and it all got rather nasty.’

‘Did you try to stop this at any point?’

‘Of course I did,’ she snapped, although this was only a half-truth. The guilt radiating from her told the rest of the story. ‘You don’t know Quentin. You don’t know what he’s like.’

Her defensive shell was cracking now. Harrison sat back and softened his tone. 'You can tell me about him.'

'He's as manipulative as they come. He makes you feel powerless. He's quite dangerous, in his own way. You may accuse me of being complicit in my daughter's abuse, and perhaps you're right, but I was frightened of him.'

'You were frightened he would hurt you?'

'Hurt me, yes. Or worse, leave me with nothing. I should have left him. I should have taken Lucy and disappeared, but I couldn't.' She closed her eyes and pressed her fingertips into them. 'You hate them, you're afraid of them, and you want them at the same time. It's an impossible thing to explain.'

'You don't have to.'

'Because you can see into my head and you already know I'm a weak-willed and pathetic excuse of a woman.'

'That's exactly what he wants you to believe. Can I ask whether your husband ever made Lucy sing for Kostas Gianopoulos?'

'Kostas!' She laughed sharply. 'Dear God, what has he got to do with any of this? He's a business associate of Quentin's. An associate, that's all. They have developed some properties together, that sort of thing.' The fear she had been giving off became tempered by jealousy. 'He and I were ... friends. For a while.'

Harrison held her gaze. 'Friends?'

Her cheeks reddened and she turned away. 'We had an affair. My husband slept with any female who was willing to lie down for him, so please don't judge me.'

'I'm not judging you.'

She softened. 'It was off and on for a couple of years. He and Quentin were working on some projects together and he came to Edinburgh most months.'

'When was this?'

'It started about five years ago, maybe?' She stared out of the window, ghostly in the fading light. 'I was in love with him. At one point I thought I might leave Quentin for him.'

'What happened?'

'He's a married man, and his loyalty to his wife won out. He broke it off in the end.'

Harrison had been pondering the wisdom of disclosing what Nessa Walker had said about Lucy being in Greece. At this moment it would bring Elizabeth more pain, but even so, she was his client. She had not hired him to hide her daughter's whereabouts.

'Elizabeth, I believe Lucy may be in Greece with Kostas now.'

Elizabeth's shoulders stooped and her ramrod spine subsided into itself. Then she took a deep breath and straightened herself. 'She may be in Greece, but she won't be with him. She wouldn't be. He's older than I am.'

'Do you really believe that would stop either one of them?'

'No.' Elizabeth swallowed the remainder of her whisky and closed her eyes. A shudder went through her body. 'How do you know?'

'Lucy's friend Tim Cartwright.'

'You've spoken to Tim?'

'No, but I've spoken to someone who heard from him recently. At the moment, we don't know where Tim is either.'

'Let me tell you about Tim. He's a slimy, money-grubbing addict masquerading as a do-gooder. It wouldn't surprise me if he was lying.'

'You met him, then?'

'Yes. The last time I saw her, she was with him. Goodness knows what she saw in him.'

'And you picked all that up from one meeting?'

'It was written all over him. I tried to tell her. Why does Tim think Lucy has gone to Greece?'

'They went together, apparently, to work in a refugee project in Athens, but they split up a couple of months ago.'

'But she's still there?'

'I can't say absolutely, but I think so.'

'Is she safe?'

'I don't know that either. Is there a reason she wouldn't be safe with Kostas?'

'I don't believe Kostas would harm her, but do you even know for sure if she's still with him?'

'No, I don't.'

She gripped the edge of the worktop, her knuckles whitening. 'Then bloody well go there and find out.'

'You want me to go to Greece. On your bill.'

'If that's where Lucy is, then I want you to go there and bring her back for me.'

'And if she doesn't want to come?'

'Then make her!'

'I can't do that, Elizabeth.'

She glared at him, then turned away abruptly and began to cry. 'I'm sorry, Harrison. I know you can't. I don't know what's happened to my life.'

He stood back and tried to defend himself against the waves of emotion coming from her. 'I'll do my best.'

She mopped her eyes with a handkerchief. 'Another thing. I'd like you to get close to my husband and see if you can figure out what he knows about my dog, or anything else.' She wrote an address on a sticky note. 'This is his office. He often leaves there around six and walks to the Guildford Arms.'

He took the note. 'Okay.'

She wouldn't look at him. 'I'd like you to go now, please.'

'Keep yourself safe, Elizabeth.'

'I'm not afraid of him anymore, you know,' she said.

She was lying.

It had started to sleet by the time Harrison found his way to the office of Merriweather Holdings, a converted Georgian house on a cobbled New Town side-street. He waited across the road, out of the circles of orange light cast down by the lamps, watching a figure moving around an illuminated room on the second floor. At a quarter past six, the light went out. Harrison pulled his hat down over his ears and drove his hands deep into the pockets of his coat. He waited close to five minutes, wondering how long it took a person to come down the stairs, before the shiny black door opened and the man stepped out. He pulled the door hard behind him, tested it, tightened his scarf and set off to the right. Quentin Merriweather carried his excess weight like an emperor's cloak, sweeping everyone out of his way as he stormed along the street.

Harrison followed as closely as he dared for a few seconds, trying to catch Quentin's vibe without attracting his attention. He felt the same writhing anger he'd perceived at Elizabeth's house, and also the kind of worry that wakes you up at night and squeezes the breath out of your lungs.

At the end of the block, he pulled a phone out of his pocket and stared at the little glowing screen as he stepped out into the traffic, ignoring the cars that beeped at him as they rushed down the hill. Harrison waited at the crossing light, wondering if Quentin was suicidal or just blindly audacious.

The light changed and he hurried to catch up with the big man. The sleet, driven hard by the wind, stung his face, but for once he was grateful for the foul weather. Quentin was hell-bent on the pub and there was little chance of him lifting his eyes or slowing his pace in this evil blast. He walked quickly and his footsteps were heavy. The heels of his leather brogues made a watery scrape on the pavement.

Quentin went into the Guildford Arms, an elegant old Edinburgh pub that retained its faded, worn-velvet Victorian grandeur. It drew a boisterous crowd of tourists, after-hours businessmen and hardened drinkers, the latter two often being one and the same. Harrison lingered outside, preparing himself for what would hit him the minute he went through the door.

If he had to describe the blended colour of all these well-dressed people's emotions, it was the shade of congealed blood: frustration and loneliness shot through with rage. It felt like the onslaught of a violent stomach flu, and knowing it was coming never made it any easier. He would have to glean what he could quickly and leave. He took a deep breath and focused on Quentin's broad back, in front of him at the bar. Quentin was fixated only on shouldering other men out of the way so he could quench his thirst.

Harrison waited behind him, allowing the crowd to press them closer together, until the damp black wool of his coat brushed the far more expensive camel wool that Quentin wore. It was risky and possibly dangerous getting this close to the man, but in here there was no other option.

Where is Lucy, Harrison thought. He asked it over and over, aiming it like the muzzle of a gun at the back of Quentin's head. Where is Lucy? What have you done to her? You know where she is. Think about her. Remember her. *Remember your daughter.*

NINETEEN

She was the most perfect peach in the orchard: a taut, warm film of skin just thick enough to contain all that perfect, honeyed sweetness. You wanted to pick her from the branch, taste her, let her juices drip down your chin and slowly consumer her. From a young age, she had just enough curve in all the right places, topped off by a glorious, shimmering tumble of blonde hair that could turn any man's eye. At twelve, she was still a child, totally unaware of her sexuality. By fourteen, she had learned how to use it.

So had he. On summer days, the North Berwick garden could be a paradise. It was the best place to broker the deals he most wanted, worth the investment of wine and meat. In winter, a fire-warmed drawing-room and brandy. Food and alcohol opened negotiations, but it was Lucy who clinched them. He brought her down to sing for directors, CEOs, provosts, heads of planning departments and government ministers, and when she sang, they were no better than sailors drawn onto the rocks. Fools of men. All men were fools when they put their balls in the driver's seat, and all the fancy tailoring and private education in the world would never change that. Quentin Merriweather understood this absolutely.

What he had failed to anticipate was where it would lead. There were things he never imagined he would do for money before he did them.

It was a foul night and he'd had a bloody rotten day, most of it spent on the phone or Skype, trying to pin down people who he knew were avoiding him. Elizabeth was clearly not going to play ball either. She could fight as dirty as he could, no doubt about that. Sometimes he had to remind himself not to underestimate her. Now was one of those times.

He bought himself a large brandy and sat alone on a red velvet bench. Charlie Prescott and Gus Rutherford were usually here by six: brothers in arms, boisterous easy company. They could talk about cars and rugby and go home drunk enough to forget everything else. Going home sober wasn't an option.

Somehow, his life had become twisted, like a gold chain thrown into the bottom of a jewellery box. Every year, it got more difficult to distinguish legitimate business from dirty dealing. These days everything felt grubby, but he had to remind himself that this wasn't his fault. The older he got, the better he understood that the whole damn show was rotten, and if you didn't play the game, you would be chewed up and spat out. Investments had consequences he never reckoned on when he was young and starting out: bankrolling an engineering project could produce a weapon and that weapon could destroy a town. An oil pipeline could destroy an ecosystem. An outsourced factory was a sweatshop, the procurement of migrant labour was the slave trade by another name. His money, his deals, had led to all of these things. You could only pretend not to be aware for so long, and you either accepted it or you cut your losses and got out.

Brandy on his tongue brought his mind back to Lucy. He missed her more than he cared to admit to himself, and in ways that shamed him deeply. He missed the smell of her, the glow of her skin. The name Lucy came from the Latin *lux*, for light. He missed the light she brought to his eyes. He missed the way he felt when she touched him. He missed her voice. That *voice.* She destroyed men when she sang, like the Sirens of ancient mythology.

There were moments when he wished for her return, as any father would, and when he wished that he was any father. Secretly, with the brandy in him, he wished that many things had not happened.

But they had, and it would be disastrous for him if Lucy ever did come back and open her mouth. That could not be allowed to happen. His insides twisted and pain spread from the centre of his chest out to his arms. You make your own destiny, he thought, and if this thing gave him a heart attack, maybe it was what he deserved. It might be better than the alternative.

He stared into his glass and waited for peace that would never come. After a moment he looked up and searched the crowd for friends. He couldn't see anybody he knew, which was strange because he knew a great many people in this city. But lately, friends had been thin on the ground. People had been avoiding him since his split from Elizabeth had become public. It wasn't beyond possibility that the bitch was putting out malicious rumours so that she could blackmail him. Some of the darker gossip had whispered its pernicious way back to his ears. Toxic knowledge had leaked out, about the fights they had had and the things he had done in the heat of the moment. If she wanted to tell people he slapped her around, so be it. But if she thought she could hang him up by telling half-truths about Lucy, or about the nature of some of his business affairs, steps would have to be taken.

Steps had been taken. The call had come around mid-morning to let him know that the job was done. The brute of a dog was dead, and it would put the fear of God into the bitch. Elizabeth knew enough to understand that silence was her only protection.

He returned to the bar and shouted for another brandy. A hand landed on his back and a voice said in a strange, mid-Atlantic accent, 'Hi Bobby.'

Quentin turned abruptly to face a tall intellectual type with glasses and a beard. 'You've got the wrong man.'

The stranger stood far closer than was necessary. 'Oh, I'm so sorry.' He patted Quentin's arm, but his hand stayed two or three seconds too long. His eye contact was intense. A strange electricity passed between them and Quentin took a step back. Damn poofs felt at liberty to come onto you wherever they liked now. Scotland had become too liberal for its own good.

'You might be better off down Elm Row, mate. The bars are more your kind of scene down there, if you get my meaning.'

'Thanks for the tip.' The tall man drifted away without ordering a drink.

Quentin paid for his brandy and drank it at the bar. There wasn't any point in going back to the booth. It was looking like Charlie and Gus had stood him up again.

TWENTY

Amy squeezed into a little table in the back corner of her favourite café on Leith Walk, making sure there was no chance that anyone could peer over her shoulder at her screen. Nerves jigged in her stomach as she typed the name Kostas Gianopoulos into Google, as if a simple web-search could make her a target. Maybe it could, she thought, glancing up to check what was going on around her.

The web presented her with several men bearing the name of Kostas Gianopoulos, and within a few clicks, it became obvious which one was her target. In between images of a twenty-something student and an overweight baldy with bad glasses, she found a man who looked like he was next in line for the role of James Bond. He had thick wavy hair, a shadow of stubble over a square jaw, and wore a tight designer suit that showed off a well-trained physique. Only a rich man could look that good in his fifties. Photographed at what looked like some high-brow social function, he stood hand in hand with an equally stunning black-haired woman. Following the links, she noted down everything that seemed important.

He was, as Nessa Walker indicated, best known for building a string of hotels dotted around the resort areas of the Greek and Turkish Aegean. He was also a noted philanthropist, celebrated for donating significant quantities of his own money to a variety of causes, including the homeless, victims of sexual abuse and refugees. Amy underlined this twice.

The woman beside him was his wife, Kaliope Maris, who turned out to be a journalist with an international reputation. As a young woman, she had covered fashion for the New York Times and then Paris Match before marrying Kostas and going freelance.

There was nothing immediately sinister about Gianopoulos or his wife, and in fact, they seemed to be respected and admired wherever they went. She wondered about the wife's part in all of this, how Kostas was keeping his affair with Lucy secret, and where Lucy was living if not with Kostas. Amy recognised the faint, high-pitched whine in her ears as her personal incoming alert. She sipped her coffee, thinking about where to look next. Rubbing sweaty palms on her jeans, she typed in Kostas Gianopoulos Edinburgh.

LEITH HOTEL PLAN VICTIM OF BREXIT, announced a small article from the Edinburgh Evening News, dated from early August. Amy held her breath and read:

Plans for a 50-room boutique hotel in Leith have been mothballed. The hotel, which was to have been part of the ongoing regeneration of the Western Harbour area, has been put on ice. Capital financier Quentin Merriweather and his partner, Greek hotel magnate Kostas Gianopoulos, have withdrawn their planning application, citing Brexit uncertainty. Merriweather, a significant shareholder in Gianopoulos's Aegean Resort Group, denied a rumoured professional split between the two men. He said, 'We have worked together seamlessly, across international boundaries, for a decade. This project would have delivered jobs and stimulated tourism in the area. It's yet another example of how the Great British public have shot themselves in the foot with this idiotic referendum.'

So Kostas and Quentin were still in touch with each other, or had been as recently as August. This meant either that Quentin knew Lucy was in Greece, or Kostas hadn't told him. It might explain the suggestion of a split between them. Amy filled the page in her notebook with questions and turned over a fresh sheet.

She searched *Tim Cartwright Greece.* Halfway down the page she found a tiny headline in the Coventry Telegraph: FEARS FOR LOCAL MAN MISSING IN GREECE.

Local Mum, Louise Cartwright, 52, has asked for information to help trace her son Tim Cartwright, a promising young singer who was last known to be working in Athens. Louise, of Kingston Road, told our reporter that the twenty-five-year-old has not been in touch since September 12th. She said, 'Tim seemed to be in a very low place last time I spoke to him. He had broken up with a girl he was seeing and didn't know what he was going to do next. We don't talk every week, but this is the longest he's ever gone without being in touch. I worry that he's done himself a mischief.' Louise has been in touch with Greek authorities, but hopes anyone with information on Tim's whereabouts will get in touch.

'Christ,' Amy muttered. It was a big step forward, although missing so much essential information. The article didn't name Lucy, for a start. It didn't mention a father and only hinted that Tim's relationship with his mother was not as close as it might have been. There was also an indication that Tim might be capable of harming himself, which didn't surprise Amy in the least. There was no mention of a response from the

Greek police, but Amy guessed that this case would not top their list of priorities.

She looked for Kingston Road, Coventry, and up popped an image of a red-brick terrace almost identical to the one she had grown up on in Belfast. So, a working-class boy without a fat wad of family cash to fall back on. He wouldn't have the funds to travel indefinitely, without at least earning a little income in some way. Surely busking couldn't cut it forever. Likewise, poor Louise wouldn't necessarily be able to fly out to Greece to search for him.

The distant klaxons were louder now, and goosebumps appeared along her arms. When she blinked, she got a fleeting impression of rippled, undulating water. She closed her eyes and placed her hands on the table, the way Harrison sometimes did, trying to tune out the café noise and listen to the things that were unspoken.

For a minute, she could hear young voices around her, conversations about parties and jobs and relationships, but then something else came, very faintly, from somewhere far away. Footsteps running, slapping on wet tarmac, and laboured breathing. A sense of panic. Someone in pursuit, bearing down, shouting in a language Amy couldn't understand. And then, the end of the road: the tarmac falling away into black water.

She opened her eyes, the voice still shouting in her ears. Her t-shirt was damp under the arms and she felt twitchy. Sometimes the past and the future crowded out the present so effectively that she began to question which of these was real. She looked around the café and tried to return herself to the present. It was getting late and she wanted to go home, but she knew from experience that she would not be able to settle for hours. She picked up her phone.

'I've found some more stuff,' she said when Harrison answered.

'So have I,' he replied. 'Do you want to come over?'

She could hear street noises behind him. 'Where are you?'

'Almost home.'

'I'll hop on the bus,' she said, and pulled on her coat.

Harrison had cleared the clutter from his kitchen table and replaced it with paper from a heavy roll. He tore off a long piece and picked up a black marker. 'What do we know and what do we only think we know?'

Amy didn't want to make a fool of herself by jumping in with assumptions. He was playing the professor again, asking her to demonstrate some level of intelligence that she wasn't convinced she had. At eighteen she had talked herself out of going to university because she didn't believe she would cut it there, among the middle-class people and their fancy words. From somewhere far away, she could hear her dad's tenacious ghost asking, *What do you need with a degree, wee girl? Who do you think you are, anyway?*

Who did she think she was? All this week, she'd been questioning the wisdom of her involvement in this case, and her friendship with Harrison. Was friendship even the right word?

It is, and stop worrying about it, said Harrison's voice in her head.

She met his eyes and he gave her a strange smile, cheeks flushing. He was embarrassed at being caught in the act. Amy cleared her throat and looked down at the paper again. 'Here's what I found out about Kostas.'

Harrison scribbled out the details that she recounted. Quickly, the blank sheet filled with names and notes, circles and connecting lines. It was a web of twisted relationships and hidden intentions.

'Good research,' he said.

'Uh huh, so there's more. Tim Cartwright's mother reported him missing six weeks ago. She last heard from him on the twelfth of September.'

'Which is the same date he emailed Nessa.'

'Yeah. Harrison, I had one of my premonitions, and I saw something. Somebody was being chased, and then he came to the end of a pier or something, and in front of him, there was just water.'

'You think it was Tim?'

'I don't know. Maybe.'

'You think something's happened to him?'

'Usually I see the future, not the past.'

Harrison sat down. 'Shit.'

'Yeah. Shit. I feel like I should send him a private message or something, and let him know, for all the good it would do. Nobody ever believes me anyway.'

'I believe you.'

Amy took a deep breath. 'Thank you, but you're not the one being hunted down.'

'Did you find him on Facebook?'

'Yeah, but I can't see past his privacy settings.'

'Okay, well let's think about that while I tell you about Quentin Merriweather. I'm pretty sure he's a psychopath, and he has money worries, bad enough to try to bully Elizabeth out of the house.'

'By having her dog killed.'

'Yes. Let's hope it's only the dog. He doesn't appear to know where Lucy is, but he's afraid of her coming back.'

'Afraid enough to hurt her?'

‘Possibly. The way he thought about Lucy was sexual.’

‘God.’ Amy paused to let this sink in, and realised that she wasn’t particularly surprised. ‘Filthy bastard. Did he do anything, or did he just fill his sick mind with it?’

‘I don’t know what he’s done, but he’s thought about plenty. He used her when he was negotiating deals. He brought her out to sing and flirt like a fucking show pony.’

She glanced at him, unused to hearing him swear. ‘Can’t we just phone the cops and get the man locked up now?’

‘Not without hard evidence. What we know isn’t provable by any means that the justice system recognises.’

Amy considered his words. ‘How confident are you, Harrison?’

‘About what?’

‘About what you do. Your abilities.’

‘I’ve learned to be confident. It’s taken most of my life. I’ve experimented a lot, and I’ve met people who have taught me things.’

‘Like who?’

‘Like…my friend Tomas in Bolivia, he was like me. There’s a mountain right at the centre of the city of Potosí, called *Cerro Rico*. Once upon a time, it was the largest silver mine in the world. It’s also known as the mountain that eats men, because of the numbers of people who have died there over the centuries. Tomas had psychic abilities. They used him to find missing miners when there were collapses. He taught me how to focus and listen, and he taught me how to journey.'

'Journey?'

'You put yourself into a kind of a trance. You can travel to other places or into the world of the spirits.'

'You talk to the dead?'

'Spirits. Death is just our construct'

Amy breathed out. 'Did you know you're batshit crazy?'

'It's been said before. Do you want me to show you?'

'Show me what?'

A flicker of a smile crossed his face. 'Come on.'

Amy followed him to the far end of the corridor, to a room she hadn't seen into before. It was just a small, square bedroom, except that there was no bed in it. There was no furniture at all, only dark blue walls, a plush red rug covering the bare floorboards, and a lot of candles. The only other contents of the room were several large plant pots sprouting some kind of herb.

Harrison touched one of the bright green leaves. 'This is *Salvia divinorum*. It's a hallucinogen, sometimes called Seer's Sage. Let's just say it helps me on my way.'

'So, it's a drug? You get high and see things that aren't real?'

'Who says they aren't real?'

'They're hallucinations.'

'I saw you, didn't I? I knew where to find you.'

'The drug showed you where to find me. Right. Are you addicted to this stuff?'

'No,' he replied, but didn't addicts always say no? It was unnatural enough to trust the things he said without knowing that his so-called vision came from a narcotic plant. And yet, he did see her.

'Is it even legal?'

'Not anymore.'

'Do you take other stuff?'

'I've tried a few things,' he said vaguely.

'What things,' she asked, although she wasn't sure she really wanted to know.

'Oh, just … the usual. Acid. Mushrooms. Coca leaves. Ayahuasca, which was crazy. Salvia isn't for everyone, but I find it works best for me.'

'It works best for you, does it?' Outside, the bare fronds of a willow whipped like snakes. 'Jesus, Harrison.' She turned briskly away from him, went back to the kitchen and filled the kettle.

'If we're done, I'm going to make myself a cup of tea and then get a taxi. Is that alright?'

'I can take you home.'

'Honestly, a taxi is fine.

'What's up?'

'Nothing.' She opened his cupboards, took down a mug and searched through boxes of green teas, chai and herbals. 'You have any black tea, or is that too normal for you?'

He stepped up beside her and took the lid off a metal tin beside the microwave. 'Here. You know you might as well say it, Amy.'

She took out a teabag and dropped it into the mug. 'Say what?' It felt like the beginning of their first argument. Deflecting a fight with denial would never work with Harrison; he would always have an unfair disadvantage. She couldn't bring herself to speak, so he stepped in.

'You're disappointed in me. You think I might be a bit of a charlatan after all.'

'The word I was thinking of was quack, but charlatan works. I even know what it means.'

He pushed up his glasses and pressed his fingers into his eyes. 'Yeah, well, I've thought it often enough. I would give this all up in a heartbeat. All I know is that the Salvia helps me make something useful out of it.'

'If I smoke that plant, what will I see?'

Surprise crossed his face. 'I chew it. You *can* smoke the leaves or the extract, but I wouldn't recommend it. I don't know what you'll see.'

'But what's it like?' she pressed.

'You dissociate, your senses work differently. You might go into surreal places or really dark places. You might feel like you're leaving your body. You can feel a bit sick afterwards.'

Amy put down the mug and switched the kettle off. 'Can I try it? I want to see where you go.'

'That's not how it works. Everyone's trip is their own. I'm not sure it's a good idea, Amy. Not after…'

'Not after I almost jumped off a bridge?' She faced him defiantly. Caroline had talked her through a lot of history she never wanted to remember, but this was different. She would have no control over where she went or what she saw. The plant could take her back to Afghanistan. It could take her home. It could take her into another horrific future that she had no power to prevent. She summoned her resolve. She'd gone unarmed into worse places than the depths of her own mind. 'I want to do it.'

Harrison paused before sighing deeply and whispering, 'Okay.' He led her back to the little room. 'It can be scary, but I promise I'll be with you the whole time.'

She bent down and sniffed the plants. 'You'll stay with me?'

'I'll be right here. I won't let you fly away, I promise.'

'Tell me what to do.'

'Take off your shoes and sit down on the rug.'

Amy took off her boots and sat down, watching as he closed the wooden blinds, blocking out the hammering storm, replacing it with yellow candlelight.

He picked a handful of leaves and sat beside her. 'Lie down. Breathe in.'

She breathed in, filling her lungs slowly as she counted to ten.

'I want you to think about being safe. You're in a place where nothing can hurt you. Breathe out. Let your body relax down into the floor.' His voice became low and toneless. 'Now, take the leaves, one at a time. Chew them as long as you can but try not to swallow them.'

He pressed a handful of the leaves into her hand. She raised one to her lips, nibbled the tip of it. It was bitter but earthy, like wet foliage after a rain. She chewed a second leaf and then a third, holding the wad in her mouth like tobacco. The juices ran down her throat. The taste grew more bitter, but she forced herself to keep chewing the fibrous leaves.

Harrison spoke slowly, a whisper barely breaking into voice. 'Imagine yourself walking. You're following a path through a forest. The trees are thick around you, and you can't see what's on the other side of them. Just keep walking. Let the path take you wherever it goes.'

She could see the winter-bare branches, a red-gold light shining through them.

This whole performance felt silly and she began to laugh. The more she tried to stifle it, the funnier it became and her body shook with laughter. Then it stopped and she lay still again, returning to the forest. A drum played in the distance. There was a march. She could hear the flutes, playing the same old cheery tunes that heralded violence and death. The notes bit her face and arms like horseflies, and she tried to brush them off but couldn't.

Then came the sound of breaking glass, except it seemed to be within her, like someone inside her body was throwing stones and shattering her ribcage. She saw fragments exploding out of her chest in slow motion. It didn't hurt, but she didn't have to listen to this shit anymore.

She began to run. The drums urged her on, half a beat ahead of her footsteps, making her faster. The trees were gone and she was running along her street. She was on the road and there were people watching as if it was a race, except that she was the only runner. There was Ricky, standing on the pavement, waving his arms and shouting.

She couldn't tell if he was shouting her over or cheering her on, but she ran past him. She ran past all the buildings and then the tarmac disappeared and she was running on dirt. Hard-packed, sandy earth. Barren, rocky hills rose steeply on both sides. The valley narrowed. A thin line of darker, damp earth snaked along it but there was no water in the stream. Everything was dry, scorched by sun and by human hand. She knew this place. It was dangerous to be here, at the bottom of this draw with the hillsides above her. Taliban hid among those rocks. They had caves up there, caches of weapons, the perfect view down to anyone moving along the bottom. In her peripheral vision she saw them sliding over the rocks like shadows. She ran faster, expecting the crack of rifle fire to echo out above her.

But it didn't come. Instead, other runners appeared. They gathered alongside her, mostly men but also a few women. She saw her mates, Sonny Wilson, Cameron Brown and Ryan McGann. But you're dead, she thought. She saw others she'd only known for a few hours or minutes. She knew each of their faces because she had knelt beside them. She had held them as they screamed in pain and died. But here they were in all their glory, running on limbs that had been reduced to shreds of flesh and exposed, broken bone. She could taste their blood as it splattered her skin.

Some overtook her, some stayed behind. They were in formation, running as a single troop, and she was in the middle, safe inside the pack. Nobody was armed. They didn't speak but it felt like they were leading her somewhere. She trusted them, and followed.

The dry, scrubby draw widened out and the landscape became greener. Grassy fields spread to her right and left, bounded by hedgerows. She was running through a field of ripening, waist-high barley, which shimmered and parted in front of her as the force of her movement had created a whirlwind. She held her arms out wide, hands skimming along the barley heads, and as she moved, more people rose from the ground. She could see them dusting themselves off and looking around, briefly confused. Then they too began to run with her.

Abruptly, she came to the edge of the land and stopped dead. In front of her was black water, and the sun had disappeared. It was night. All of the dead people stood behind her, gathered in a tightly-packed crowd. They were urging her on, into the water, but they were not coming with her. She looked down and saw only the opaque depths.

A large form began to rise up to the surface. It was a man, floating slowly up from below, his eyes wide open and staring at her through the water. His face was familiar, but she couldn't place him. He reached up toward her and spoke, but his voice was distorted by water and she couldn't understand him. His hand reached out of the water and closed around hers, and his touch was ice cold. She resisted. He was going to pull her under, and all of those people who she thought were here to protect her were just going to watch. Amy dragged herself backwards, but his fingers were clamped around her wrist. Her feet slipped toward the edge. She struggled, but her limbs felt weak. The ghosts behind her began to move toward her. They were going to push her in. She opened her mouth to scream but no sound came out.

The man raised his face from the water and shouted, 'I have to tell you! Listen to me! Please!'

They were pulling against each other, evenly weighted, deadlocked. She called for the ghosts over her shoulder. They stood close but didn't help. She screamed again, as her feet slipped off the edge and she plunged down into the water.

Hands closed on her shoulders and someone said her name. 'Amy. Come back now. I've got you. It's okay, come back.'

She felt herself fall backwards. The jolt of the impact went through her body and she opened her eyes. Harrison was sitting at her head, one hand on each of her shoulders, peering down at her.

'Fuck.' She dragged in a breath, sat up quickly and whirled around to face him. Behind him, she could still almost see the crowd of people she'd gathered. The smell of the sea was in her nose and her wrist throbbed where the man in the water had gripped it. She rubbed her hands on her jumper, surprised to find it completely dry.

'You're back,' Harrison said. His hand was resting between her shoulders and she could feel its warmth through her clothes.

She was caught between two worlds now, and could still hear the man calling up from the inky water, as well as a faint echo of her cry. 'Did I scream?'

'You shouted *help me.*'

'Shit.' She was out of breath and sweating like she had run for miles. The hair around her forehead was damp and her face was pulsing with heat. He offered her an empty cup and she spat the bitter wad of chewed leaves into it, then shuddered and wrapped her arms around her knees. A wave of nausea came and she breathed it down.

'It's normal to feel a bit sick.' He kept his hand on her back, reassuring her that this room was the reality. His brown eyes were full of worry and questions, and she could tell that, at least this one time, he wasn't reading her at all. She had wondered if he might be able to see what she was seeing, but evidently not.

'I'll get you some water,' he said, and took the cup away. 'Just stay there and take a minute.' When he came back, he turned on the overhead light and the room shifted back into a plain, square box. The images began to fade, although there was still a sensation of someone pulling at her, trying to drag her into the water.

She drank, grateful to rinse the taste of the Salvia out of her mouth. 'I may puke.'

'You need a bucket?'

She attempted a laugh, but it came out as a wheezy gasp. 'No, but … Jesus, that was horrible, Harri.'

'Are you alright?'

'I don't know.'

He stood up, held out his hand and helped her to her feet. 'Hold on to me if you're dizzy.'

She steadied herself on his arm for a couple of seconds. 'I'll take that cup of tea now.'

'I'll make you something to eat. It brings you back to earth.'

She followed him back to the kitchen and sat while he made tea and toast. He brought out butter, jam and cheese and set them all out in front of her. As the smell of toasting bread reached her, the walls became flat again and the last echoes of that other world faded. Her face still stung and she felt it with her fingertips. 'I feel like I've got bugs crawling on my skin.'

'Yeah, that's normal.'

'You have a very strange definition of normal. Harri, why are you doing all of this for me?'

'Because you asked me to, remember?'

'You could've said no. I mean, you don't take people into your life very easily, do you?'

'No.' He looked up and took a breath. 'I don't.'

'So, why me?'

'Because you're just like I was, and I needed someone to help me too.' He smiled with his eyes before turning his attention back to the food. Maybe it was the weird distorting effect of the Salvia leaves, but he looked different tonight. Less bookish and awkward, more…

She cut the thought short, hoping he hadn't read her mind. There was no privacy in the company of Harrison Jones.

He piled the slices of toast on a plate and she ate as if she hadn't eaten all day. Her muscles felt like jelly.

'I saw people,' she said, after five or six large bites.

'You don't have to tell me.'

'I want to. I saw … the people I've lost. The ones I haven't been able to save. They were all dead, but they were running with me and they were protecting me. It was …' She shook her head because she didn't know the word. 'It was kind of beautiful.'

Now that the dizziness had subsided, a strange power flowed through her. Those spirits had come to her side to keep her safe. They weren't angry, they weren't lost or damned, they were grateful. Even though she hadn't been able to keep them alive, they were grateful that she had tried. They hadn't spoken any words at all, but she knew they wanted to return the favour. They wanted to serve her. It was humbling, and it was also a thrill.

'But then ... he tried to pull me into the water, and I got scared.'

'Who tried to pull you into the water?'

'A man. He was in the water, and ... he wanted me to come with him. I've seen him before, I'm sure.' Then it dawned on her. She knew exactly who he was. 'Harri, I think it was Tim Cartwright.'

He put down his mug and combed his fingers through his beard. 'Right ... okay.'

'He was trying to take me to her.'

'He was in the water?'

'Yeah. I want to go back,' she said. 'Tim was trying to show me where Lucy is. I know he was.'

Harrison considered her words with a mouthful of tea. If he had thoughts about what she'd seen, he wasn't giving them away. 'Not tonight.'

'I don't want to lose it.'

He sighed. 'You've seen enough for one night. Besides, you don't always get to control where you go. Tell me what you remember about where he was.'

She closed her eyes and tried to focus on the details. 'It was dark, I didn't see very much. It was like ... a pier, or a quay. It just came out of nowhere. There were lights in the distance, out on the water.' Some possible pieces clicked into place. 'I think Lucy might be on a boat.'

'What makes you think that?'

'I had a dream a few days ago that I was sneaking onto a boat like some kind of commando. It was a yacht, a properly enormous floating palace. Maybe I was there to rescue her. I should have told you before, but I didn't think anything of it. I didn't think it was connected.'

'Could you tell where you were?'

'Some Mediterranean port. Not a big place.'

'Somewhere in Greece?'

'Possibly. I've never been there, I wouldn't know.'

'Would you recognise it if you saw a picture?'

'I'm not sure, Harri. I mean you can't just go chasing off somewhere you've seen in a dream, can you?'

‘Why not?’

Sometimes his questions were so naive that they threatened to undermine every assumption she’d ever made about anything at all. It was like he’d never learned the rules. Or more likely, he had decided to rewrite them.

TWENTY-ONE

Later on, Amy called herself a taxi and left Harrison alone with a tumbler of whisky and his doubts. He hadn't expected her to have such a powerful vision her first time. It indicated ability far beyond what he'd first seen in her, and he worried about unleashing it further. It would change her life, and not necessarily for the better. There were so many things he hadn't told her. How you could never really be alone in your head again. And how at the same time, you could never really be open with anyone. How you had to unlearn everything you had been taught about science, about life and death, about reality. How easy it was to lose touch with yourself because you could no longer tell your own emotions from everyone else's.

How ordinary relationships were impossible. These days, he rarely allowed himself to think about his years with Sophie, who had given him more than half a decade of her young life, believing him to be the person she would grow old with. He had allowed himself to believe that too, but to stay the course, love needed privacy. It required tactful dishonesty, and Harrison was incapable of giving those things. That lesson had proved exquisitely painful, for both of them.

He had to talk to Amy and make her understand these things before he let her chew the Salvia leaves again.

But he was thinking too much and losing valuable time. It seemed obvious now that Tim and Lucy were in danger, or soon would be, but he was doubtful whether a warning from a stranger via social media would do anything to keep them safe. He could feel the shadow of something much bigger and more ominous hanging over this whole affair, but couldn't yet see any detail.

Right now, he needed guidance. He picked more leaves. One of the plants was starting to look a bit depleted, and it would be much harder to replace them now that Salvia had been criminalised. He had to tend them carefully and keep them alive. It was time to lay off the stuff and let the plants and his brain cells regenerate.

He lit two candles and sat in their dim flickering light, thinking as hard as he could about Tomas. He closed his eyes and listened to the cadence of his own heart. It began to echo, as if his body had been hollowed out. He was following it down a tunnel, into the Cerro Rico. He'd never been here before.

The walls were crumbly and unstable, held up by rickety wooden supports. The only light was a tiny beam on the dirt floor directly in front of him. The ceiling lowered and he had to bend almost in half to move through it. He listened for the voices of men working and the clink of picks against rock, but all he could hear was his breath and the boom of his heartbeat. Every pulse felt like an explosion deep underground. If he wasn't careful, he'd bring the mountain down on top of himself.

'Tomas!' he called into the darkness. His voice echoed back at him, repeating endlessly like reflections between two mirrors.

He began to run, still hunched over, one hand over the top of his head to protect it from the low beams. The tunnel descended more sharply now and gravity felt stronger than normal in here. He couldn't stop or turn around if he wanted to.

His foot caught on something and he pitched forward. He was falling down a chute. The walls lit up with seams of gold and silver, which blurred like lights inside a road tunnel as he fell past them. Precious metal blades protruded from the walls and scored his skin. He was being flayed alive.

He landed in a bloody heap and the wind was knocked from his lungs. Gasping like a landed cod, he pushed himself to his knees and stared blindly into the darkness. His hands felt wet and he could hear his blood dripping onto the hard-packed floor.

'You spend too much time with dead people, brother.'

He tried to speak. His lips made the shape of Tomas's name but no air moved through his larynx.

'Relax, *compadre*. You know this is not the place of your death. It is mine.'

At last, Harrison's lungs inflated. He sucked in as much of the hot, sulphurous air as he could and squinted toward the source of the voice. As his eyes adjusted, he could see that they were in a chamber, scarcely bigger than a tomb. Indeed, a tomb was exactly what it was.

Tomas was a shadow, sitting with his back against a shimmering wall. His face was blackened with dried blood. He swept his hand wide, showing off a gleaming seam of silver.

'How do you like that? I died a rich man.'

'Fat lot of good it did.'

'Watch what you say or I'll keep you here to share the wealth.'

'Why did you bring me here?'

'To tell you something you need to know. These tunnels were made by slaves.'

'I didn't need to fall down a hole to know that. Tell me, Tomas.'

‘You must free the slaves, Harri. That is what you must do.’

‘What are you talking about?’

‘Free the slaves and you will find the gold.’

‘You never used to talk in riddles when you were alive.’

‘I am giving you the answer, my friend.’

The ground beneath Harrison’s knees began to rumble and dust began to fall from the ceiling. ‘Tomas, what’s happening?’

‘The mountain is hungry.’

Stones began to shower down on him, tiny ones at first and then larger ones. He shielded his head with his arms and curled up as tightly as he could. The rocks pelted his spine, his hands, his legs, breaking his bones, paralysing him. He couldn’t move his arms or legs. The rocks delivered crushing blows to every part of his body except his skull. He was going to be fully conscious until the end. The mountain’s roar became louder and the chamber collapsed on top of him.

He woke up face down on the rug. Slowly, he pushed himself up. His body felt bruised and pummelled, and his head was pounding. That was how Tomas died. Painfully, brutally, fully aware of what was happening to him. Harrison had never allowed himself to visualise it before. Tomas wanted him to see it.

It was hard to breathe. He put his palms up to his eyes and they came away wet. How could Tomas go to work every day, six days a week, knowing what could happen at any moment? How could a man with a wife and four children, a man with so much love of life, get up every morning in the dark and walk into that hole?

Because he had no choice.

Free the slaves. That's what Tomas said. But which slaves?

The pain in his bones was still receding and he got up slowly. The Salvia hadn't mixed well with the whisky and he felt nauseous. The corridor in his flat still had a distinct downward tilt, and the rotten egg smell of the mine was still in his nose. Even with the lights on, he could feel the rumbles coming from deep within the earth. Doing his best to ignore them, he cleaned up the remnants of their food and washed the dishes. It was late and he needed sleep, but if he went to bed with the Salvia still working through him, he'd go straight back into that awful place. It had been a long time since a vision had been so frightening and so visceral. Even Tomas was telling him to give it a rest.

And yet ...

The word slave repeated in his head.

He made himself a cup of tea, sat at the table and studied his hands. It was hard to believe they were clean and intact. In the mine, they were so black they looked like they had been burnt.

He studied the timeline that he and Amy had been working on. *Free the slaves and you will find the gold.* He remembered the vision of Lucy in that room, singing for those men who all coveted her sweet body and shimmering, golden curls. The question was, which one was she: the gold, or the slave?

And could it be there were others?

The office of LASAR-Net was open but empty when he arrived the next morning. A buzzer bleeped as he pushed the door open, and Nessa Walker shouted from somewhere in the back, 'I'll be right with you.'

As he waited, Harrison read the posters and leaflets on the notice board. They promoted English classes, training courses and women's charities. One leaflet said in large black letters: Human Trafficking and Enforced Labour: Report It! Beneath that, there was a helpline number. Harrison took a copy.

'Oh ... it's you.'

He turned around. 'Can you spare a minute?'

'Aye.' Nessa pulled the door to the back room closed behind her and looked him over, a good deal less suspiciously than she had when he'd been with Amy. 'I haven't heard any more from Tim, if that's why you're here.'

'My partner found an article in the Coventry Telegraph. Tim's mother has reported him missing in Athens.'

'Oh my God.' She covered her mouth with her hand. 'I knew something like this would happen.'

'We don't know what's happened yet,' he said, trying to sound reassuring. 'This might sound strange, Nessa, but have you got anything here that might have belonged to Tim or Lucy?'

'Like what?'

'Anything. Clothing they might have left here? A scarf, a book, any old thing.'

Nessa sneered. 'What are you, like a dog trying to catch a scent?'

'You're more or less right.'

'So, you're a psychic detective, then?' She was amused and curious, but mostly just making fun of him. Thankfully she didn't give him time to answer. 'I'd have to look around. There might be something. Where's your partner today?'

'Amy's working on another line of inquiry.'

This elicited a grin. 'You make that sound quite exciting. So, are you two like ... a husband and wife team?'

'We just work together.'

The more she wanted to know, the more open she became. If he went with it for a few minutes, she might give away something else. He ran his fingers through rain-soaked hair and wiped his hands on his coat. 'It's awful out there today. I hate this time of year.'

'It's lonely for a lot of people.'

'Aye, it is,' he said, and sighed for effect. Then he shook his head. 'Sorry. How did you get into this work, Nessa?'

'I fell into it by accident. I went to uni to become a teacher but I got ill and dropped out. Eventually, I started volunteering for a mental health charity that helped me, and then I got a job there, and I've been working in the voluntary sector ever since.' She paused with her mouth half-open, as if she was afraid of saying too much. 'I love this job, but it's hard. The people's lives ... the things that have happened to them are like nothing I've ever heard. I don't know how I haven't cracked up yet.'

'Anyone who spends their life helping folk in need earns my respect.'

She beamed, inside and out. Harrison got the impression she wasn't used to receiving praise. 'Thank you. That's awfully kind of you. You don't need to hear my life-story. I can't think of anything Lucy or Tim might have left here. Sorry.'

‘It’s fine. I’m sorry for taking up your time. I’d better make a move.’ He made it sound like he’d rather not.

‘Hang on.’ She reached out for his arm. ‘I’ve just remembered, I have something in the back that I think might interest you. Stay here.’ She hurried away and came back with a small frame. ‘This belonged to Kostas Gianopoulos.’

It was an icon on a small panel of wood, perhaps three inches by five: something you might buy in a Greek souvenir shop. It depicted Mary and the baby Jesus with passive moon-shaped faces, gazing at each other against a background of bright gold. Harrison took it between his hands and studied it. Desire and frustration shot through it like opposing magnetic charges.

‘This is a strange thing to leave here.’

‘It is, aye. He gave it as a gift to this young Iraqi Christian woman we were helping. I don’t know why. She’s a bonny girl, so maybe he was trying to get in with her. She didn’t want it. I never knew what to do with it, so I just stashed it at the back of a storage cupboard.’

Harrison closed his eyes for a couple of seconds. He saw Kostas trying to force the icon into the woman’s hands, saying, ‘Please, take this as a token of our friendship. I can help you.’ A heated exchange passed between them, but he couldn’t make out the words. Kostas was angry that she wouldn't take it. Women didn't often refuse his advances.

'Mr Jones, are you alright?'

He forced his attention back to Nessa. 'The woman he gave this to. Do you know where she is now?'

'Aye, Maryam's still around. She volunteers with us and she's applying to university. She's one of our successes.'

'Do you think she'd be willing to speak to me?'

'What about?'

'About Kostas.'

'She might. Is it relevant to your case?'

'Aye, I think it might be.'

'What were you doing just there, praying to it or some bloody thing?'

Harrison pretended he hadn't heard her question. 'When is Maryam next in?'

'This afternoon. She can be intimidated by men she doesn't know. I won't bother telling you her story, but if you know anything about the recent treatment of Iraqi Christians, you can imagine.'

'I can imagine all too well. Would she prefer to speak to Amy?'

'Probably.'

‘Okay, we’ll pop in. We’re not going to scare her or cause her any trouble, I promise. You can sit in, if it would reassure her.’

‘I’ll see what she says.’

‘Once again, Nessa, thank you.’ He held up the icon. ‘Can I take this until later?’

‘Keep it if you want. I’ve got no use for it.’

TWENTY-TWO

Nessa Walker left Harrison to man the front office and showed Amy into the back room. It was a windowless square containing a meeting table, six dirty chairs, bookshelves with over-stuffed file boxes, and a row of grey metal filing cabinets. A corner of the ceiling was water-stained and sprouting black spots of mould, and the carpet didn't bear scrutiny. Amy had a brief moment to wonder what it would be like to spend your working life in this squalid, musty place, before Nessa came back in with Maryam.

Amy smiled at Maryam, trying to hide her shock. The girl looked about thirteen, though was likely to be nearer to twenty. What had happened to her family? Amy knew without having been told that they had fallen victim to one of many possible fates, and that Maryam had reached Scotland alone.

She had the kind of effortless, natural beauty that would make any man turn his head. Her striking green eyes were very round, and her expression serious but calm. Amy recognised it immediately: she was assessing her situation, reading the signs, watching for the first hint of danger. It was the expression of a soldier.

'Maryam. It's nice to meet you.' she said as calmly as she could. She wasn't sure whether it was appropriate to shake hands, so instead, she motioned to one of the chairs. 'Thank you so much for agreeing to speak to me.'

Maryam glanced at Nessa for reassurance before sitting down.

Nessa sat, and said, 'Feel free to ask Amy anything you want, love.'

Maryam sat down. 'Are you from the police?' She had already acquired a slight Scottish accent.

'No, I'm not. And I promise you're not in trouble. I only wanted to ask you what you remember about the man who gave you this.' She slipped the little icon out of her handbag and passed it across the table.

Maryam's fine dark brows arched upward. 'I had forgotten about this.' She took a deep breath and thought for a moment. 'A Greek man. He was a wolf in the clothing of a sheep. Is that the way you say it?'

'Yes, it is. Do you remember his name?'

'Kostas. He was kind and handsome, but he was bad. I have met many men like him. They pretend to be your friend and they offer to help you, but you are not a human being to them.'

'What did he say to you. Did he threaten you?'

'He offered me work. He said he knew a place where I could work and be paid a lot of money. I came here, I had nothing. Only the clothes on my back. Most of us are the same. Some girls would be tempted, but I have met his kind before. The girls go and you never see them again.'

'What kind of work did he offer?'

'He could never put it into words. Kostas must keep himself clean, you see? But I know what kind of work.' She glanced at Nessa. 'The kind where you must lie with men.'

'Sex work?'

'Yes. But they do not give you a choice.' She turned the icon over and pointed to a blurred mark on the wood. 'You see this? He told me to call this number. He got angry when I told him no.'

Amy squinted and saw something that neither she nor Harrison had noticed previously: a mobile phone number written in tiny, faint pencil script on the bottom left corner.

'Did you call it?'

Maryam shoved the icon away forcefully. 'No, never.'

'I wish you'd told me,' Nessa said.

Maryam's eyes flickered toward her, full of shame. 'I was afraid. I did not know who to trust. If he found out I told anyone, he would have made things bad for me. This is the way it works.'

'You thought I was in on it?' Tears formed in the corner of Nessa's eyes. 'How could I be in on something like that?'

Maryam only shook her head.

Amy answered for her. 'Because sometimes friends aren't really friends, and sometimes all you can trust is what you know in here.' She thumped her fist over her heart.

'You understand,' said Maryam meekly. 'Thank you.' She turned to Nessa. 'I am sorry. I hope you are not angry with me.'

'Of course not,' Nessa said, but her face had drained of colour. She stood up and paced back and forth at the end of the table, rubbing her hands over her face, apparently on the verge of a full-on anxiety attack. 'I can't believe I let him in here. I can't believe I was so stupid.'

Amy ignored Nessa's attention-seeking behaviour, and tried to reassure the girl. 'Maryam, I promise you, your name will never get back to Kostas or anybody else. He's not in the country anymore, so don't worry about him. I only want to make sure nothing happens to any other girls. Is there anything else you'd like to tell me?'

'No, that's all. I never saw him again.'

‘Okay. Thank you.’ On impulse, she reached across the table and squeezed the girl’s hand, wondering if she’d feel any tingling messages coming through her skin like Harrison would. But all she felt was warm, soft, sweaty skin. ‘God bless, Maryam. I wish you well.’

In the car, she showed Harrison the phone number on the back of the icon. ‘Should we phone it and see what happens?’

‘No way.’ He touched the number with his finger tip, as if it might tell him something. Amy noticed that his hand was shaking.

‘You don’t look so hot, Indiana.’

‘I don’t feel so hot either, to be honest.’

‘Are you coming down with something?’

‘Just my usual pre-Christmas depression combined with overwork, mental overload and sleep-deprivation. Nothing a bottle of whisky won’t cure.’ He chuckled to himself. ‘Or at least make me forget. I’m going to speak to Colin Muir, my mate in CID. The icon is one for him, not us. I need to figure out how we get closer to Lucy.’

‘Let me journey again and find Tim.’

‘Amy ...’

‘He’ll tell us where she is.’

‘No.’

‘Why not?’

‘You don’t know what you’re getting yourself into.’

‘Then why did you let me do it last night? Why did you let me into this at all?’

‘I don’t know if I should have.’

Amy crossed her arms and watched him drive. ‘Harri, I grew up in East Belfast. I’ve been to Afghanistan twice. It’s my job to scrape casualties off the streets of Edinburgh. There isn’t much that can shock me anymore. I’m not weak and I don’t need you to protect me from anything.’

‘I know. But when I met you, you were suicidal and I don’t want to be responsible for ...’

‘I am perfectly capable of taking responsibility for my own life. Anyway, you’re the one talking about depression.’

‘That was a joke.’

‘You think you’re the only one who can read people? You’re an open book.’

He smiled. ‘It’s just a seasonal thing.’

‘Right.’ They rolled to a halt on Minto Street. The road was torn up for the renewal of gas pipelines, and the queue of taillights ahead of them stretched into the distance. Pedestrians left them in the dust. They were going to be stuck in this uncomfortable conversation for quite a while longer. ‘What do you do for Christmas, anyway?’

He shrugged. ‘Just try and survive it, like most single people.’

‘I mean, where do you go? You stay at home?’

‘My mum lives in Glasgow. Sometimes I go there, or I spend it with some friends from work. What about you?’

‘My mum’ll expect me to go home, but to be quite honest I’d rather sit in my flat alone and stick toothpicks under my fingernails one by one.’

Harrison winced. ‘That good, huh?’

‘Festive as a crematorium on a rainy day. It’s the same every year: overcooked turkey, EastEnders and the usual chorus of, *It’s not the same since Dad and Ian died.* My mum doesn’t ascribe to the notion that life goes on.’

Harrison said nothing. Amy shivered although the heating was on full and she was sweaty in her damp coat. Inside her head, a little door opened and from the other side, she could hear someone shouting. Her stomach began to flutter.

She shifted in her seat and looked out the window. The wipers clunked back and forth and they rolled slowly toward the city centre. Out on the street, people were already leaving work and scurrying for buses. Afternoon drinkers were emerging from pubs, blinking into a blur of headlights and rain.

Thc voice was still shouting. It was Ricky, in a state of lonely desperation. In what seemed like a flash of lightning, she saw him holding a rope, forming a hangman’s noose. She thought for a moment about what she had said to Maryam, and she knew she had to follow this, even if it proved to be a mistake.

True to form, Harrison glanced at her with a curious expression. 'What is it, Amy?'

'Oh my God. Can you not just switch that off sometimes?'

He braked hard as the traffic in front of them came to another abrupt halt. 'Believe me, I wish I could. Is it Ricky?'

She cringed. 'I need to go see him.'

Harrison stared straight ahead for a moment, the red gleam of the traffic lights reflecting on his glasses. 'Tell me where to go.'

'You don't have to do this. Drop me off and I'll walk from here.'

'I'm taking you.'

Gratitude almost overwhelmed her. 'He's in the flats at Dumbiedykes. You know the ones down Holyrood Road?'

'Aye.'

'I wasn't sure how well acquainted you were with Edinburgh's juicier addresses.'

'I've had occasion to visit one or two of them.' He indicated right to turn down Infirmary Street. 'And no, to answer your question, I'm not completely clueless, even if I did go to private school.'

Amy stared at him for a couple of seconds. 'I'm sorry for whatever I just thought.'

‘That I’m a clueless private school toff and that when Ricky sees me coming, he’ll think I’m a social worker.’

‘You scare me, you know that?’

‘Do I really look like a social worker?’

‘Do you really want me to answer that?’ She fell silent for a moment as they turned onto Dumbiedykes Road. The estate was a curious island of social housing that survived from the time when this was an industrial part of town, tucked between the touristy Old Town and Holyrood Park.

‘He’s in the one at the far end.’ She motioned for Harrison to continue driving along the curving street. ‘It’s not his flat, he’s crashing with his mate Geo. He’s been on the housing list since he moved out of my place, but there aren’t many one-bedroom places around. They offered him something on the fifth floor of a block out in Granton, but the lift was broken and with his leg ... I don’t know, he probably should have taken it. It meant they put him to the end of the list again.’

‘What’s wrong with his leg?’

‘He survived an explosion that killed four men in Helmand. You know when you see the leg of a cow hanging in the back of a butcher’s lorry? That’s what his looked like when I got to him. Half the skin was gone, the bones were shattered; it was full of metal, some of which is still there. By some miracle, they patched things up well enough for him to keep it, but it'll never be right.'

'Some way to meet a guy.'

She laughed softly. 'We were already together before that happened. He's a changed man, though. He hasn't coped well at all with Civvy Street. Pull in here, it's that one.' She pointed to the grey three-storey block at the end. 'Will you come in with me?'

'Do you want me to?'

'Yes,' she said, not bothering to hide the fear in her voice.

The stair buzzer was broken and the door was banging on its hinges. She pushed it open and they went up one flight and along the landing. Amy thumped on the door to the flat with her fist and called 'Ricky!' through the shiny PVC. There was no answer, so she banged again. 'Ricky, it's me. I know you're here.'

When he appeared, he was so drunk he had to hang onto the doorframe. His mouth twisted into a lurid grin. 'Hiya Doc.' He wobbled and tried to straighten himself up. His finger stabbed the air as if it was trying to point at a buzzing fly. 'Nice of you to stop by.' He looked Harrison up and down, eyes screwed up as he tried to focus. 'Who the fuck's this?'

‘Harri and I work together,’ Amy said. ‘We were passing and I had a bad feeling, Ricky. I just wanted to check you’re okay.’

Ricky ignored her concern and squinted up at Harrison. ‘This your new boyfriend? He’s no your type, hen.’

‘I just said, we work together, that’s all.’

‘That really is all,’ Harrison added for emphasis.

‘It better be,’ Ricky threatened, though at this point he didn’t look like he could land a punch on a bag. He turned and limped back into the flat. ‘You wantin’ a cold one?’

‘No thanks. Everything alright, Rick?’ There were no suspicious lengths of rope or other obviously dangerous items in sight, and she wondered if she’d over-reacted.

‘I’ll make us some tea,’ she muttered, and filled the kettle. The kitchen was as she expected it to be: a sticky demonstration of the fact that man can, for some time, live on beer alone. ‘Geo not here, Rick?’

‘Naw, he’s ...’ Ricky’s face went blank as he tried to remember, ‘I’ve no seen him in ... four, five days. He’s got a bird somewhere. It’s good of him to let me stay here, eh?’ He turned to Harrison again. ‘Without him, I’d be on the street, eh? Thanks to this one, here.’ He jabbed his finger toward Amy.

‘Oh, for the love of God, Ricky,’ Amy blurted. The same old anger filled her. She should have learned by now not to get into it with him. ‘Will you give me a break? I came by because I was worried about you. You know how I get a feeling about things?’

Gratitude crossed his face for less than a second, followed by anger. ‘You came by to gloat, you wee bitch.’ He took a step toward her and she turned her back protectively. ‘You came by to rub my nose in the shite.’

‘No, I didn’t.’

‘Well take a good look around. You like this place? Consider yourself lucky you don’t have to stay here.’ He took another step toward her, and she refused to back away.

‘Blame the Man, Ricky, not her,’ Harrison said, stepping between them. ‘None of this is Amy’s fault.’

‘What the fuck you know about it, pal?’

‘I know you’re hurting. I know it feels like the whole planet’s against you, and I know that even after everything that’s happened, Amy wants to help you because she’s that kind of person and she can’t leave somebody alone when they’re in pain.’ He paused while Ricky goggled at him. ‘And you’re right, nothing in this world is fair at all.’

Ricky opened his mouth and looked for a moment like he was ready to fight. Then he crumpled like a pair of cast-off jeans, dropped his head onto the table and started to cry noisily.

'Oh, for the love of Jesus,' Amy muttered, as the mood swung from threat to humiliation. She slipped the can of beer out of his hand and poured it down the sink. 'Ricky, get a grip.'

'I can't sleep,' Ricky bawled. He lifted his red, slimy face and tried to fix his eyes on her. 'I haven't slept in days, Amy. I don't know what to do with myself. I wish you'd stay with me, just for one night. Just stay here tonight, Amy. I'd sleep if you were beside me, I know I would. Please, hen. Just one night, please.'

'No.' Amy kept her distance, standing behind him clutching the warped worktop. She bit her lip and took a breath before speaking. 'I'm sorry life feels so bad right now, Rick, but I can't do that.'

Ricky's shoulders shook. He bolted out of the kitchen, knocking his chair over in the process, and they heard him retching violently in the bathroom.

'Poor bastard,' Harrison said.

'You should have had a career as a bomb disposal expert.'

'Amazing what a little empathy can do. Let's just see if we can get him into his bed.'

When the sounds of vomiting died down, they ventured into the bathroom to find him sitting on the floor beside the toilet, head in his hands. Amy filled a cup of water and made him rinse his mouth, and he barely noticed when they hoisted him under the arms and steered him onto the mattress he slept on in the spare room. They settled him on his side and he lay submissive and barely conscious, muttering pathetic words of love and apology.

Amy stood up and straightened her jumper. 'Let's go.'

'Don't leave me, Amy,' Ricky moaned, struggling to sit up.

Harrison gently pushed him by the shoulders back onto the mattress. 'Just relax, mate. You're all right. Just close your eyes and get some sleep.'

'Amy ...'

She came back to the mattress and sat down beside him. 'I'm here, Ricky.' She took his hand, watched his eyelids grow heavy and felt the coiled tension in his muscles relax. Minutes went by and everything became still and peaceful. Even the voices and music from the neighbouring flats died away, and eventually all Amy knew was the steady cycle of her breath.

She was nearly asleep by the time Harrison placed his hand on her shoulder.

'He's out for the count. Let's leave him to it.'

'Gladly.' Amy pulled the covers over Ricky and looked at him for a moment. His creased face had relaxed and she could almost see the features she had once fallen in love with. It had been a lively, handsome face before the war made it ugly. They left him sleeping off the foul cocktail of liquor and bad spirits. Harrison drove her home through the now relentless rain.

'I'm sorry about that,' she said after several minutes of awkward silence.

'Don't be.'

'I hope you know I'm not as fucked up as that.'

Harrison laughed softly. 'Thanks for the reassurance.'

'Could you…see anything? About him ... and me?'

'I saw enough to know that it took some guts for you to go over there tonight.'

She looked away for a moment. It was hard to remember the pain of Ricky's fist on her face anymore, but what she would never forget was that first sight of herself in the mirror afterwards: the eyes swollen nearly shut, the bruises spreading along her cheeks and mouth, the blood drying on her lips. He had gone for her face because as much as he wanted to hurt her, he wanted to humiliate her even more. He wanted to shame her and make her afraid to go out, and he wanted to make her believe she deserved it.

'It only happened the one time,' she said, hoping he wouldn't look on her as a victim. The humiliation was still there.

'I can't imagine you'd be the kind of person to allow it to happen more than once.'

'No, I'm not.' Receiving no response, she continued. 'He used to be alright, you know. He's smart as a whip, and he used to be such good fun to be around. I don't know if he changed after his injury or if he always had it in him to be like this. Maybe I'm not as good a judge of character as I used to think I was.'

Her voice broke and she swiped tears with her palms. 'I thought I could help him. To see him now, it's ...' She took a deep breath, unable to finish the sentence. Sometimes she wondered if would have been better for Ricky if he'd died in that explosion.

'You helped him tonight, when he has no right to expect you to.'

'Thanks for coming with me. You didn't need to.'

'I wanted to.'

She stared at him. 'Why?'

Harrison didn't answer.

'To protect me?'

'Maybe. Was I wrong to do that?'

'I don't need protection against him.'

'I know you don't,' he said, and it sounded like a lie.

Amy mopped her nose with the sleeve of her parka as they turned into her street, wondering if he was this protective of all his friends or if she was a special case. ‘Well, thank you anyway.’

‘You’re welcome.’

TWENTY-THREE

This really was getting too big for him now. He had never seen it as his job to dole out justice, and his cases rarely involved the police. With resources so thin on the ground and new forms of threat materialising every few months, the police were less concerned all the time about reopening stone-cold missing persons cases. But occasionally he had reason to call them in, and even more occasionally, they had reason to call him.

He pulled up the number of the one cop who he knew wouldn't automatically write him off as a quack. Detective Inspector Colin Muir was a psychic in denial, a man whose hunches were legendary and who regularly seemed to know things he shouldn't. He refused to acknowledge any special capacity in himself but he had quietly brought Harrison in to crack several dead-end cases. It had been more than a year since they'd last spoken.

He was almost surprised when Colin answered. His voice was ragged. 'Harrison Jones, the wandering shaman. Does normal timekeeping not apply to you?'

Harrison glanced at the clock. It was nearly eleven. He had fallen asleep on the sofa after dropping Amy off, and now suspected he was going to be up half the night. He cringed. 'Sorry, Colin. Listen, can you spare an hour tomorrow morning?'

'Aye, what's it about?'

'I've got a bad feeling about something I'm working on.'

'And that's meant to be news?'

'Worse than usual.'

'Right. Meet me at the usual place, ten o'clock. If something comes up and I can't make it, I'll let you know.'

'Thanks. Apologies for waking you.'

'Ach, never mind. The list of things keeping me up nights is getting longer by the minute.' Colin never told him the details of his life outside of work, but Harrison had picked up enough to know they weren't the happiest. Par for the course.

'Sorry to hear that, Colin. Hopefully see you tomorrow.'

'Aye. Go to bed, Jones.'

Colin Muir had gained weight and lost hair. He was in his mid-fifties but looked well older, and he had pouches under his eyes where he appeared to store all the bad things he'd seen during a career in the force. He emerged from the door of St Leonard's Police Station with an e-cigarette already sticking out of his mouth. It released a puff of candy-sweet vapour into the dank air.

'Jones.' He shook Harrison's hand and took the measure of him. 'Not you and all.'

'What?'

Colin rubbed his chin. 'Every man and his dog want a damn beard these days. My laddie's been growing his for six months and still looks like he's got ginger pubes stuck to his face. Filthy things, beards, if you ask me.'

Harrison instinctively raked his fingers through his, hoping there were no crumbs left over from his breakfast. 'It's my winter insulation.'

'As if you needed it, up there in your ivory tower.' Colin scrutinised the ceiling of cloud and haar, hanging somewhere between the top of the crags and the summit of Arthur's Seat. 'We might get half an hour before it starts pissing down again. We walking?'

'Aye.' They headed up St Leonard's, toward the steps that would lead them down into Holyrood Park. 'You well, Colin?'

Colin blew a wry breath of laughter through his nose and sent out a ripple of jaded anticipation.

'You don't really need to ask, do you, Harrison? So, what's on your mind?'

'You familiar with a guy called Quentin Merriweather?'

'Merriweather? Christ.' Colin's laugh turned into a wheezy cough. 'He's your typical crooked developer, though if you asked him, he'd say he was the property king of Edinburgh. Famous for wining and dining the politicians and the planning officials. Backhanders for consents that should never be granted, building reg violations left right and centre, you name it.'

'You never pinned him though?'

Colin shrugged. 'White-collar crime isn't really my department. Shit doesn't stick to guys like him; you know that. It's always somebody else's fault. What's he to you, anyway?'

'His wife hired me. Soon to be ex-wife, I should say. Their daughter Lucy's missing.'

'Oh aye?'

'Well, I say missing ... She's taken herself off somewhere and cut herself off from her parents. I am pretty sure she's out of the country, most likely in Greece.'

'And?'

'And she's hooked up with a Greek hotel tycoon called Kostas Gianopoulos. That name mean anything to you?'

'Nada.'

‘I was hoping you might check him out. He’s got his fingers in things over here and has connections with Quentin Merriweather. I think he may be involved in some pretty heavy stuff, Colin.’

‘Such as?’

‘Such as human trafficking. The sex trade. He was sniffing around a refugee charity here in town last year, picking out young women. An Iraqi girl I met there yesterday named him.’

‘That’s a serious allegation.’

‘Too right it is. I want to know if it’s just him or if Merriweather has some hand in it.’

Colin walked silently for a moment, vaping like a cherry-flavoured steam engine. ‘I’m going to need something more to go on than the word of a refugee girl.’

‘Why, because her word isn’t as legitimate as anyone else’s?’

‘Ach, don’t go all bleeding-heart precious on me, Jones. I doubt this girl’s going to want to go public with an accusation and all that entails.’

‘I doubt it too.’ He took the small, wooden icon out of his coat pocket and handed it to the detective. ‘She said Gianopoulos gave her this. If you look closely, you’ll see there’s a number on the back. He told her to call it if she was looking for work.’

‘And you know it’s that kind of work.’

'No, I don't. Not for sure.'

'Did you call it?'

Harrison laughed. 'I'm not the cop here. I'll leave that to you.'

Colin inspected the icon and turned it over, squinting at the tiny pencilled numbers. 'How long ago did he give her this?'

'A year and a half ago, roughly.'

'It's unlikely the number's even still live, but I'll check it out.'

'Anything you can get me on Kostas Gianopoulos would be a help. Addresses, connections to the Merriweathers, anything. There's one other thing. Lucy had a boyfriend called Tim Cartwright, from Coventry. His mother has reported him missing in Athens. She's called Louise Cartwright.'

'And you know that through your ... own sources?' Colin glanced at Harrison.

'No, my partner dug that off the internet.'

'You have a partner? You mean to say there's another guy like you out there?'

'Woman. She's called Amy.'

'Oh aye.' Colin raised an eyebrow. 'She got a beard and all?'

'No.'

They walked for a couple of minutes beneath the crags, carrying their thoughts silently like satchels of stones. Gulls cried into the winter sky and tyres hissed on the wet tarmac. Colin screwed his face against the weather and inhaled deeply, then started coughing, a sustained fit that doubled him over and turned his face a vicious shade of purple.

'You alright, Colin?'

Colin shook his head and waited for the coughing to subside. 'Jesus,' he whispered. 'I think I'm fucking dying here.'

'I'd know if you were dying.'

Colin responded with a grunt of a laugh. 'I'm due to retire next year,' he said, making it sound like a terminal diagnosis.

'That's not a good thing?'

'I've got no idea how me and the wife are going to tolerate each other when I'm not working all the hours.' He shook his head. 'But you didn't come out in this shite weather to hear about my domestic malfunctions. We've got a Merriweather, Gianopoulos and a Cartwright. I'll check them out.'

'There's a bit more to it. Elizabeth Merriweather claims Quentin abused both her and Lucy.'

'There's not a lot we can do about that unless she reports it to us and wants to press charges. Getting a conviction ...' His words disappeared into a stifled cough.

'A conviction would be highly unlikely, I know.'

Colin flapped his hands in defeat. 'We heading back?'

They turned around and walked back in the direction of the station. Harrison shortened his stride, drove his hands deeper into his pockets and tried to tune out Colin's discordant psychic drone. A life spent following criminal trails had taken its toll: in Colin's personal universe, all roads led to hell. Half an hour in it was more than enough.

They shook hands at the door of St Leonard's and Harrison walked back to George Square. He taught his afternoon seminar on autopilot, legs twitching beneath the table as his students debated the existence of the supernatural. He maintained the pretence of listening while he thought about Colin Muir, and why a man would secretly convince himself that dying young was preferable to facing retirement with his wife. He thought about Ricky, who had been broken by other people's battles. And he thought about Amy.

He thought about Amy a lot.

Harrison wished more of his students and colleagues approached their work the way Amy did. He thought about how his colleagues would judge her if they met her. They'd judge her by her accent and by the directness of her questions and by the fact that she'd never read Levi-Strauss or

Foucault. Yet Amy Bell understood other people better than the whole of the social anthropology department, with all of their theoretical weaponry, put together.

What she wanted to know – what Harrison still couldn't explain to her – was why.

Coming up the stairwell to his office, he bumped into Lara and Jonathan Weaver. They were clattering down the steps in a hurry and laughing richly at something.

'Oh, hullo Harri,' Jonathan muttered.

Harrison would have preferred to let them go past without a conversation, but Lara paused. Her cheeks flushed. Embarrassment swelled in her and overflowed from her mouth. 'Hey,' she muttered.

Jonathan cleared his throat. 'I'll wait outside.'

'I'll be two minutes,' she said, waving him away before turning back to Harrison. 'How are you?'

'Fine,' he replied. His voice sounded colder than he had intended it to, but she had an awful way of prizing him open by any crack she could find. 'How's the book coming on?'

'Slowly but surely. Listen, I hope this isn't awful for you, seeing us together. It isn't my intention to hurt you, or ...'

'People move on, Lara.'

'Have you moved on?'

He smiled. 'I'm not pining for you, if that's what you want to know. I have other things in my life at the moment.'

'Oh,' she said, and for a couple of seconds, her mind was absolutely open to him. She wanted to know what those other things were, and who they involved. She wanted to know if he still had feelings for her, and she wanted to tell him that Jonathan was only a rebound romance and that she already knew it wasn't for the long-term.

Harrison broke eye contact and looked down at the scuffed green linoleum beneath his feet, trying to close her out. 'You still have some stuff at my house. You might want it back.'

'I can pop by.'

'I'll put it in a bag and bring it into your office next week.'

'That's fine.' She deflated like a balloon. 'Harri, Jonny and I are ... it's nothing serious.'

'You don't have to explain anything to me.'

'So, I don't have to explain that being with you feels like being naked all the time? It takes some getting used to.'

'So, it wasn't about meat after all.'

'You know it wasn't.'

He lifted his hands in a helpless gesture. 'That's life, Lara. That's me. I can't help it. Don't leave poor Jonathan waiting down there too long, eh?'

‘Right,’ she said slowly. Then she nodded. ‘Okay. I’m sorry. Listen, you take care.’ She patted his arm.

‘You too.’ He side-stepped her and continued up the stairs.

Reaching the safety of his office, he locked the door and sat down. Two-dozen new emails flickered into his inbox. He scanned their headings and turned away from the screen without reading further. Aziza Maalouf would be turning up for her supervision session soon, and he needed a clear mind for that. He took off his glasses and let himself drift a little. He wanted to go back to that rope bridge in the jungle, but hadn’t been able to since he met Amy and the Lucy Merriweather case kicked off. There was a sense of someone waiting for him just on the other side of that bridge, and it frustrated him that he couldn’t see who it was. The tiny beacon of hope he tended for his dad flared whenever he thought about it.

He was juggling too many balls and soon they were going to come crashing down around him. Lucy Merriweather was taking too much of his energy. She would have to be his last case. He would bring her home and then he would draw a line under it, for real this time.

TWENTY-FOUR

Elizabeth poured her second large whisky of the night and drew her pashmina closer around her neck. The sea was thunderous tonight, and the trees were creaking and tossing themselves about like frenzied dancers. With Simba gone, she was truly alone in the house for the first time in her life. It had become a cold, frightening place, full of dark corners and unexplained noises. She couldn't settle with a book, and she was afraid that if she turned on the television or the radio, she might not hear the sound of someone coming up the drive or trying to break in. She moved through the rooms, touching things the way Harrison Jones had done, trying to pick up some echo of Lucy. Some distant whisper of her voice, or the tiniest flush of warmth. From Lucy's bedroom window, she looked out over the back lawn, watching the patterns of moonlight stretching and disappearing as the clouds tumbled across the sky. With every shadowy motion, she thought she saw a figure sneaking toward the house. There was no-one except the phantoms projected by her mind.

They would come for her, eventually: Quentin's phantoms, Lucy's phantoms, or her own. They would punish her for her complicity in crimes she barely had words for.

Jones knew more than he was letting on, she was sure of that. But what did he know? There was so much more she should have told him, but she couldn't bring herself to speak it. He would think she was as guilty as Quentin, and she wanted him to think well of her. And not just for the purposes of bringing Lucy home. Beyond the psychic abilities which intrigued her, Harrison Jones was exceedingly intelligent and not unattractive.

It was pathetic, allowing herself to think of him that way. She'd hired him for a job, that was all, and he would be, no doubt, far too ethical to dally with a client. She was too quick to fall for any man who spoke kindly to her; this had always been her biggest problem. Quentin had been kind to her too, in the beginning.

Elizabeth looked around the room, her breath bottled up somewhere between her lungs and her throat and a sickening pressure building up behind it. She sat on Lucy's bed and squeezed the pillow against her chest. It smelled a little dusty, but there was nothing left of her girl. Her beautiful baby girl.

A child who was forced to become a woman too soon, if only on the outside. Lucy might have been nine or ten the first time they asked her to sing at one of their gatherings, although her voice was already mature and clear. Elizabeth couldn't remember whose idea it was, that first time. It would be easy now to blame Quentin, but perhaps she'd thought of it first. It didn't matter; it had been innocent then. They stood her in front of a light, so that it illuminated her halo of golden curls and made her look like she'd been painted by Michelangelo. She had such an effect on people; it was almost magic, the way she drew them in and rendered them helpless. That night, Quentin secured the financial backing he needed to build an office complex on greenbelt land to the south of the city. Lucy had been a lucky charm. Was it wrong that time? Or the times after that?

Elizabeth remembered all the dresses she had bought Lucy, all the times she had done her makeup and told her how to walk, how to talk, how to flirt. Was it wrong then? She was not the first mother in history to teach her daughter how to use her assets. It had never been her intention for Lucy to sleep with these men.

Maybe it had only crossed the hazy line between showing off a talented daughter and exploitation when Lucy began to resist. Quentin was the one who wanted her to keep singing, and once Quentin had an idea there was no turning him from it. His anger was sickening to witness. He didn't just shout at Lucy, he bellowed and blew like a bull in a ring. He called her names that no girl should hear, and he threatened her with worse. He threatened to turn her out into the street. Elizabeth had only dared to intervene once, and that night in their bedroom he had strangled her to the brink of passing out. After that, she let Lucy fight her own battles.

In the end, it was Lucy who turned herself out into the street.

Elizabeth pressed her face into the pillow and let out a wail. Her whole body strained, trying to force the anguish and self-loathing out like sickness, but she couldn't rid herself of it. Images flickered inside her eyelids, blue negatives of Lucy, permanently burnt into her vision. Lucy sticking her finger down her throat, forcing herself to vomit. Lucy with red lipstick smeared across her cheek, a twisted echo of the joyful little girl with spaghetti sauce on her face. Lucy in a blind rage, spitting curses and accusations.

Elizabeth pressed the pillow as hard as she could over her mouth and nose. She wanted to suffocate herself, but she couldn't make herself do it. Maybe Lucy was right. She was selfish then, and she was selfish now. She had been frightened, but as much for her status rather than for her life. That was the most shameful thing. The pillow fell onto the floor and she dropped down onto it, curled onto her side and cried.

When the tears finally stopped, she felt dried out as old leather. She gathered herself off the floor and scrubbed the smeared mascara from her cheeks with the heels of her palms. She had to pull herself together and make a decision. She could not allow herself to be the victim any longer.

She went downstairs and opened her laptop. Elizabeth had been writing for years, silly romantic stories and novels that she never finished or allowed anyone else to read. It was time now to write a different kind of story.

TWENTY-FIVE

They gave Lucy as much wine as she wanted, and as many pills. They eased the seasickness and calmed her when the walls of her cabin started to close in and the fear crept toward her. The pills whispered in her ears like tiny angels, hushing her, singing lullabies, easing the panic in her belly so that she could lie back down on her bed and sleep.

There were fleeting moments of clarity, but these were terrifying and so hopeless that the only thing she knew how to do was take another pill. As long as she took the pills, she was alright. She could pass the time and she could do what she was asked to do.

Sometimes memories came, but they were all broken and disconnected. She couldn't quite piece together how she'd come to be living in this tiny, windowless, wood-panelled room where she always felt sick. She was on a boat; that was why she felt sick. That's right, she reminded herself, Victor's three-decked luxury yacht. It was luxurious and tacky, kitted out with marble and mahogany and chrome, but everyone who came on board exclaimed over its beauty. Just like they did over hers.

They had still never given her any money to top up her phone, and lately, they had started to confine her to her cabin when she wasn't required. At night, Agata would come for her. She would be taken to sing as Victor and his associates discussed business in the stateroom. She had no way of knowing what their business was, because it was always conducted in Greek, Turkish or sometimes Russian. After she had finished singing, they would take her to a cabin much larger than her own and make her wait. Then a man would come and she would allow him to kiss and suck and poke her where he wanted. Victor had said it would only be a rare occasion, but now it was every night.

The men were mostly in their fifties and sixties, with dyed hair and breath that smelled of wine and cigars. They spoke to her in different languages but sometimes she couldn't tell what it was. They were always kind to her. They didn't hit her. One old bugger liked to give it up the arse, and that hurt even though he was gentle and used about half a tub of Vaseline. Some of them were so fat and drunk they couldn't manage at all.

When they were done with her, Agata would take her to a small bathroom, wait with her while she showered, then take her back to her cabin. Her rucksack, passport and all of her clothes were still in the wardrobe, but she couldn't imagine picking them up and walking out of here.

They sailed sometimes, but because they rarely let her see above deck during the daytime, she had no way of telling where they were. Time stretched, collapsed in on itself, lost all meaning. She no longer knew for sure what day it was, or even what month. The yacht pitched around in storms and the gusts of wind coming in from the deck were cold.

Lucy tried to remember how long it had been since she boarded the yacht. Sometimes it felt like days, other times it felt like she'd been here for years. It was only meant to be for a few weeks, a special private tour for Victor and his friends. She was going to be wined, dined and royally paid.

It had been longer than a few weeks and she was still being royally paid. So they assured her, even though she never actually saw any money and had no idea where it would be going. Maybe they'd set up a bank account for her somewhere. They gave her plenty to eat and the food was good, although she was rarely hungry. Nobody had asked her to pay a penny for her accommodation.

Nobody was forcing her to take the pills.

She was here by choice.

Wasn't she?

This wasn't what she thought it was going to be. She couldn't remember exactly when or how it had changed.

When the drugs wore off, she realised that nothing had changed at all. This had been the trajectory of her life since that first time her parents made her sing at a party. There wasn't much difference between singing for men and screwing them; in one case they wanted to buy her soul and in the other her body. She'd been eighteen the first time she slept with a man for money – or at least for money of her own – and it hadn't felt as dirty as she'd thought it would. It was worth it to buy her freedom.

Freedom she had now surrendered to keep the favour of a man who could never be hers. Worse than that: a man who had promised love but traded her away like a commodity. Kostas was no better than her father, and she had been conned. This prison was punishment for her stupidity, and the only thing she could do was curl up and cry. She cried for everything she'd had and lost, and she cried for Tim, and she cried for the future she now knew she would never see. On the worst nights, when the sea was rough and she spent hours huddled beside the toilet, she cried for her mother.

TWENTY-SIX

Amy woke after a dream and lay in bed for a while, until she knew that trying to get back to sleep was an exercise in futility. The flat was cold, so she wrapped a blanket around herself, went to the kitchen and filled a cup of milk. Caroline had suggested she should keep a journal beside her bed, to write down the dreams and worries that came for her in the night. What could she possibly write about the things that had happened these past couple of weeks? It would seem like the raving of a mad woman.

The microwave beeped and she took out the cup of milk, stirred a little honey into it and held it between her hands. She sat down with it, blew a ripple of breath across the foamy top, and took a sip. She closed her eyes and tried to remember her dream. She was almost certain it had been the same yacht she'd dreamed about before, moored in the pretty harbour alongside smaller cruisers and fishing boats. The town huddled over the water, white and grey buildings climbing the hillside, red-tiled rooftops, an old clock tower, the lights dancing on the water. It all looked very Greek.

She switched on the laptop and thought for a moment. If Lucy was with Kostas, it seemed likely that they would be near Athens. On Google Maps, she scanned pictures of the Athens ports, but they looked wrong: too urban, too modern, too seedy. The place she had seen was quaint and quiet. Unusually quiet.

There were no cars.

Amy typed in 'Greek port near Athens no cars.'

Google gave her a name: Hydra. It was a small island, a favourite weekend retreat of affluent Athenians, just over an hour by sea from the port of Piraeus.

She scanned the images, and there it was: the crescent-shaped harbour, the hilly village, the clock tower. There were a couple of large yachts on the seaward side of the long stone quay, well away from the fleet of much smaller craft. She looked through photographs and felt like she'd been there, though of course she hadn't. At least, not yet.

Adrenaline flooded around her body, followed by fear. A night commando raid on a boat was not exactly her speciality. Maybe that part was optional. If Lucy was on the boat, there had to be another way to get her off.

If she was even there. If the boat was even there. If any of this was more than a fantasy. So many ifs, so many assumptions, and none of them rational.

She picked up her phone and sent Harrison a text message: *Hydra Island, nr. Athens. Call me when you get up.* Half-hoping the phone would wake him, she went to the window and peered out at the dark, damp street. It wasn't raining, and a strong northerly breeze had blown the clouds away, revealing a faint pinprick of stars. A canny city fox paused to sniff at an old takeaway box, then trotted on. A man followed in the same direction, stumbling over his own feet. Amy wondered about Ricky. He had gone quiet in her head, which she hoped meant that he was no longer in the same state of crisis, or had at least temporarily backed down from it. She wished she could put him out of her mind completely. He should be nothing to her, but she didn't know how to make him nothing. She had literally held his life in her hands, and once you had done that for someone the connection between you was permanent.

As night turned the corner into early morning, she packed a towel and a swimsuit into a light backpack, dressed and went out into the cold winter pre-dawn. She ran to the top of Easter Road and down Abbeymount into Holyrood Park, made a circuit of Arthur's Seat and arrived at the Commonwealth Pool just as it was opening. Instead of going to the gym, she swam forty lengths of front crawl and came out to a message from Harrison: *Ya beauty!* It was so unlike anything he would actually say that she laughed out loud.

She rang him back and he picked up after only one ring.

'Where you at?' He sounded very Canadian, as if the excitement had brought him back to boyhood.

'The Commy Pool.'

'Come over. The coffee's on. Did I tell you you're brilliant?'

'You didn't have to. I'll be there in ten.'

She jogged slowly along the still-dark streets, dodging the early morning dog walkers. If anything, it was colder now with the approach of dawn than it had been earlier, and a light frost glittered under the streetlights. The winter solstice was only a couple of weeks away and the wind carried the smell of snow. She crossed Minto Street and headed for the Grange, hoping she wouldn't be too sweaty again by the time she reached Harrison's house.

He answered the door in a pair of cotton joggers and a heavy orange and red wool jumper with alpacas on it. Amy snorted. 'Nice. Is this what passes for fashion in ... where is it again?'

'Potosí. Rosa makes these, so I had to buy them for everybody I know. I might have a spare somewhere, if you want one.'

'No thank you.' She followed him into the kitchen. 'Did you not fancy going somewhere warm? My image of an anthropologist is a sweaty Englishman in a pith helmet, squatting by a campfire in the jungle somewhere.'

'I'm not a big fan of heat or jungle spiders.'

'You'd want to have seen the size of the spiders in Afghanistan, by the way. I still can't put on a pair of boots without shaking them upside down first.' She quite enjoyed seeing him cringe. 'Anyway, it's too early in the morning to talk about that place. Where's that coffee you promised?'

He poured her a cup, then took four pastries out of a paper bag and put them on a plate.

Amy helped herself. 'Thanks.'

'So, Hydra. I was looking at it online. You're pretty sure it's the place?'

'I can sort of feel it. Have you been there?'

'No. I haven't been to Greece since I was a kid, trailing around archaeological sites with my parents.'

She imagined him as a gawky, bespectacled child, kicking stones behind parents who wore matching khaki shorts and socks with sandals. 'I can just picture that.'

'I would rather have gone to the beach.'

'My parents took us to the beach. It was a caravan on the Antrim coast, or if they were feeling particularly flush, we made it as far as Blackpool. Once we went to Benidorm, but Dad got the shits really badly and they never went abroad again.' She chose the least cluttered place at his big table, sat down and selected a croissant. 'Are we going to Greece?'

He sat down across from her, slouched back in the chair and stretched his long legs out. 'I may have to. I can't pick up any real sense of Lucy from here.'

'So…no idea if she's alive or dead.'

'No. But at least you've given me a place to start looking.' He sighed and stared up at the ceiling. 'I can't really afford to take the time off right now, but ...'

'But?'

'Something tells me I don't have a lot of time. I think I have to go.'

'You have to go? You mean we, right?'

'No, I mean I.'

She laughed, then stood up. 'Oh no, don't you dare.'

'I'm not going to put you in danger.'

She turned and jabbed a finger toward him. Anger flooded out of her. 'You couldn't fight your way out of a paper bag, Professor. You need me. I'll pay my flight if that's what you're worried about.'

'It's not about money, Amy.'

'Then what is it about?'

He didn't respond. Her fury had shocked him into silence. She glared at him and waited. His unspoken answer rippled through the still morning air. He turned away from her while she breathed it in. Understanding came like a clearing of the fog. She knew why he still did this. All the lost souls he brought home were just proxies for his father. The only missing person he truly cared about was the one he couldn't find, and for all his outer confidence, there was a great black hole of doubt right in the middle of him. He didn't want her to see him fail.

But he didn't want to do this alone either.

'Harrison …'

'What?' he asked abruptly.

'Look at me.'

He stood up and faced out the window. 'Amy, just leave it. I'm sorry I got you into this.'

She rounded the table and stood beside him. 'I'm not. Are you listening to me? I'm not sorry, and I'm not walking away now. We're going to find her, alright? If she's out there to be found, we're going to find her.'

He said nothing, so on a whim, she took his hand and squeezed it. A little ripple of surprise went through him and he looked down at their entwined fingers. His brown eyes were wide and full of questions, and Amy realised that everything about their relationship had turned inside out.

For a couple of seconds, they faced each other, poised like raindrops on a blade of grass. Then he took a deep breath and nodded.

'You'd better go home and pack some things. I'll see if I can get us on a flight tonight or tomorrow.'

'Thank you. Oh, and Harri?'

'What?"

'Please tell me you're not going to take that jumper to Greece.' She sat down again to finish her croissant and coffee. 'It's truly awful.'

TWENTY-SEVEN

Harrison printed the boarding passes for a flight to Athens, leaving from Edinburgh airport in less than twenty-four hours, sent a text to Amy and then began packing a small selection of clothes into a rucksack. They would have to travel light and fast. His best hope was to get near enough to Lucy to pick up a clear image of her, and then hand the rescue – if indeed that was what it was – over to local police. But it didn't always work out that way, and the possibilities troubled him. Amy's insult still stung, even if it was wrong. He could fight his way out of plenty more than a paper bag, but he didn't relish it. There was at least one very mean bastard behind this situation, and likely more than one.

His neck began to prickle as he rolled a couple of spare shirts, and then his mobile started to ring. 'Colin,' he said, without even looking at the name. 'How are you?'

'Still shite, Jones. I'll give you two guesses who we got a call from this morning.'

'Elizabeth Merriweather.'

Colin made a wheezy sound into the phone. 'This game's rigged. Got it in one. Seems that somebody has broken into her house and poisoned her dog.'

'I am aware of that. She phoned me just after it happened. An enormous brute of a thing that she doted on. She's properly heartbroken.'

'Why didn't she contact us first? Why you?'

'I asked her that and she thought you wouldn't be interested.'

'What's she hiding?'

Harrison wondered how much to share. 'Quentin had somebody do it. He's trying to intimidate her out of the house.'

'How do you know it was him?'

'I just know. Obviously, I can't prove it. She's frightened of him.'

'Or she's been protecting him.'

'I don't think so. The man abused her and their daughter for years. I suspect the dog has been the final straw. Have you taken a statement from her?'

'Some of the local boys are there now. They knew I was checking into the Merriweathers, which is why they let me know about the call. I can't piece much together yet but I have a feeling there's a lot more to this bugger than we know.'

‘Your feelings are usually right, Colin. Keep going with it.’

‘Alright, well listen. The phone number on the back of that wee picture has been deactivated, but I did find something that might interest you. Kostas Gianopoulos and Quentin Merriweather are the joint owners of a property down in Newhaven. It’s a block of serviced apartments, Western Harbour Terrace is the address. Number eleven. You know where I mean?’

‘Roughly, aye. Those ugly new places down past the Ocean Terminal?’

‘Those are the ones.’

‘Right, thanks for that. I think I might just take a run down there this afternoon.’

‘Watch yourself down there, I mean it, Jones. Don’t give yourself away. If you see anything amiss, call me. Anything at all.’

The Western Harbour was a development of modern apartment buildings on a spit of reclaimed land that jutted into the steel-grey Forth, between Leith and Newhaven. He parked around the corner from the address Colin had given him and walked along, scanning this strange, cold environment. An icy wind howled off the water, biting his cheeks and flattening the long brown grass and weeds in the area of waste ground across the street. A beer can clanked down the otherwise deserted street and gulls keened over this hard, new habitat. Across a narrow stretch of water, coloured pennants fluttered on the Royal Yacht Britannia, and Christmas shoppers spilt out onto the balconies of the Ocean Terminal. The raw energy of Edinburgh's old port didn't reach the Western Harbour. This place felt like an outpost on the moon.

Number Eleven was a block six floors high, with a small sign above the lobby door labelled International Luxury Serviced Apartments. Behind the wall of shiny glass, a woman sat at a high-gloss black desk, clicking on a mouse with red-tipped fingers.

He buzzed for entry and she let him in.

'May I help you, sir?' she asked, in a European but unidentifiable accent. He paused for as long as he dared, gathering what he could from her. She wore a form-fitting suit, a sleek bun and blood-red lipstick. The getup seemed excessive for manning a concierge desk alone on a Saturday afternoon, but university dress standards left him in no position to judge.

He placed his hands on the desk and allowed it to convey her emotions. She was bored and vaguely suspicious of men, but in no particular distress. He summoned the haughtiest tone he could manage and said, 'Is there an apartment available for viewing?'

'Yes, of course,' she said. 'We have two apartments available at this time. How long will you require to stay in Edinburgh?'

'It'll depend on business,' he replied. 'I'd like to see the apartment, please.'

She took a bunch of keys from a drawer and stood. 'Of course, sir. Please come with me.' She led him to the lift. 'All of our apartments are furnished to the very highest standards; with everything you need for your comfort. We provide all cleaning and laundry services for your convenience, and if there is anything else we may do for you, you must only ask. What is the nature of your business?'

'Marine engineering.'

'Ah, very interesting. You must travel extensively.'

'I am rarely home,' he said, glancing at himself in the mirrored interior of the lift. He had traded the alpaca jumper for a suit jacket and trousers, and gelled his hair into temporary tidiness. More gently, he added, 'My wife has forgotten the look of me, I think.'

She glanced back at him in the mirror. 'You must get lonely sometimes.'

'My work keeps me busy. May I ask your name?'

'I am Tamara.'

‘Pleased to meet you, Tamara.’ he said, ready to supply a pseudonym if she asked. She didn’t.

Her smile flickered, then disappeared. The lift doors chimed open. ‘Here we are. Number six is the Penthouse. Our finest property.’ She unlocked the apartment door and he followed her into a stylish and clinical open-plan flat with a view sweeping across the Forth and down over the harbour toward Leith. The furniture was shiny and mostly black: black marble, black glass, black lacquer, all free of dust and fingerprints. The only softness in the place was a pristine white sheepskin rug over the high-gloss floor. The vibrations hit him as soon as he stepped through the door: loneliness, shame and the dull, constant ache of a fear that never went away. His palms began to sweat.

‘Very nice,’ he said. ‘I’d like to have a look around.’

‘Be my guest,’ she said, sweeping her hand toward the room. ‘You will find everything to your liking, I am sure.’

He moved through the apartment, occasionally pausing to touch a surface or lift an object. Everything he touched gave off the same midnight blue shimmer of worry. It was particularly strong in the master bedroom. He peeled back the quilt from one corner of the king-sized bed and ran his hand over the starched white sheet. A smell of bleach rose up and somewhere in his mind, a woman moaned in pain and wept for her home. The hairs on the back of his neck stood up and a wave of nausea coursed through him. He replaced the quilt and took a deep breath.

Tamara was still waiting by the front door. 'It is elegant, is it not?'

'It's… got a certain style.' Harrison cleared his throat and fought the desire to bolt. Free the slaves, Tomas had told him. The slaves were right here. It was like walking through a portal into an Edinburgh in a different, darker universe. He had to do this. 'This may be an awkward question, but I was led to believe that there might be certain other services available to … gentlemen in my position.'

Her eyebrows lifted, but he detected no real surprise in her. 'Ah, of course. Please, say no more. Yes, we can help in that regard. We are very discrete, of course, and our girls are all very beautiful.'

'Not Scottish, then,' he said, and gave her a wink.

She giggled and placed her lacquered fingertips over her mouth. 'Of course, the Scottish women are beautiful too, but our girls are mostly of a Mediterranean complexion. Dark and … delicious.'

'Just what I like,' he said. Gordon Leigh-Davies would be happy here, at least. 'Are any of the young ladies here today? I'd like to see what else I'm buying before I commit.'

He used the word deliberately, to gauge her reaction. Tamara hesitated for a moment but did not dispute the nature of the transaction. 'That service has an extra cost, of course.'

'I understand that, thank you.'

'We have someone here. If you wait here, I will get her for you.'

'You're very kind.'

She left him and came back several minutes later with a girl following behind.

'This is Valentina. You will have to forgive her lack of ... preparation. She appears to have slept late.'

Valentina wore only a negligible black dress and a pair of spiky heels on her bare feet. She tried to hide her bare face behind a veil of dark, wavy hair. She radiated shame like a pulsing crimson aura, but she was as striking as he had expected her to be.

'She is more beautiful without makeup. I'm very pleased to meet you, Valentina. Would you give us a moment alone, Tamara?' Harrison asked.

He could tell that Tamara wanted to refuse. 'If you want a service now …'

‘Like I said, I want to see before I buy. A couple of minutes are all we need. You can wait outside the door.’

‘Very well.’ Tamara backed out the room and snicked the door shut gently.

Harrison smiled at Valentina and took a step toward her. ‘I’m not going to hurt you.’

‘You may do as you wish, sir. What would you like?’

‘I would like you to tell me how old you are.’

‘Twenty-four.’

‘No, you’re not. You’re what, sixteen? How long ago did you leave Syria?’

Her eyes opened wide in surprise. ‘I am from Spain, sir.’

He didn’t try to dispute her story. ‘Can you tell me anything about the men who brought you here?’

‘I am here by my own free will,’ she asserted, but she was staring him full in the face now, crying silently for his help.

‘Can I hold your hands, Valentina?’ Even as he said the name, he knew it wasn’t really hers.

She nodded.

Harrison took her hands and held them gently between his own. He closed his eyes and waited for the details to come. She trembled but didn’t try to remove her hands.

There were bombs and there was hunger. There were two boat journeys: one overcrowded, cold and wet, and the other hot and sickening. There were many dark hours on the move, in a windowless van or the back of a lorry. Terror every step of the way, regret, sometimes anger and sometimes acceptance of a fate worse than death.

He could see a festering ball of green-black energy inside her and he let himself go toward it, tap it, draw it away. She shuddered and dropped to her knees.

Harrison knelt in front of her and had to catch his breath before he could speak. It felt like he had been punched in the stomach. 'Rima. Is that your name?'

'How do you know that?' she whispered. 'What did you do to me?'

He swallowed hard. 'I want you to stay here, Rima. Do not tell anyone about this. Don't tell Tamara, don't tell anyone. Help will come for you. I promise, help will come for you.'

'There are other girls.'

'I know.' He stood and helped her up. 'Don't say anything to them until someone comes for you.'

'Please, I don't want to be deported,' she said.

A deep, grinding ache was travelling through his bones. His ribcage felt like it might crush inwards. There was no way to make things right for her, but he had to get her away from here.

'I know you don't,' he said. He couldn't bring himself to make her a false promise.

On the landing, Tamara radiated a seething haze of suspicion and seduction. 'Valentina is to your liking, yes?'

'Valentina is very lovely.' Saying the words made him feel sick.

She pressed the lift button. 'If you would like to come downstairs, we can complete the reservation for you, Mr… I'm afraid I didn't catch your name.'

'Davies. Gordon Davies.' The name came to him in a moment of spite.

'I'm pleased to meet you, Mr Davies.'

He wanted to run down the stairs, but forced himself to smile and wait calmly beside her. As the lift descended, he stared straight ahead, refusing to make eye contact. Back at the front desk, she presented him with a form. He made a show of glancing over it.

'I'll hold off just now, if you don't mind. I have another apartment I'd like to look at before I commit.'

'I see,' she said, with some surprise. Immediately the colour of her mood darkened and questions began to tumble out of her. What had Valentina said to him? How did he know about the girls? 'Was there something wrong with the apartment?'

'On the contrary. Everything was ... just as I expected it to be. Tamara, thank you for your time. I'm certain I'll be back.'

Leaving the apartments, he felt so bruised and battered he could barely move his legs. He managed to steer the car safely away from the Western Harbour, but the pre-Christmas Saturday evening traffic was bad and his eyes weren't fully focusing in the dimming light. His head was beginning to pound.

He made it as far as Albion Road, where he pressed Amy's buzzer and dragged himself up the stairs.

TWENTY-EIGHT

She wasn't the only girl on the boat. Sometimes Lucy heard voices in the cabin next to hers, and occasionally they saw each other in passing, but their minders made sure they didn't speak to each other. Every few days, one girl would disappear and another would arrive. They were in transit: being picked up and delivered to different places for some special purpose. It didn't take much to work out what that purpose was.

Every so often, a girl would try to break away. There would be banging and screaming, and then silence. Lucy never knew who escaped, who submitted and who was forcefully subdued. Maybe they were killed.

She stopped taking the Valium they gave her, and as the fog in her mind began to clear, she understood the full horror of her circumstances. There was no bank account. Whatever contract she had signed had long since expired. She was being held captive. The warm, languid days with Kostas were long gone now. Her heart ached for him, for the shame he would feel if he knew what he'd signed her up for.

But of course, he did know. She had only been pretending to believe otherwise to protect her heart, but it was a dried black thing now and not worth protecting.

There was no way to fight them, so she forced herself to perform as she had been doing all along. Alone in her tiny cabin, she tried to work out a plan. The only time they didn't watch her with hawkish attention was when she was with one of the men. Sometimes the men would leave her for a few minutes, while they washed themselves or went to empty their bowels. The cabin they used for these pleasures had its own private door onto the rear deck. She would have no time for hesitation. There was no way of knowing where she might be plucked out of the water, or if she might fall into the hands of men who treated her as badly, or worse. She would have no money, no identification and no sensible clothes. But surely somebody would help her.

Surely.

Her chance arrived late at night, when the old man who came for her was so drunk that he stumbled away to be sick after his climax. As soon as he had pulled the bathroom door closed, she slipped on her bra and panties, peered out onto the deck and saw nobody. That didn't mean she wasn't being watched from some unseen position, but just maybe there was time to make it over the railing. She took a deep breath and hesitated. Water ran in the bathroom. It was now or it was never.

Lucy threw the door open and launched herself for the railing. It was a longer-way down than she'd imagined, but by the time the shouts came behind her, she was in the air. She dived as far from the boat as she could and plunged deep into the black, cold water. It took a lot longer than she expected to kick for the surface. When she got there, she stole a single desperate breath and swam as hard as she could for the opposite side of the harbour.

It wasn't that far; she should be able to swim this. But she'd done no exercise in weeks now. She'd barely walked the length of herself since she'd come onto the boat. She'd done nothing but eat, drink, take the damn pills and lie on her back. After only a few furious strokes, her legs began to cramp and the cold began to seep into her blood. She stopped for a moment, treaded water and tried to catch her breath. Somebody was shouting at her from the pier. A man was waving his arms and shouting in Greek for her to swim toward him. She didn't recognise him as anyone from the boat, so she swam toward him. Maybe they would simply let her go and replace her with someone else.

There had to be an endless supply of girls. Surely, she wasn't worth a fight.

When she got near enough, the man on the pier threw in a life ring. She heaved herself onto it and kicked weakly while he dragged her in. By the time his hands closed around her wrists, she was shaking violently and almost too weak to climb out of the water. The man was wearing a uniform—police or coastguard, she wasn't sure. Relief flooded into her and little lights swam in front of her eyes. He was speaking rapid-fire Greek, questioning and scolding and exclaiming over her state of undress. She shook her head and tried to tell him she couldn't understand, doubled over with fatigue and cold.

'Help me,' she said, but her voice came out in a whisper. She tried again. 'Help me. I have to get away.' Clearly, he couldn't understand her any better than she could him.

She tried to step around him and run, but he grabbed onto her arm. She screamed and wrenched herself away. The man clung onto her. In her desperation, she dragged him along the pier.

He only let go when two men from the boat caught up with them. One of them placed a thick dressing gown around Lucy's shoulders and held her tightly, while the other offered some apologetic explanation to the man. All three of them laughed heartily. Lucy wanted to fight, but she was too weak and too tired. A tunnel closed in around her head and her legs drooped. She sagged in the man's arms and felt him catch her. She was barely conscious of being lifted and carried back onto the yacht.

Sometime later, Victor sat on the edge of her bed, stroked her and spoke in soothing tones. When she opened her eyes, he switched to English.

'That was a very silly thing to do, my beautiful flower. And very, very dangerous. There are so many wicked people these days. All of these refugees. They are desperate, my darling, and you are so very young and beautiful. What do you think would happen to you? Do we not treat you well here? Here you are celebrated and loved and admired. We don't want to lose you, my dearest Lucy.'

She opened her mouth but her tongue felt coated with fur and was incapable of making the right sounds. They had given her more drugs. Victor watched her trying to speak, and then placed a meaty finger over her lips. 'Don't upset yourself, my darling.'

'I want to go home.' Hot tears leaked out from the corners of her eyes and ran into the pillow. 'I just want to go home.'

'When you are rested, we will discuss the terms of your contract. But not tonight. Tonight, you must rest.'

'What happens to the other girls? Where are you taking them?'

'There are no other girls. Only you.'

'I've seen them.'

'You are having bad dreams. You have been very sick. Look how skinny you have become. You must eat more.'

Lucy turned away, closed her eyes and pretended to go to sleep. She had clearly seen the girls. She'd heard them shouting and crying in the night.

She could have been dreaming. This whole thing could be a bad dream that she couldn't wake up from. She couldn't tell what was real anymore.

Victor sat for a little while, stroking her hair and her back. Eventually, he got up and pulled the door closed behind him. Lucy listened to the familiar clunk of the lock on the outside and knew there was only one other route of escape left to her. She took a bottle of wine out of the little refrigerator under her dressing table, opened it and drank straight from it.

TWENTY-NINE

Amy buckled herself into the seat and looked out the plane window at the lights shining on the wet tarmac. She had been up for four hours already, and the only suggestion of daylight was a timid pink glow on the south-eastern horizon. Beside her, Harrison crossed his arms over his chest and looked claustrophobic. His knees were wedged tightly against the back of the seat in front of him.

Amy tried to joke. 'You have clearly exceeded the optimal height for budget airline seats.'

'No comment,' he muttered through his teeth, leaning toward her as the inflated backside of a man protruded into his space. Amy bit her lip as she watched the hefty man trying to force his suitcase into an already packed overhead compartment. The plane smelled of dirty plastic and wet wool, and was nearly full. It was surprising how many people wanted to fly to Athens on an early December Sunday morning.

‘Are you okay?’ she asked. Yesterday he had let his guard down for her, just enough to let her see the true weight of his so-called gift. Being trapped in a flying metal tube with dozens of people and their unstated terrors would be a unique brand of torture. ‘Do you want to try to sleep?’

‘The only way I can sleep on a plane is if I drug myself. There’s no point on a short flight.’

‘Do you mind if I sleep? I’m cream-crackered.’

‘Go ahead.’

Facing three hours in this seat, her body had started complaining like an exhausted toddler. Her stomach was churning and her eyelids felt swollen. She had tossed and turned much of the night, her mind in a spin of confusion about what had already happened and anxiety about what was to come. Harrison’s appearance at her door last night, just as she was sitting down to an early tea, had spooked her badly. He’d been pale as a ghost, sweating like he had a fever and unsteady on his feet.

She had sat him on the sofa and forced a mug of sweet tea between his hands.

‘I hate this, Amy,’ he had said, and crumpled forward, palms pressing into his eyes. Instinctively, she had tried to put her arm around him, but he had pulled away as if her touch had burnt him, saying, ‘Don’t.’

‘Harri, I’m sorry,’ she had said, only half understanding what she was apologising for. The intense loneliness of his existence had finally started to dawn on her, and as she thought back to their meeting on North Bridge, she wondered if maybe she had rescued him rather than the other way around.

After ten minutes he’d recovered enough to get his phone out and make two calls: one to his mate Colin Muir in CID and one to Nessa Walker at LASAR-Net. Then he told Amy the story of the International Luxury Serviced Apartments at Western Harbour, and a sixteen-year-old Syrian girl called Rima.

The airline staff performed their usual safety routine and the plane rolled back from the terminal. Within a couple of minutes, they were juddering into the turbulent winter sky, bouncing away from the cloudy dawn before banking sharply to the left. Amy looked at Harrison. His arms were still crossed, his hands tucked in tightly. His eyes were closed and he appeared to be asleep, but she knew he wasn’t. She made a pillow with her jacket, pressed it between the window and her cheek, and closed her eyes.

When she woke, much later, they were cruising in the blue sky above a layer of billowy white cloud.

‘Good sleep?’ Harrison asked.

'Was I out long?'

'Couple of hours.'

Amy checked her watch. 'So… what's our plan?'

'We get into the centre of town and find someplace to stay, then I thought we'd check out this co-operative that Nessa mentioned. It's possible Tim's gone back there.'

'What about Hydra?'

'I think we may be too late to get the boat there today.'

'Tomorrow, then?'

'Probably. Depending what else we turn up.'

Amy looked down, trying to catch a glimpse of land between the broken clouds below. There was a shimmer of golden light rippling over a dark blue sea.

'I owe you an apology about yesterday,' he said, without warning. 'You didn't need to see me in that state.'

'I've seen a lot of folk in a worse state than that, believe me.'

'I guess. Well, anyway, I'm sorry. Sometimes it all gets a bit ...' He finished the sentence with a grimace.

She glanced around to check that none of their fellow passengers were listening in, but they were all distracted by laptops or magazines, their voices lost behind the engine noise. 'You actually looked like you were in physical pain.'

He nodded. 'When I connect with someone with so much trauma inside them, it feels like going twelve rounds with a psychopathic kickboxer. I got my black belt in karate at school, but no fight ever hurt as bad as that. Rima was one of the worst I've met.'

'This is why you didn't want me to touch you.'

'I'm sorry, Amy. I know it's a difficult thing to understand. I'm not ... I wasn't ... trying to reject you.'

'And I was only being a friend. We're clear on that point, right?'

'We are.'

'You really have a black belt in karate?'

'I had a black belt once upon a time. I try to keep my skills up. Every once in a while, it comes in handy.' A sad smile flickered onto his face. 'Do you want to know the back story?'

'Only if you want to tell me.'

'To cut a long story short, my parents split up because of how I was, and my dad walked away and never came home. My mum couldn't stand to have me around after he left. She sent me off to boarding school, where I got beaten up on a regular basis until I finally took it upon myself to learn to fight back. Hence ... the karate. I was good at it. It helps keep me sane.'

'I get that.' This time, for once, she wasn't teasing. 'So, your parents didn't know what to do with you either.'

'That surprises you?'

'I thought for sure your folks would be of a more open-minded and tolerant breed than mine.'

'Only about some things. If I'd been gay, they would have been perfectly fine, but they took this personally. They're both scientists and sworn atheists, and this thing shook their world view. It was like I'd been handed the power to undermine everything they knew, as well as their authority over me. And when they realised it wasn't going to go away, they turned on each other. I came away from it all believing neither of them ever really wanted a kid in the first place.'

'And you have no idea at all where your dad went?'

'We think he went back to Canada right after he left, but after that it's like he vanished off the face of the earth.'

'Why would he do that?'

'I've been asking that question for thirty years.'

'And you never pick up anything from him?'

'No.' His blunt tone indicated that this was an unwelcome line of questioning.

‘God.’ She took a deep breath and thought about all he’d said. ‘It’s a weird old life, Indiana.’

‘Are you ever going to stop calling me that?’

‘Just accept it. I only give nicknames to people I like.’ The engine noise changed tone, and the plane tilted into a decline. She looked down at a wrinkled, arid coastline in front of them. ‘Three weeks ago, I hadn’t met you.’

‘A lot can happen in three weeks.’

‘And you can have months on end when nothing happens. Since I split up with Ricky, I’ve been in limbo, waiting for something to happen without knowing what. And now this, and it feels like everything has changed.’

‘In a good way?’

‘Mmm,’ she breathed, considering his question. ‘I’ll answer that if we survive the next couple of days.’

He glanced at her. ‘Are you scared?’

Most likely he could tell exactly what she felt, but she didn’t want to say it. It was the same feeling she had before going on operations: not fear, exactly, but anticipation and the kind of excitement that filled your legs with a fierce heat. Danger was an addiction worse than any drug she knew, and once it was in your blood you never really got rid of it.

‘I’m alright. You?’

‘I am…somewhat anxious.’

She laughed. 'Relax, Jones. I've got your back.'

They took a taxi from the airport to the centre of Athens, a sprawling city under a layer of winter smog. Signs of Greece's recent economic troubles were visible everywhere: potholed roads, broken pavements, graffiti, people huddled like stray dogs in squares and small parks. Fashionably-dressed people went about their business, barely noticing them. Compassion can only stretch so far, Amy thought silently, as they rolled on through the traffic. Sometimes there were just too many people to help.

As they neared the city centre, the Acropolis rose like a massive stage set above jumbled streets of ordinary apartment blocks, shops and offices. The bleached stone of the Parthenon shone a pale pink in the filtered light. The taxi left them in front of a Novotel close to Syntagma Square, where, to Amy's relief, Harrison booked them into two single rooms. They took the lift to their respective rooms and agreed to meet in an hour. She locked the door behind her and looked around the room: it was clean and so generic that you might walk into this room in Athens and walk out of an identical one in Bangkok. Car horns and scooter engines rose from the street, four floors below. She looked out for a couple of minutes, watching the patterns of this new place.

She closed the curtains, peeled off her sweaty clothes and stood in the shower for a long time, leaning against the tiles while the hot water cascaded over her. She closed her eyes and imagined herself holding Lucy Merriweather's guitar, feeling the curved wood against her belly and the strings pressing into her fingertips. Without the benefit of the Salvia leaves, she pictured herself walking back through the woods, moving out of this beige hotel bathroom, looking for the clearing and the door.

Where are you, she thought. I'm looking for you, Lucy. *Where are you?*

She was in a room with no windows. Walls of reddish, glossy wood, a bed, a small dressing table. Lucy lay under a white sheet, her hair splayed across the pillows. She was in a state of deep, dreamless sleep. A drugged, unnatural sleep. Amy tried whispering Lucy's name, but the girl didn't respond.

Amy needed to see out. She needed to find her way out of the room. She touched the wall and began to move her hands up it. And she climbed, as easily as a spider, up the wall and across the ceiling. Unseen, she slipped out the door and along a narrow corridor. At the far end, there were steep steps leading up. At the top of the steps, a metal door with a round portal. She moved through this, out onto the yacht's lower deck. For just a moment, she was able to hover above the boat. They were in port. It was night, and the lights of the little town glittered on the water. A man patrolled the deck, walking stiffly forward and aft, then climbed the stairs and went into an upper cabin. Amy moved toward the stern of the boat. She read the name Circe in black letters.

She felt herself falling, and then she was spluttering in icy water. Her eyes popped open and she was crumpled in the tub in the hotel bathroom, legs bent under her. The water had run cold.

'Ow, shit,' she muttered, slipping and bumping her elbow as she reached for the tap. She turned it off and dried herself as quickly as she could in the steamy room, repeating the name Circe so that it would not disappear from memory. The little port was Hydra town. She had spent hours studying the place on Google Street View.

Filled with a sense of giddy triumph, she threw on her clothes, ran along the corridor to Harrison's room and banged the door with her fist. He peered out, then slid the chain to open the door. He was dripping and wearing only a towel around his waist.

'Amy. You alright? What's happened?'

'Oh, God ... sorry. I'm fine, I was just ... Do you ... want to get dressed?' The towel barely covered him. Trying to keep her eyes above waist height, she discovered a pleasantly-formed chest, lightly covered with damp brown hair, and a belly that was still flat. For a man who liked his food, he was surprisingly fit. He smelled of perfumed hotel soap.

'Hang on.' He closed the door and opened it again a few seconds later, still shirtless but with a pair of jeans on. 'Come in.'

He turned away from her and dug in his backpack. An Andean condor stretched its wings between his shoulder blades, at least twelve inches from tip to tip, outlined in black and decorated with brightly coloured geometric patterns.

'Oh my God.'

'What?'

'That is some tattoo.'

'I forgot you hadn't seen it.'

'I haven't seen you with your clothes off before.'

'Right enough. Sorry, that was a stupid thing to say. I got it after Tomas died; I guess I wanted something permanent to remind me of him. Do you like it?'

'It's ...' she cleared her throat, caught off guard by his question, 'a work of art. I didn't think you were a tattoo kind of person.' His back itself wasn't bad either, now that she had the opportunity to study it. It was smooth, tapering down to a neat waist. She fought down the urge to run her hands along the condor's wings. For a couple of seconds, it almost felt like he wanted her to.

'I wasn't, until then. Anyway.' He pulled a black t-shirt over his head, depriving her of the view. 'What's up?'

'I saw Lucy on the boat. The boat is called Circe. It was in port, in Hydra. I'll recognise it. I saw it, Harrison, clear as anything.'

'How?'

'I don't know. I was in the shower. I closed my eyes and tried to send myself there.'

'Right,' he said slowly. 'Are you sure it wasn't ... a dream or ...'

'How do you tell the difference?'

'I just know.'

'Well, I just know too.'

'Fine. I believe you. What about Lucy? What did you see?'

'She's in a cabin with no windows, below decks. She was asleep, but she looked ... drunk, or drugged. I think they're guarding her.'

'So, they're definitely holding her against her will?'

'I think so.'

'Was it Kostas? Did you see him?'

'No, I didn't.'

'You were able to move around the boat? In your vision?'

‘Yeah. It was like I could fly.’

‘That’s handy,’ he said, and sounded impressed. ‘So, assuming what you saw is the reality, we aren’t going to be able to sneak on or off without a fight.’

‘I did have that dream about a commando raid ...’

He held up a finger. ‘No way. Don’t even joke about that.’ He rubbed the towel over his wet hair and dug in his rucksack for clean socks. ‘We get the first ferry over there in the morning, scout things out and come up with a plan.’

‘We could just go to the police when we get there.’

‘I’m not sure about that.’

‘You don’t trust them?’

‘Think about it. It’s just a wee island. Somebody knows exactly what’s going on and is choosing to look the other way.’

‘So ... what are you saying? We don’t involve the law?’

He made a noncommittal gesture. ‘We need to be very careful who we trust.’

‘So how do you propose to get her off?’

‘We’re going to have to use what we know against him.’

‘You mean ... Maryam and the Western Harbour? Isn’t that blackmail?’

‘Yep.’

Amy watched him lace up his boots and considered the implications of what he'd just said. 'Harri, the man is a criminal. You think he's just going to let you away, knowing what you know?'

'You remember what Maryam said to you. Kostas has to keep himself clean. He's not going to do anything to ruin his reputation.'

'Maybe not, but he can get someone to do it for him.'

'Then I suggest we watch our backs.' He stood up, pulled a black woolly hat onto his head, and slipped photographs of Tim and Lucy into the inside pocket of his coat. 'Are we ready?'

THIRTY

The humanitarian co-operative where Tim and Lucy had volunteered was a twenty-minute walk from the hotel. They wound their way through streets crowded with tourists, passing countless shops selling leather goods, traditional knitwear, jewellery and food. The psychic traffic was also busy. Harrison did his best to tune it out, but he was tired and lightheaded from hunger, which always made him more receptive. After passing five or six shops selling greasy gyros and souvlaki, his stomach started to grumble.

'I have got to eat something.'

'Food is quite the priority in your life, isn't it?'

He glanced down at her. She was honed and wiry, with no spare fat anywhere on her body, or at least on the bits of it that he had seen. She was the kind of person who ate out of necessity rather than pleasure, and never more than she needed. 'It's kind of important, isn't it?'

'Yeah, but ...'

'But nothing. If I don't eat, I can't concentrate.' He stopped in front of a takeaway window and said a polite, *'Kalispera,'* to the man at the counter, and ordered gyros in a pitta. 'You want something, Amy?'

'I'll have the same, I guess.'

He asked the man behind the counter for a second order and paid for the food. They walked along to a bench in a green square on the next block. Amy sat next to him. The bench was small and she sat so close that their elbows touched and he could smell the fruity scent of her shampoo, mingling with the smell of the food. The clouds had broken to allow a gentle warmth through. For a minute or two, he allowed himself to enjoy being here beside her, in a city that was new to them both. She looked like a young traveller, lively and open, a different person completely from the one he'd first met on North Bridge.

As their arms brushed, he could sense excitement running through her like an electric current. The contact seemed to complete a circuit between them, so that it went through him too. It was the thrill of discovery, of new-found power, and of desire. He felt it too, and it was unsettling. He wasn't supposed to enjoy this.

He took a bite of the salty, delicious meat and said through a mouthful, 'Oh God, this is good.'

Amy laughed at him and picked the meat out of the pita with her fingers. She gave it an experimental taste. 'I didn't know speaking Greek was one of your many talents.'

'A few words, that's all.'

'Everybody here seems to speak English.'

'And why would I be so arrogant as to assume they should speak my language when I'm in their country?'

'Did you speak the language when you lived in Bolivia?'

'My Spanish is good. I learned enough of the indigenous languages to get by. It's important, you know. You can't really get inside a place or its people if you don't understand their language.'

'Well, *you* can.'

'Feelings and thoughts are different things. We all have the same human emotions, but culture and language shape how we explain these.'

She looked up at the passing people for a few seconds, chewing thoughtfully. The sun lit up her eyes like aquamarines. 'I'd love to do what you do.'

'You could.'

'Not likely. I'm not even close to clever enough.'

'What gives you the idea that I'm any cleverer than you?'

She didn't answer his question, and there was something about her smile that made him curious.

He swallowed a mouthful. 'What?'

'You learn a lot about people when you travel with them.'

'What have you learned about me?'

'Mmm. I'm still gathering evidence.'

'Okay then, fair's fair. Let me gather some of my own. Show me your tattoo.'

'Who says I have one?' Amy pretended to look shocked.

'I think you do.'

She arched her right eyebrow at him. 'You got x-ray vision now as well?'

'No, but you're a millennial ex-squaddie. I'd put money on it.'

'I might have one.'

'Do I get to see it?'

She laughed. 'No.'

'You've seen mine.'

'Because it's on your back, and now that you mention it, you were quite happy to show it off. Are you flirting with me, Indiana?'

His face warmed. 'No.'

'Well good, because that would be weird.'

'Weird how? Am I too old for you?'

'How old are you?'

'I turned forty at the end of October. I did not enjoy it.'

'Well if it's any consolation, no, you wouldn't be too old for me. It's just ... well ... just because. I don't know. I think of you as a workmate now, or a teacher or something. Maybe a big brother, except I like you better than my brothers.'

'Okay.' He shook his head, wondering where all of this had come from. 'I'm sorry, forget I said any of that.'

'No, it's ... okay, it's just ...' She took a deep breath. 'We're here to find Lucy and Tim. It would overcomplicate things. It's not that I don't like you, because ...'

'Because you do.'

'You can feel that?'

'Obviously.'

'For Christ's sake, is nobody allowed to have any privacy around you?'

He looked up into the watery sunlight, smiling sadly. 'You can see why I'm single.'

'Have you ever had a long-term relationship?'

'One.' He looked out across the square, watching pigeons squabbling over a McDonald's burger box. The six years he'd spent with Sophie now felt like a chapter written into his life-story and subsequently cut from the final draft. 'Like you, I was engaged, for a while.'

'What happened?'

‘Everything and nothing. We found it impossible to live with each other in the end. It’s the way it goes.’

‘Oh, Harri ...’

‘You and I need to keep things professional,’ he said, with a mixture of regret and relief. ‘Do you agree?’

‘Absolutely.’ She held up her half-eaten gyros. ‘You want the rest of this?’

‘Sure.’ He downed it in three bites and took a deep breath, feeling more solid than he had been a few minutes ago. The city’s emotional din was less overpowering. ‘Okay, I’ve put this off long enough. Let’s go.’

Following the map on his phone, they found their way to the former office building that housed the co-operative. The lobby was busy with people coming and going, speaking languages he couldn’t immediately identify, carrying bags of clothing, boxes of food and musical instruments. Harrison picked up a strong sense of comfort—this was clearly a place of refuge and respite—though, beneath that, there was a keen, relentless drone of frustration. Here people on the move could rest, but they didn’t want to stay too long. Some had been here far longer than they wanted to be.

Lucy’s residual psychic signature was here too, though it was faint enough to suggest that she hadn't been here for some time. Behind that, very faintly, was a dissonant hum of menace.

He greeted the woman at the front desk in Greek.

'How can I help you?' she replied, in North American-accented English.

'I believe you've recently had a couple of British volunteers working here? Tim Cartwright and Lucy Merriweather?'

'Oh, uh ...' She looked behind her, as if seeking permission from someone who wasn't there. 'They don't work here anymore.'

'Would you be able to tell us where they might be now?'

The woman's smile faded and she hesitated. She gave off pulses of annoyance. 'I don't know.'

'Do you have any information about them at all? Because it's possible they're in some danger.'

'Well, that wouldn't surprise me. Who are you? You're British, right? Are you relatives?'

'We're investigators, from Edinburgh. We've been hired by Lucy Merriweather's family.'

'Investigators,' the woman repeated. 'Can you ... wait for a few minutes? I'm going to get somebody to come down and talk to you.' The woman picked up the phone and asked somebody called Maya to come downstairs, her tone secretive and urgent. 'She'll be down as soon as she can,' she said, hanging up the phone. 'You can have a seat right over there.'

Amy and Harrison sat on plastic chairs. She read an English leaflet that described the co-operative's work.

'This puts Nessa Walker's operation to shame.' She passed Harrison the leaflet. He read that the co-op provided immediate humanitarian assistance to refugees, migrants and homeless local people in the form of food, clothing and shelter. It also ran classes, support groups, cultural activities and gave access to legal advice and medical care. Volunteers did the best they could to confront problems governments would rather ignore.

A Muslim woman sat three seats along, comforting a fussing baby while a toddler clung to her leg. Her face was haunted and she was numb inside and out, drained of emotion and defeated.

'How can we live with ourselves?' Amy asked quietly, after a moment.

Harrison could almost hear her guilt, and it wasn't the familiar, generalised political guilt of a well-intentioned British citizen. It was specific and all her own. Their connection was getting so close now, he could feel what she felt almost like it belonged to him.

'This isn't your fault.'

Their eyes met and then broke apart. ‘For all I know, the man I killed could have been that woman’s husband.’

Harrison knew better than to offer hollow words of comfort. He placed his hand momentarily on her shoulder, and the scene flashed like a movie trailer inside his mind. Their patrol unit was ambushed. While she tended a wounded man, they came under fire from a Taliban fighter on a suicide run. She had no choice except to snatch up the wounded soldier’s rifle and shoot.

That gunshot still woke her up at night, shattering the cool darkness of her bedroom.

‘That’s them,’ he heard the North American woman say. A formidably tall and broad-shouldered woman moved toward them. There were silver streaks in her tightly knotted hair, and her brightly coloured skirt dusted the floor.

Harrison slipped his hand away from Amy’s arm and stood up. ‘Hello.’

‘Would you come with me, please?’ She wasn’t interested in pleasantries.

They followed her through a door to the side of the front desk, along a corridor and into a private office cluttered with stacks of paper and cardboard boxes. ‘I am Maya Retsikas. Lisa told me you are looking for two of our former volunteers.’

Harrison shook her hand before introducing himself. She bore the weight of responsibility for other people's lives with authority, and she wasn't best pleased with being diverted from her task.

'Thank you for taking the time to speak to us. I'm Harrison Jones and this is my partner, Amy Bell. We've come from Edinburgh.'

She gave a knowing nod. 'For Lucy Merriweather and Tim Cartwright.' She motioned toward the chairs beside a small, round table. 'Please sit down.'

'I take it you know them,' Amy said, sliding onto a chair. There was an edge of military aggression in her voice. Harrison shot her a look and thought the word *easy*.

Amy sat back in her seat and glared at him.

'Of course, although as Lisa told you, they are no longer here.'

'Are you the manager here?' Harrison asked more gently.

'We have a co-operative management structure. I am the coordinator of the volunteers. We have people working here from all over the world. Some of them have very specific skills to bring, others just want to do what they can. Tim and Lucy did what they could, although they ...' she hesitated, choosing her words carefully, 'caused us a few problems.'

'What kind of problems?'

Maya pressed her fingertips deep into her fleshy jowls. 'They took drugs. They behaved let's say inappropriately. They argued with each other. I can't prove it, but I think they stole from us.'

'How long ago was this?'

'They were here until early September, when we asked them to leave. We have very many traumatised people coming to this centre, and this needs to be a place of calm and safety. Who are you working for?'

'Lucy Merriweather's mother employed us to find them. She hasn't seen or heard from her daughter in over a year.'

Maya shrugged. 'I'm sure that is distressing for her. We have people in this centre who have not seen their families for much longer than that. Many daughters go missing.'

Rima came immediately into Harrison's mind. 'Is Lucy one of those daughters?' he asked, more sharply than he intended to.

Maya was nonplussed. 'I do not know where Lucy is.'

'Do you think she got into some kind of trouble?'

'That is possible. If she was buying drugs, you never know who she got mixed up with. It is likely she just got bored and moved on. Maybe she met another boy, I don't know. There was something not right with her, but I don't have time to think about that. I need volunteers who can work without being constantly told what to do and how to do it. I told the same thing to Tim, when he was here looking for her last week.'

'Last *week*?' Harrison leaned forward, not sure he'd heard her correctly.

'Yes. It may have been ... Tuesday or Wednesday?'

'Do you know if he's still in Athens?'

Maya shrugged. 'I have not seen him again.'

'Do you have a phone number for him?'

'If I did, I wouldn't be allowed to give it to you.'

'And you haven't any idea where Lucy may be now?'

'No. Like I said, we asked them to leave. I had to repeat that request to Tim when he came. He was abusive to some of our people.'

'Abusive how?'

'Angry. Shouting.' Her head nodded with each point. She brought her hands together in a praying gesture and pointed them toward him. 'I understand he is upset that Lucy has left him, but I think he is also mentally ill.'

'Maya,' Amy cut in, 'can I ask whether you've met a man called Kostas Gianopoulos?'

'Kostas? Of course, I know Kostas Gianopoulos very well. He is one of our most generous patrons. He is outspoken about the plight of the refugees.'

'Is he really?'

'Oh yes, he has given us money. He helped us get this building. He is a very wonderful man. Why do you ask about him?'

Harrison glanced at Amy. He could tell that Maya believed this to be true, and that she thought of Kostas as a friend. He didn't believe she was complicit in Kostas's crimes, but asking any more would raise her suspicions.

'He's friendly with Lucy's parents. We thought he might have some idea where she is.'

Maya shrugged again. 'He is very busy and I haven't seen him for a couple of months.'

Harrison moved on. 'Could we look around and see where Tim and Lucy worked?'

'I can give you a tour of our centre, if it will help you.'

'It would. Thank you.'

'Come with me,' she commanded, and she swept back along the corridor. 'We serve over two hundred people every day. Men, women and children.' Her voice boomed as she led them around the building's four sprawling floors. There were classrooms, makeshift medical and dental clinics, and art studios. The top floor had been converted into dormitories. Conversations drifted around in many languages, bursts of laughter echoed up stairwells, children ran along corridors.

'Impressive,' he said to Maya.

'We work around the clock, every day of the year. Because war and persecution do not stop. We have at least forty volunteers per day. You understand, I work very hard and it can be difficult. I don't personally get to know all of the volunteers as well as I would like.'

'But you knew Tim and Lucy.'

'I knew them because they caused a lot of trouble, as I told you. I'm sorry to say, some young British people are like babies. They come here for selfish reasons and they understand nothing.'

'What did they do while they were here?'

'Most of the time, they worked in the cantina or the storehouse. I will show you.' She took them to the cantina first, a sunlit room on the first floor, thick with the smells of coffee and cooking food. People sat at long trestle tables, talking and laughing. 'They helped in the kitchen, cooking and washing dishes.'

Harrison walked slowly behind her, allowing his fingertips to brush the tables and work surfaces but failing to pick up anything significant. Leaving the cantina, they followed Maya to the storehouse. It was a cavernous basement filled with stacks of donated clothing, blankets, dishes, cookware, sleeping bags, tents and medical supplies. The room was windowless, badly lit and filled with a restless, seething fear. It raised the hair on the back of Harrison's neck. He paused and looked at Amy, wondering whether she felt it, but she walked straight past him.

There were seven or eight people working, sorting through piles of clothing, noting down sizes and hanging them on rails.

'This is a big job,' Maya said. 'We are given many things, all mixed up, and it all must be sorted. Greek people are very charitable. Sometimes too much.' Her laugh echoed against the concrete walls. 'Tim liked to come down here. Sometimes I caught him smoking hash in the back there. Lucy, I don't know. She just ... drifted around. She never went where you told her or did work for more than a few minutes. A strange girl. Do you know her well?'

'I've never met her,' Harrison said. He barely got the words out. At the mention of the names, it felt like somebody had cleaved his skull open. The floor tilted steeply away from him, pulling him forward. He took a step back, leaned against the wall and forced himself to stay upright. The pain was so violent that he raised his fingertips to his forehead to check for blood. Maya had turned away to speak to another woman, but Amy hurried to his side.

'Harri?'

‘That guy over there,’ he whispered. ‘At the back.’

Amy looked around. The young man in question had curly black hair and a handsome, clean-shaven face. He was on his knees, folding children’s clothes. ‘What do you want to do?’

‘Let’s go. He’ll follow.’

‘Right,’ Amy said, glancing over her shoulder. The man wasn’t looking at them, but he was poised and listening.

Harrison said abruptly, ‘Maya? Thank you for showing us around. We have some other places to try, but would it be okay to come back if we need to?’

‘I’m sorry I can’t help you more,’ Maya replied. ‘I don’t know what good it would do to come back.’

‘We may have a few more questions. But thank you again.’

She had already dismissed them. ‘You can find your way out?’

‘Yes, thank you.’

They slipped out into the corridor and he placed his hand against the wall to steady himself. After a couple of seconds, he gathered himself together and took a deep breath. ‘Talk about the evil eye.’

‘Are you alright?’

‘Yeah. Come on.’

They hurried upstairs and out into the street and waited just to the side of the doorway. Harrison's skin prickled as he could feel the man approaching. As soon as the door opened, he turned and stepped into the man's path.

'Where are they?' he said, with more force than he felt capable of acting on.

Spooked, the younger man tried to sidestep him. 'I don't know what you mean.'

Harrison blocked him, and Amy moved onto his left, trapping him against the wall. 'Yes, you do, or you wouldn't have followed us out here.'

'Keep your hands where we can see them,' Amy ordered, as the man's right hand crept toward his pocket.

He lifted his palms toward her. 'I don't know who you are, but you need to leave this city. If you ask any more questions, it will not go well for you.'

Boldly, Harrison grabbed a fistful of the man's sweatshirt and drove him into the wall. 'We came here to find Lucy Merriweather and Tim Cartwright, and you're going to tell us where they are.'

For a couple of seconds, the man was too shocked to struggle. His mouth opened and he betrayed himself without uttering a word. He had been hired to kill. 'I can't,' he choked. 'I don't know.'

That much was the truth.

'Who are you working for?'

'You are safer not knowing.' Kostas Gianopoulous.

'Fine. We'll know if you try to follow us.' Harrison released him. 'Go.'

The man slid beneath his arm and bolted around the corner. Harrison moved in the opposite direction, stretching his stride as far as he could without breaking into a run, aware that Amy was practically jogging to keep up with him.

His skin was still prickling, as if the black-haired man was somewhere behind them. He glanced around but could see only a sea of strangers. 'Keep an eye out.'

'Who was that?'

'He works for Kostas. Kostas knows Tim is here, looking for her, and he's paid this guy to get rid of him.'

'And has he?'

'Not yet. As soon as Maya mentioned Tim and Lucy, he wanted to kill us.' They turned around a corner and found a busy coffee shop. 'In here.' He pulled her inside and they made their way to a tiny bench table at the back. 'I'll get coffee. You keep your eyes open.'

The café was overheated and he had started to sweat inside his coat. The pain in his head had dulled to the level of a particularly vicious hangover. Standing in the queue, he fought down nausea and tried to grasp any residual intent from the man in the storehouse. It was fear more than hate; he was a reluctant hitman, forced into it by circumstance, and he had a knife at his own back. He had been charged with a task he was afraid of fulfilling. That fear might come in useful, at some point.

He bought the coffees and brought them back to Amy.

'No sign,' she said softly.

'Good.' Harrison peeled off his coat and sat beside her, also facing out. Amy shifted restlessly, legs jiggling and eyes darting through the crowd. Before even touching her coffee, she stood up.

'I'll be back in five minutes.'

'Where are you going?'

'I want to have a look in a shop we passed.'

'You want to go shopping?'

'There's something I need. It's ... just girl stuff.'

He knew she was lying, but felt too queasy to try to read her. 'For Christ's sake, be careful out there.'

'Yes sir.' She touched her fingers to her forehead. 'I will be right back.'

He sipped his coffee and scanned the café, feeling conspicuously foreign and alone in this crowd. Amy was as good as her word and back within five minutes. She eased back into the seat with a paper parcel crinkling inside the deep pocket of her parka.

‘Got what you needed?’

‘I hope so,’ she breathed, her cheeks flushed with the cold. ‘No sign of our friend, and now my coffee is just the right temperature.’

‘It’s gone cold.’

‘It’s just right. How are you?’

‘Better.’

‘Harri, you know that vision I had of Tim? In the water? Do you think it’s going to happen?’

He studied her, hearing echoes of past traumas. There seemed little point in offering her false reassurance.

‘It might.’

‘And there’s nothing we can do about it.’

‘We can still try. Tim’s around. I can feel him. I’m sure he’s still in Athens. He’s determined to find Lucy and I doubt he has any clue how much danger he’s in.’

‘We *know* where Lucy is.’ She pulled out her phone. ‘He might just come to us if we message him and tell him that.’

Harrison chuckled. ‘He might.’

She cringed. ‘Go ahead, tell me all the reasons why that’s a really stupid idea.’

‘No, it’s not. It’s worth a shot. Try, and see what happens.’

She paused, her cup halfway to her mouth. ‘What ... now?’

‘Yes, now.’

Amy took her phone out of her pocket. ‘Where should I say to meet?’

‘Here. Right here. Café Stelios.’ He passed her the menu card. ‘Here’s the address. Tell him we’ll give him two hours max.’

‘You want to sit here for two hours?’

‘If we have to.’

‘Right, okay.’ She sighed, and her thumbs began tapping on the phone.

Hello Tim, she wrote. *My partner and I are private investigators from Edinburgh. We’ve been hired by Elizabeth Merriweather to find Lucy. We know you’re looking for her too. We believe we know where she is, and we need your help to bring her home. Please, come and meet us at Café Stelios...* She paused to check the spelling of the street name.

‘Do I tell him to watch out for that guy?’

‘We don’t want to scare him off. Just tell him to get here fast.’

...by no later than 4pm. Please trust us, and don’t mention this to anyone else. Come straight here as fast as you can. Amy Bell.

‘Good,’ Harrison said, reading over her shoulder. ‘Send it.’

She pressed send and put the phone down. ‘What now?’

‘Now we wait. Why don’t you go online and see what you can find out about the police and emergency services on Hydra, just in case.’

‘Good idea. By the way, tomorrow’s Monday, right? What are you going to tell the university?’

‘I was going to phone in sick first thing tomorrow and hope to God we make it home by the end of the week.’

‘Hope to God we make it home at all, more like. I guess I’ll have to do the same.’

‘You say that with some relish.’

‘It feels like skiving school all over again.’

‘You were a tearaway, weren’t you?’

She smiled. ‘I had my moments.’

‘I can tell. You want a cake or something?’

She laughed. ‘Oh my God, you never stop. Where do you put it all?’

‘Hollow legs.’ He stretched them out under the table and crossed his ankles. ‘I’ve always been able to eat as much as I want.’

‘A man your age ought to be careful.’

‘A man my age?’

‘Middle-age spread and all that.’

‘Bugger that, I’m in Greece and I’m getting some baklava.’ He got up.

When he came back to the table, with two sticky pieces of baklava on a plate, she slid her phone toward him. Harrison read the message from Tim:

I will be there as soon as I can. Wait for me.

THIRTY-ONE

Amy recognised Tim Cartwright the moment he walked in. He was tall, slouching and pallid, with shaggy dark blond hair that didn't appear to have been washed anytime recently. It was impossible to guess what a girl as stunning as Lucy had seen in him.

Tim paused and looked around. She caught his eye and raised her hand, palm out. He approached cautiously, glanced over his shoulder and slid into the seat across from them. He smelled of body odour and cigarettes, even over the heavy wafts of perfume and strong coffee.

'I'm Amy and this is Harrison Jones.'

'Alright?' Tim asked. His voice had a smoker's croak. 'Who are you, like? How do you know Lucy?'

'Elizabeth Merriweather hired us to find her.'

Tim's lip curled into a sneer. 'Elizabeth Merriweather doesn't give a rat's arse about Lucy. That bitch is rotten to the core.'

Amy felt strangely compelled to jump to the defence of a client she'd never met. 'She is Lucy's mother, whatever you think of her.'

'Lucy and I came here to get away from her.'

'And you left Lucy alone here.'

'She kicked me out.' He shrugged away any responsibility. 'You said you know where she is?'

'We do.'

He started to push back from his seat. 'Well let's go, then.'

'Stay there, Tim, it's not that simple,' Harrison said. 'She's not in Athens and we can't get there until tomorrow. There are some things you need to know. People know you're sniffing around, and we bumped into a guy who is going to do his best to stop you from finding her. Do you take my meaning?'

Tim's face indicated that he did not. 'Who?'

'Your friend Kostas has paid someone to keep you away from Lucy.'

Tim snorted. 'She's not with him anymore. He doesn't know where she is either.'

'I think you'll find he does.'

'Let's just ask him.' Tim looked over his shoulder again, and this time he waved at a smartly-dressed man who had just come in the door. Amy felt Harrison tense beside her, and her hand went into her pocket, fingering the paper-wrapped parcel inside. They were trapped in the bench against the back wall, and the café was too crowded to make a run for it now.

'Tim, you stupid bastard,' Amy muttered. 'I told you to keep your mouth shut.'

'He agreed to help me find her.'

'I fucking bet he did.' She glanced at Harrison and read his expression all too easily.

The man sauntered over in his long grey coat. He had dark golden hair and a face that should have been carved by a master sculptor. He offered his hand to Harrison, who shook it uncharacteristically, and then to Amy. 'I am Kostas Gianopoulos. Tim tells me that Elizabeth Merriweather has sent you.'

'That's correct,' Harrison replied.

'And you are not police.'

'No.'

'In that case, my car is outside. My friends, perhaps you would like to accompany me to my apartment so that we can speak openly.'

'We can speak here,' Amy said, spreading her hands on the table.

'Miss Bell, I understand your concern. I assure you, no harm will come to you in my company. We want the same thing, which is to ensure Lucy's safety. So, you believe you know where she is?'

'We're led to believe she's on a yacht, on the island of Hydra. Your yacht.'

Kostas smiled. 'She is indeed there, but it's not my yacht. She is working for the man who owns it. I believe together we might be able to negotiate the termination of her contract.'

Harrison gave Amy a look of mingled triumph and admiration. 'You're trying to tell us you can't do that yourself?'

'What the fuck?' Tim was spluttering, more to himself than to any of them. He turned on Kostas. 'What the fuck, man?'

Kostas waved him away like an irritating bluebottle. 'It's ... a little bit complicated.' His voice was velvety and earnest. 'I will show you the hospitality of my home, and I will have my driver bring you back to your hotel.'

'We're not going anywhere with you,' Amy said.

Harrison nudged her. *He's telling the truth.*

He's evil.

But we have to use him.

'Jesus bloody Christ, you lied to me.' Tim's voice broke in desperation. 'You said you didn't know where she was. I asked you for help. Do you know how much pride I had to swallow to do that?'

'It is not about pride,' said Kostas, kindly. 'It is about Lucy. A beautiful young girl, with her whole life in front of her. We have used her badly, both of us. Sometimes men learn these lessons only when it's too late. I speak only for myself, of course.'

Amy felt like an incendiary device, quivering at the point of explosion. Harrison touched her arm and met her eyes for no more than a second. She took a deep breath and relaxed.

'We'll come with you,' he said to Kostas, 'for one hour only. You can tell us what you know, and we'll be on our way.'

'Of course. I thank you. Come, please.'

They followed Tim and Kostas outside. 'What are you thinking?' Amy whispered through gritted teeth.

'Trust me,' Harrison replied. Then, abruptly, he caught her hand and held it tightly. 'And keep that thing in your pocket. That's not how this is going to happen.'

The ferocity in his voice was something she hadn't heard before. Anger flared like a gas flame. She should have known it was impossible to hide anything from him for more than a few seconds.

He smiled and released her hand. 'Come on.'

They followed Kostas to a black Range Rover and sat in the back with Tim, while the driver snaked his way through congested traffic and falling darkness.

'Have you been to Athens before?' Kostas asked pleasantly, turning around in his seat.

Shadows fell over him, accentuating his cheekbones.

'I came as a child with my parents,' Harrison replied.

Kostas nodded. 'I'm afraid our city is not as beautiful as it used to be. The economic crisis has taken its toll on everybody and everything. Nothing is ever fixed, nothing is cleaned, there is no pride anymore. So many people can only think about survival these days. Hardship breeds anger and other dangerous things. Of course, I have been very lucky. I must remind myself of this every day.'

'Britain isn't much better.'

'No, it isn't. The policy of austerity is all wrong. I believe that to truly succeed as a society, we must invest in people, especially the ones on the lowest rung. I see potential in everybody. This is why I support the Refugee Co-operative and many other charities.'

'This is why you ...' Amy started. Once again, Harrison's fingers gripped her skin. She broke off.

'I'm sorry?' Kostas said.

'This is why you groomed Lucy the way you did,' Tim said, rousing himself from a stale silence.

'I didn't groom her, Tim. I gave her an opportunity. I gave her a start. She has such a talent; I truly believed the world deserved to hear her voice.'

'But not mine. You didn't care if I sank like a stone while your little bird was singing.'

Kostas only shrugged. 'I'm very sorry about that, Tim. Hers was the brightest light. You ... were the accompanist, that's all.'

'I made her. I got her gigs in Edinburgh. She would never have done that without me. She was singing my bloody songs!'

'I must give you credit for that,' Kostas accepted. 'We are nearly there.' He turned around and faced front again before Tim could say anything further. Tim slumped back against the seat and gave off a sour, unwashed smell.

They had entered a wealthier neighbourhood, with tree-lined streets and pale, clean stone Victorian houses. The driver turned under an archway and parked in a courtyard set back from the street. Through the darkness, Amy could see olive trees and planters with flowers still in blossom. Kostas unlocked an arched wooden door and led them up a flight of stairs and through a second locked door. The lights flickered on to reveal a soaring studio apartment with minimalist decor: quirky, ultra-modern furniture and art pieces. It was immaculate and looked practically unlived in.

'I must apologise,' Kostas said, slipping out of his coat and draping it over the back of a sofa. 'The place is cold and not well equipped for guests. I spend most of my time in my country house outside of the city, and only come here when I am in town for business. My wife Kaliope insisted on buying it. The art is all her choice, not mine. Of course, she has much better taste than I do.' He laughed. 'I will turn the heating on and see what I have to offer. There is wine, at least.'

'Will your wife be joining us?' Harrison asked.

'I am afraid that you will not have the pleasure of her company. She and I are currently estranged.' He shrugged. 'We both travel so much; we are like ships in the night. It takes a toll on the marriage. I am hoping that in time ...' He lifted his hands and let them fall. 'Who knows? She has every right to be angry with me.'

'Do you have any children?' Amy asked, almost feeling sorry for him all of a sudden.

'None. It is a source of great sadness for us both. Please make yourselves comfortable. Perhaps while I get some food together, Tim will tell you how this all began. Tim, stick to the facts, if you don't mind. These good people are more than capable of forming their own judgements about me.'

He spoke with such gentility and grace that it was almost possible to believe that their assumptions about him were wrong. She wanted to follow him into the glossy marble kitchen and coax a tale of lost love and misunderstanding out of him, rather than listen to sweaty, shifty Tim.

The man was a silver-tongued snake, she reminded herself. He was deliberately manipulating her emotions into a softer place, as if he could see into her the way Harrison did. She turned away from him, sat beside Harrison on a cream leather, L-shaped sofa, and said to Tim in her most unadulterated Belfast, 'Right then, boyo, let's be hearing it, and don't you be selling us a line of shite, because we can sniff it a mile away. You understand me?'

Tim propped himself on his elbows and ran his fingers through greasy hair. 'I don't know where to start.'

'At the beginning,' Harrison said. He stretched his legs out and waited, looking relaxed as a master interrogator. Tim, on the other hand, looked terrified and trapped.

'Lucy and I met in Edinburgh. I was volunteering at a charity called LASAR-Net and doing a few gigs around the place. She got up to sing at this open-mic one night and she had this incredible, high, pure voice, like ...' He drifted for a second, then brought himself back. 'Anyway, we got talking and we decided to try to put some songs together. A couple of weeks later we got together ...'

'What did she see in you?' Amy asked.

'That I respected her,' he shot back angrily. 'I wasn't trying to use her or exploit her like everyone else had done.'

'Everyone who?'

'Her parents, for a start. Other men. When I met her, she was sleeping around for money, so she didn't have to take anything from her parents. That's how bad it was.'

'What do you know about her parents?' Harrison asked.

'Lucy's dad used her to seal business deals. When she was nine, ten, I don't know, they started bringing her out to sing whenever he had his associates round. When she got a bit older, it went further than that.'

Amy glanced at Harrison, who asked calmly, 'Further how?'

'They dressed her up, made her play the cocktail waitress. Got her to chat-up all these fat old blokes, stroke their egos, make them feel good about themselves. You get the idea?'

'Did it ever go beyond that?'

Tim took a deep breath. 'She let one of her old man's associates talk her into going to bed with him when she was fourteen.'

'Do you know who?' Harrison leaned toward Tim and held his gaze.

Tim squirmed but seemed unable to break away. After five or six seconds, he physically covered his eyes with his hands. 'How the fuck would I know who? She didn't tell me his name.'

'You're lying,' Harrison said.

'What the fuck is going on here, man? What's your game?'

Harrison didn't move. He sat like a cat watching a wounded mouse scurry back and forth against the base of a wall, going nowhere. Amy had not thought him capable of this understated cruelty.

Tim made a noise like somebody was crushing his windpipe, then looked up.

Kostas arrived, carrying a large tray with a bottle of white wine, four glasses, and a plate of olives and stuffed vine leaves. He set this onto the marble coffee table between them and sat down. 'The dolmas are not homemade, but they are good. The wine is made by a friend of mine. I believe you will find it to your liking.'

He poured the wine, handed out the glasses without ceremony and took a sip of his own. The silence of an unspoken truth hung over the room.

'I made love to Lucy when she was fourteen,' he said. 'She told me she was sixteen, and at the time I believed her. I had only recently met her parents.'

Harrison nodded, apparently satisfied. 'And were you the one who got her pregnant when she was seventeen?'

'No.'

'Okay. You realise that you've just admitted to the statutory rape of a child.'

'Of course I realise that, but we are trying to prevent a greater crime now, are we not?'

'Unless we're too late. However, ... Tim, please, carry on.'

Tim snatched a glass and drank greedily. 'When I was working at LASAR-Net, Lucy showed up one day and she had Kostas with her. She said Kostas was interested in what happened to the people who finally made it to Britain.'

'I wanted to make a very large gift to a refugee charity in Scotland, and I wanted to see their work before I did so.'

'And did you?'

'Yes, I gave LASAR-Net a sum of fifty thousand pounds. It was enough to secure their operations for a year.'

'Nessa Walker mentioned this when we spoke to her,' Amy interrupted. 'She didn't say it was that much.'

Kostas shrugged. 'I am privileged to be able to help.'

She wanted to ask about Maryam and the icon, but Harrison silenced her with a glance.

He turned back to Tim. 'What made you and Lucy decide to leave Edinburgh?'

'She was being harassed by her mother. Threatened with being cut off, cut out of her will, called a slut and a bitch and all sorts. Elizabeth got drunk and set her abusive texts. Completely mental, mate. The woman is off her trolley.'

Kostas showed no reaction to Tim's description of his former lover. Whatever he may have felt for Elizabeth in the past, he had no interest in defending her now.

'Did Lucy have any contact with her father during that time?'

'Fuck no,' Tim spat. 'Anyway, we packed up and left. We travelled around Europe for six months before we got here.'

'What did you do for money?' Amy asked.

'We busked. Tell you what, as soon as Lucy opened her mouth, the money flooded in. She kept saying she wanted to come to Athens. For weeks, it was all Athens, Athens, Athens. It was all about him.' He glanced at Kostas. 'You were the only reason she wanted to come here.'

Kostas made an innocent, helpless expression.

'Was she in touch with you during this time?' Harrison asked Kostas.

'No. It was only after they arrived in Athens, she made contact. Of course, I invited her to my estate. I organised a house concert for them, and invited my closest friends, including some people in the music industry.'

'Tim, Maya Retsikas told us she asked you and Lucy to leave the co-op. She said that you argued in front of the clients, and she suspected that you had been stealing? What can you say about that?'

'We were pretty skint. We had stuff to buy. We were just a bit desperate. That place is rolling in money, I didn't think they would miss a few old mobile phones and that kind of shit.'

'You stole from a charity to buy drugs,' Amy said.

Tim nodded. 'It sounds pretty shit if you put it that way.'

'What drugs?' Harrison asked.

'Just hash. Honestly, that was it ... at first.'

'At first?'

'There was plenty more on offer at his parties.'

Kostas shrugged. 'Some of my friends do things that I don't fully approve of, but this is life. I never forced Tim or Lucy to take anything.'

Tim closed his eyes, and the words poured out of him like water. 'I knew Lucy was falling for him. She got closer and closer to him, and more and more distant from me. We started bickering all the time, and finally she just ... snapped. She attacked me, like, physically battered me. She's a big strong girl; it bloody hurt, you know? Finally, I lost it and slapped her. Then she said she wanted me to leave, so I did and that was it. I haven't seen her since.'

'Did she come to you?'

'Yes, she came to me,' Kostas said. 'And she asked me if I would pay for Tim's flight back to Britain. So, I bought him a ticket and sent my driver to pick him up and take him to the airport.'

'That's what happened, Tim?'

'Yeah, that's what happened, except I didn't get on the plane.'

'Why not?'

Tim squirmed. 'Because I wanted her back.'

'So where have you been staying since then?'

'Different places. Crashing on sofas and stuff.'

'Your mum has reported you missing to the police, here and in the UK. Why haven't you been in touch with her?'

This merited only a shrug. 'Dunno. My mum's a pain in the ass.'

Harrison turned to Kostas. 'Did Lucy stay with you after that?'

Kostas put down his glass and combed his hair with his fingers. 'This is where it becomes rather embarrassing. Lucy stayed with me for a short time. Less than two weeks. And then my wife came home early from a business trip and found her there. There was a scene, and we all said some things that should not be repeated. Lucy came back to Athens and asked me for some money. She didn't know what to do at that point. Of course, I wanted to help her, so I ...'

'Can I ask you something, Kostas?' Amy interrupted. 'Did you love Lucy?'

'Everybody loves Lucy.'

'That's not what I asked. Did you really care about her?'

Kostas sighed and stared at the wall above Amy's head. 'If you want the truth? She turned me on. I wanted to sleep with her. I wanted to help her establish her singing career, and I didn't want to hurt her. But I didn't love her. Is that a crime as well?'

'Maybe it should be,' Amy muttered. 'How did you try to help her?'

'I introduced her to a man I know, Victor Mikos, and he offered her a job on his yacht. He likes to provide entertainment for his friends and associates. As you know, Lucy had some experience ... along those lines.'

'What kind of entertainment, exactly?'

'Singing, of course. What else?'

'Not sex?'

‘I would never have knowingly put Lucy into that situation. She’s the daughter of a business partner, after all.’

‘But now you aren’t so sure,’ Harrison said.

Kostas looked momentarily surprised, then nodded. ‘Now I am not so sure. Some stories have recently reached me through sources I would rather not disclose.’

‘What stories?’

‘About a pale-haired angel on Victor’s boat, and the things she does.’

‘Have you tried to get her back?’

‘At first, I tried to deny what I had heard. I felt so guilty, I pretended it must be someone else. It was only when Tim called me and asked if I had heard from her, that I ... began to think about what to do. Victor is ... not a man to be toyed with. Lucy entered into a contract with him.’

‘Without knowing the terms,’ Amy said.

Kostas took a drink and swallowed heavily, ‘Listen, we all know that this is an unsavoury business, and that I have not acquitted myself ... honourably. But whatever you have heard, I hope that you agree that we are allies. For Lucy’s sake.’

Harrison took one of the vine leaves from the plate, bit into it and chewed thoughtfully for half a minute. ‘You’re right, this is very good.’ They all waited while he ate the rest of it. ‘This is what we’re going to do. In the morning, all four of us are going to take the ferry to Hydra. You're going to get us on board Victor's boat ... what's it called?'

'Circe, after the –'

'The enchantress who held Odysseus and his men captive on her island and made them into sex slaves. How very appropriate. You and I are going to go see Victor, and you'll do what you need to do to negotiate Lucy's release.'

'You seem to assume Lucy is being kept on board against her will?'

'We have information of our own, which you have very helpfully confirmed,' Harrison said. He put down his glass and looked at his watch. 'That's your hour. We'll meet your car tomorrow morning at ten at Café Stelios.' He stood up and retrieved his coat. 'Otherwise, we can have the police in Edinburgh into your apartments at the Western Harbour tonight. You get me? I assume that is agreeable?'

Cracks were now showing in Kostas's glossy exterior. 'I suppose it must be. I will have my driver take you back to your hotel, and meet you there in the morning. It will save time.'

'We can make our own way. One more thing, Kostas. The man you have looking for Tim? Call him off.'

'I have no idea what you're talking about.'

'Then you have nothing to worry about.' Harrison walked toward the door, motioning for Amy and Tim to come. Tim remained fixed to the white leather sofa.

Kostas followed them to the door and dropped his voice. 'I think you understand that there are more lives at stake than just Lucy's.'

Harrison placed his hand deliberately on Kostas's arm. 'I've been hired to ensure Lucy's safety. Nothing else.'

'Then you will use only the information you must, and leave the rest. You must give me your word.'

'If we get Lucy off that boat, then yes, I give you my word. And we will see you at ten tomorrow morning.' He dropped his hand and looked around Kostas. 'Tim, you come with us.'

Tim levered himself off the sofa, snatched his coat and trailed them down the stairs like a sullen child. It was an almost silent taxi ride back to the hotel, with Tim staring at his fingernails and jiggling his leg. Amy turned to search the traffic behind them every so often, but there was no way of telling which of the glaring headlights might be following them.

The woman at the hotel desk informed them that there was a conference in the hotel and there were no vacant rooms.

Harrison sighed, not managing to hide his frustration. 'Right, Tim, you'll have to bunk in with me.'

'He can have my room, Harri,' Amy said, before she had a chance to consider the implications. 'You need your sleep, and this one looks like a proper pain in the arse.'

'Are you sure?'

'Yeah.'

Upstairs, Harrison waited while Amy gathered her bag.

Tim sat on the bed, chewing his cuticle. 'How do I know you're on my side?'

'It's called trust, Tim,' Amy said. 'I'm sorry if you don't know how to do that. I promise you, Harrison and I just want to get you and Lucy home safe. That's *all*.'

'I don't have to stay here, you know,' he said. 'If I want to take off, you can't stop me.'

'Let's get one thing straight,' Harrison snapped. 'Kostas Gianopoulos is a dangerous bastard. If you're too thick to figure it out, I'll spell it out to you in two words. Human trafficking. Do you know what that is?'

'Yeah, but ... Kostas isn't involved in that…is he?'

'This thing is a hell of a lot bigger than you know. He has a man out there…' he pointed to the window, 'looking for you. He didn't want you getting near Lucy or finding out what he's up to. He would have had you killed if we hadn't got to you first. How much money did he pay you to leave Greece in September?'

'He didn't…'

'Don't lie to me.'

Tim shook his head, mouth slightly open, as if the denial had caught in his throat. 'Couple of grand.'

'A couple of grand that you've been pissing away, pretending to look for your girlfriend but really just taking drugs and sleeping most of the day. You think he's going to let that go unpunished? You're here for your own safety, so you will stay in this room with the door locked, you will stay sober, and you will be ready to leave here tomorrow at nine. Do you understand me?'

Tim said nothing.

'They *will* kill you, Tim,' Amy added. She had to say it. Whatever came of it, her conscience demanded this. 'They will dump your body at sea and you'll disappear forever. It'll be like you never existed. Listen to me. Don't give them the chance.'

Tim laughed. 'You seem to know a lot about their plans.'

Amy looked at Harrison. 'He doesn't believe me.'

'It's up to him.'

‘Fine,’ Tim huffed. ‘Whatever. I’ll stay here, alright? Thanks for the room.’

They left Tim Cartwright to his less than sweet dreams and headed along to the far end of the corridor.

Harrison unlocked the door of his own room, and for a couple of seconds they both stood staring at the one double bed.

‘Well now, how did we get ourselves into this situation?’ Amy let out a laugh. ‘You want me to sleep in the bath?’

He pulled off his boots, hat and coat, and collapsed onto the chair by the window. ‘I don’t know about you, but I’m too knackered to even think about doing more than sleeping in that bed. You’ll be safe enough.’

‘That’s good to know.’

He got out his phone. ‘I’m going to phone Colin. Maybe he can get us some information on Victor Mikos.’

‘This thing stinks, you know that? The man should have been arrested by now.’

‘Even so, he’s our ticket on and off that boat.’

‘How’s this going to work tomorrow, Harri?’

‘I’m still trying to work that out.’

‘That doesn’t fill me with confidence.’

‘Nor me. I’ve never had to do anything like this before. I’m kind of making this up as we go along.’

'Now he tells me. God help us.' She took off her shoes and massaged the underside of her foot. Anticipation jittered through her. 'I'm going to get changed and have a wash.'

She dug her pyjamas and wash bag out of her rucksack and went into the bathroom. While she was in there, she heard his voice in muted tones through the door, but couldn't pick up any of the words. By the time she emerged again, he had finished his call and was lying on the bed, staring at the ceiling, arms folded behind his head.

'Did you get him?'

'Yeah. Hopefully he'll have some more information before we go tomorrow.'

'Okay.' She slipped into bed and lay beside him for a few minutes, feeling dizzy with fatigue and adrenaline. A lifetime had passed since yesterday morning, when she'd appeared at his house with little more than a dream to go on. Maybe this whole thing was a dream, and they weren't even here. Maybe she would wake up in her flat, back in her quiet little life, and find that this whole fantastical adventure had been wishful thinking.

Harrison let out a snore. It defied belief that he could fall asleep so fast. She nudged his arm. 'Harri.'

'What is it?' he murmured.

'Do you really want to sleep in your clothes?'

He roused himself only long enough to strip down to his t-shirt and boxers and brush his teeth. They lay side by side under the covers, like brother and sister forced to share a bed on holiday.

'Are you okay with this?' he asked.

'Yes. Quit reading my mind.'

'Sorry.' He turned his back to her and lay on his side. 'Night, then, sis.'

Amy rolled away and turned off the light. 'Goodnight, Indiana.'

THIRTY-TWO

Harrison woke in the dark, the echo of a voice still ringing in his ears. There was an unfamiliar smell in the room and a symphony of strange clunks and whirs. For a bewildering moment he couldn't remember where he was. Then the person beside him in the bed murmured and turned over, and it all came back.

It was a little before five am, he was still wearing yesterday's shirt, and Amy was dreaming. She was twitching and making little noises, and he resisted the urge to touch her and bring her out of it. After perhaps thirty seconds, she sucked in a deep breath and sat up.

'You okay?' he whispered.

She whirled toward him. 'Oh my God, Harri. You gave me a fright.'

'What were you dreaming about?'

'Mmm,' she rubbed her cheek and the reflection of the traffic light from outside moved across her pale skin. 'Tim. I dreamed that the bastard did a runner.'

‘That’s not good.’ Harrison bolted out of bed, suddenly wide awake. ‘Where did I leave my specs?’

‘Right here.’ She took them off the single bedside table and handed them to him.

‘Thanks.’ He pulled on his jeans. ‘Did you keep the spare key for that room?’

‘Yeah, it’s ... in the back pocket of the jeans I was wearing. Oh shit , you don’t think ...’

‘Yeah, I do think. I’m going to go check.’ He switched on the light, found her jeans draped across the luggage rack and pulled the key card out of the back pocket. ‘Stay here.’

He opened the door and scanned each direction down the long corridor. It was dimly lit, empty and silent. He ran along the carpet as lightly as he could, landing on the balls of his bare feet and hoping he wasn’t going to wake the whole hotel. Holding his breath, he inserted the card into the lock, waited for the green light and pushed the door.

The security chain had not been fastened. Harrison gritted his teeth and stepped into the room. Even without turning on the light, he could see that the bed was empty.

‘Idiot,’ he muttered. ‘Tim Cartwright, you absolute prick.’ He turned on the light and searched the room. Tim had left nothing behind.

The bed was still made. He was hours gone already.

Harrison felt a surge of anger at Amy for suggesting giving Tim the room on his own. Then he turned it back on himself. This wasn't Amy's fault. He'd agreed to it, at least in part because the prospect of sharing a bed with Amy was preferable to the alternative. He braced his hands against the desk and fought down the urge to kick something. Anger wasn't going to help the situation. They had tried to help Tim and he'd chosen to throw himself to the lions.

To what end? What could he possibly hope to achieve on his own? Harrison waited for a few minutes, hoping that some lingering intention might come to him. There was no sense of a struggle or forced entry into the room. All he could feel was a vague, confused need to move on, like that of a drunk man trying to find his way home. Tim Cartwright's motivations were not even known to Tim Cartwright.

He walked back along the corridor and slipped into his room. 'Well, Amy Bell, once again your dreams prove prophetic.'

'Oh, you are kidding me. He's gone? Honestly?'

'Looks that way. The bed's made, so either he didn't sleep in it at all or he took the time to make it before he left. I'm guessing the former.'

'Why? Where would he go?'

'To get a fix? To play the hero and rescue Lucy on his own? To piss off back to England? Any or none of the above. Who knows? Nothing's coming to me.'

She got out of bed and peered down at the street. 'To get himself whacked.'

'Quite possibly.'

'Shouldn't we go look for him?'

'Is there any point?'

Amy hesitated. 'If something happens to him, it's our fault. We should have kept watch over him.'

'We should have, but it's not our fault. He chose to leave.'

'And so my vision is going to come true? He's going to end up in the water somewhere and there's nothing we can do about it? This is just like all the other times that ...' she broke off.

'Just because you've seen the future doesn't mean you have any power to change it. Just ask Oedipus about that one.'

'Who?'

'It's an ancient Greek story. My school was big on the ancient Greeks. You remember what I said when this all started, right?'

'You said that not everybody is alive when you find them. But we found Tim alive and we lost him.'

'No, we did not lose him. We warned him, but he still left of his own free will.'

'Nobody ever fucking believes me. What's the point of this, Harri? What's the point of having this thing nobody else has, if I can't do something good with it?'

'Maybe the point is that there is no point. You want a cuppa?'

'Might as well. I won't be going back to sleep now.'

He filled the little kettle and set it on to boil, then went into the bathroom to brush his teeth and consider the day ahead. He didn't want to say it to Amy, but things might be less complicated today without Tim in tow. At least nobody would have to be assigned to babysit him. Still, he had no clue how it was going to play out. He could visualise how he and Kostas were going to talk their way onto the boat, but how they were going to get off again with Lucy – maybe a drugged and dozy Lucy – was another matter entirely. He had to believe that Kostas would be willing to do what he had to do, or pay what he had to pay, to negotiate her release. Kostas knew that Harrison was holding evidence against him, like a gun at his back. The man had a lot more than his reputation at stake.

He scrubbed his face and wondered what state Amy would be in when he came out. She was pouring hot water into the mugs and stirring the instant coffee granules. He could still feel the clamour of conflicting emotions in her, but they were tempered by acceptance. This reassured him that she was not about to melt down.

'It looks like it's going to be a nice day, at least,' she said.

He looked out the window. Above the glow of the streetlights, he could just make out a few stars in the clear sky. An orange glow had started to creep up the side of the buildings across the street.

'That's a relief. Are you okay?'

'Yeah. You are right, he made the choice all by himself.' She handed him a mug and studied him.

'What?'

'So ... I was just wondering if you brought any nicer clothes with you. Because they properly dress up here, and Victor is going to smell a rat if you turn up in jeans and a shirt that looks like it's been slept in.'

'That's because it *has* been slept in. I had the same thought.' He took a sip of coffee and pulled his tweed waistcoat and trousers out of the rucksack. They were badly creased.

Amy nodded toward the small wardrobe recess. 'You'll be pleased to know there's an iron. You'll look like a proper professor in those. A Scottish one at that.'

‘I don’t want to look like a professor. Lara said they made me look hipster.’

‘Who’s Lara?’

‘My ex-girlfriend.’

‘Well, I suppose they’re better than the alpaca jumper.’

‘No comment.’ He shook out his shirt and tie. ‘What are you going to wear?’

‘Nothing special, you’re going on the boat without me. We need one person keeping watch from the shore, and it makes the most sense for that to be me. I’ll find a place to hole up and wait, and do what I need to do if it all goes a bit pear-shaped.’

‘What, buy yourself a cappuccino and pretend you don’t know us?’

‘No, like play frogman and haul your sorry butt out of the water, Indiana.’

‘Good to know you’ve got this all planned out.’ He was starting to mind less when she teased him. In fact, he was almost starting to like it. ‘You’re talking to the karate master, don’t forget.’

‘Karate master my arse. Let me see your moves.’

He laughed. ‘You want to see my karate moves?’

She stood up and squared off in front of him. ‘Go on then, Jones, take your best shot.’

‘Okay.’ He took off his glasses. ‘I’ll try not to hurt you. There’s this ...’ He swept his foot toward hers, making the briefest contact with her skin before pulling back. ‘Or ... this is *Kin Geri*, the groin kick. Can be painful.’

She danced backwards, sniggering.

‘Or there’s this ...’ He spun and kicked his foot toward her face. This time, instead of backing up, she caught him by the ankle, gave him a shove and sent him sprawling backwards onto the floor. He had half a second to think about the jolt of pain that went through his hip before she lost her balance and fell on top of him.

‘Fucksake, Amy, are you trying to cripple me before the day even starts?’

‘Oh Jesus,’ she gasped, ‘I didn’t mean to do that. Sorry.’

Without his glasses on, all he could see of her face was a pleasing rosy blur. Her weight on him was warm and he was in no hurry to move out from under her. He let his head fall back onto the carpet and, without thinking about it, brought his arms up around her. She relaxed against him and placed her head on his chest. He could feel her breath quickening and her heart beating too fast.

‘Oops.’ She pushed herself up onto her hands, kissed him on the lips and lingered there. ‘That’s to say thank you, in case it all goes pear-shaped today.’

He allowed himself a few seconds to imagine the possibilities that could unfold from here. 'It's not going to go pear-shaped today, and you don't have to thank me for anything.'

'This isn't very professional of us, is it?' Her breath was warm against his cheek.

'Not very.' He lay a moment longer, fighting to stop himself from sliding his hands under her top. 'I didn't expect this.'

'I'm sorry.'

'It's nice to be surprised. It doesn't happen very often. However, you're right. Not very professional.' He eased himself out from beneath her and got up. The hip he'd landed on gave a twinge of protest, and he rubbed it as he put his glasses back on and returned to his cooling coffee. 'So … let's talk about the knife you bought yesterday.'

She sighed and picked herself up off the floor. 'Ooh, now there's a mood killer.'

'I'm sorry. Amy, please don't bring it today. I don't want ...'

'Harrison, I'm bringing it. You won't talk me out of it, so don't try.'

A chill travelled like icy fingers up his spine. 'What have you seen? Do you know something?'

'I don't know anything, but I have a feeling.'

'What kind of a feeling?'

'I have a feeling I may have to use it.'

THIRTY-THREE

'Where is Tim?' Kostas asked as they climbed into the Range Rover. He looked approvingly at Harrison's tweeds and less so at Amy's parka and jeans. She met his gaze defiantly and decided that in the bright light of morning, he wasn't as good looking as he was in photographs. The skin around his eyes was artificially tight: probably Botox.

'Our friend Mr Cartwright is feeling unwell,' Harrison answered smoothly. 'He decided to stay in the hotel today.'

Kostas accepted this with only a flicker of the eyebrows, and they rode quietly to the port of Piraeus. Amy watched Kostas shift around in his seat and rub his hands nervously on the legs of his trousers. He was twitching with anxiety. After a couple of minutes, he withdrew his phone from his pocket and tapped in a text message.

Amy glanced at Harrison. His face was grim, but he remained silent.

Kostas said, as if trying to convince himself out loud, 'I'm positive that if Lucy is content to leave the boat, Victor will release her from her contract.'

'For your sake, I hope that's true,' Amy replied. The morning's information from Colin Muir was that Victor Mikos was suspected of involvement with any number of organised criminal activities, but that there had never been a convincing enough case against him to make any charges stick. Muir thought it highly likely that he had at least some of the local law under his thumb.

At Piraeus, a narrow strip of tarmac between two quays was occupied by a collection of blue and green pup tents. Refugees sat on blankets looking out, hung up wet clothes to dry in the cool sunshine or walked aimlessly around their camp.

Kostas dragged in a dramatic sigh. 'There were thousands here before the authorities moved everybody on. You see why I must help.' Still trying to win their sympathy, despite what they knew about him.

Amy met Harrison's eyes. He looked back, and it didn't take any psychic effort at all to know that he wasn't paying the slightest bit of attention to Kostas.

Hydra was a shock after the bustle of Athens. Under a bright blue sky, it looked exactly as it had in the pictures Amy had studied: pale grey or whitewashed stone houses with tiled roofs, stacked steeply up the hillsides around the half-moon harbour. The pictures had not prepared her for just how quiet it was. Everything moved slowly. Donkeys, evidently the island's main vehicle for the transportation of goods, waited patiently and stomped their hooves. Feral cats stretched languidly on sun-warmed stone. You could hear the slosh of water against the hulls of the boats, children playing in one of the courtyards, the scratchy chatter of a radio.

It ought to be the kind of place where people could leave their doors unlocked and where no violent or dishonest act would ever be committed, but still, it was home to a man like Victor Mikos. She couldn't believe nobody here knew what his business was.

Or maybe they did.

As the crowd of passengers dispersed and the hydrofoil left on its return journey to Piraeus, they walked around the harbour. Most of the craft were small: power cruisers, sailboats and fishing boats lined up neatly in the inner harbour, but there were two much larger yachts on the far side of the outermost stone pier. One of them, gleaming white with tinted windows, was the Circe. Seeing it there made Amy's stomach twist around on itself.

Pretending to be tourists, they strolled toward it. There was nobody visible on deck, but equally no way of telling who might be peering out of the blacked-out windows. When they got close enough, Harrison paused and closed his eyes for several seconds.

'What are you doing?' Kostas asked.

'She's definitely in there,' Harrison said, ignoring him. 'Come on.' He indicated for them to follow him away from the boat, and said, 'Kostas, if Victor doesn't agree to let her go freely, I want you to offer to buy Lucy for me.'

'Buy her? For ... how much?'

'As much as it takes. Do you want to put a value on this girl's life the way you do all the others?'

'No, of course not. I care about her.' Amy noted that he didn't acknowledge the second half of Harrison's question. The lack of denial was as good as a confirmation.

'Fine then. This is my plan.' He spelt it out for them. 'Are you clear what you need to do?'

Kostas nodded, then leaned in and spoke very quietly, 'You must understand that if I am compromised in any way, none of you will make it back to Scotland.'

'We do,' Harrison said. 'Which is why you have nothing to worry about from us. We're doing you a favour, are we not? If Merriweather finds out what you've done with his daughter …'

Kostas raised his hand to cut him off. 'He has no reason to find out.'

‘Well then.’ Harrison looked content. ‘Make the call, if you’re ready.’

Kostas withdrew his phone from his pocket and hesitated for a moment, glancing at Harrison first and then out toward the Circe. Then he took a deep breath and placed the call to Victor Mikos. Several seconds passed, and then he gave a boisterous greeting in Greek. The conversation contained what seemed to Amy an ominous amount of laughter. They could be saying anything, and she and Harrison would be none the wiser.

Eventually, he tucked his phone away. ‘He is expecting us.’

Harrison took Amy’s hand and squeezed it hard. She could feel a rapid pulse, but couldn’t tell if it was his or her own. In her head, she heard him say, *Keep watch. You’ll know if I’m in trouble.*

She nodded to indicate that she understood, and said aloud, ‘Good luck. And be careful.’

She watched them stroll along the pier, chatting like old friends. Waiting was always the worst thing. There had been so much waiting in Afghanistan. Waiting at bases, waiting in trucks, waiting for men, waiting for all hell to break loose, waiting to see who would come back in one piece and who would come back in pieces. It had been the most difficult skill to learn: far worse than running into a firefight or the aftermath of an explosion. However high the butcher's bill, it was always better to know than not.

Harrison and Kostas disappeared around the far side of the Circe. Amy wandered in a leisurely way around the harbour, peering at Christmas decorations for sale at an outdoor market stall. She found her way past the office of the port police, upstairs from the island museum. It was reassuring to know where to run, in case it came to that.

After half an hour, she strolled along the pier toward the Circe, taking pictures as she went. She found a place to sit at the far end, where she could watch the yacht while pretending to watch the sunlight playing on the water. She took off one trainer and dipped her toes into the water, testing its temperature. It was cool, but bearable in comparison with the North Sea this time of year. In other circumstances, she could spend a happy week here, swimming in the sea and running along car-free roads into the scrubby hills.

With the sun on her face, she allowed herself to imagine putting Lucy on the hydrofoil to Athens and staying here with Harrison. They could stay right through Christmas. They could disappear.

She sent her thoughts toward the yacht. *Are you okay?*

Nothing came back.

THIRTY-FOUR

'Victor, my dear friend!' Kostas held his arms wide to embrace a potato-faced man with artificially black hair. After the ritual cheek kissing and back-slapping, Kostas introduced Harrison.

'I would like to introduce you to Alastair McKenzie, my friend and associate from Scotland.'

'Ah, Scotland,' said Victor, pumping Harrison's hand so heartily it hurt. Harrison steeled himself for the shock waves, but received next to nothing. The man was emotionally dead; it was the signature of a psychopath. Psychic trickery would never work on him. 'Just like our precious young lady.'

'Alastair met Lucy at my home in the summer,' Kostas said. 'He has not stopped talking about her since. I couldn't deny him the chance to see her today. I do hope Lucy will consent to sing for us this afternoon.'

'Of course, of course.' Victor nodded and led them to the ship's stateroom: an opulent chamber of leather upholstery, gleaming wood and brass. 'She is below decks, warming up her voice as we speak. I cannot tell you, Kostas, what an asset she has been to me. Although,' he chuckled, 'she did suffer badly from seasickness at first. Do sit down, gentlemen. What do you care to drink? I have the most excellent single malts, which may be to your taste, Mr McKenzie.' He held up a bottle. 'For example, this thirty-year-old, limited edition Talisker which I acquired recently.'

'Who am I to refuse such a generous offering?' Harrison said.

Victor poured three glasses of the whisky and brought them to the table. 'To your health. Yamas.'

'Yamas,' Harrison repeated. 'In Scotland we say slainte.' He brought the glass to his lips and took a sip of the most expensive whisky he'd ever tasted. And because Victor was obviously awaiting a verdict, he said loudly, in the most bullish aristocratic voice he could produce, 'God, that's bloody good.'

'Excellent!' Victor laughed. 'Please, have more. Mr McKenzie, what is the nature of your business?'

'I manage my family's estate in Argyll,' Harrison explained. 'My parents have both passed on, and I'm the sole heir. The place is quite frankly a ball and chain around my ankle. With regret, I've decided the time has come to sell the estate. Kostas came to stay last year, and do you think I could get him to leave?' He slapped Kostas between the shoulder blades and fear reverberated up his arm. Although he hid it well, Kostas was terrified. 'He fell arse over tit in love with the place.'

'Like you have fallen in love with Lucy.'

Harrison allowed himself to reveal a sheepish grin.

'I have a vision for a beautiful, exclusive Highland retreat,' Kostas said. 'Peace and quiet, the ultimate getaway, with of course the finest food and spa, and ...'

'And women ... Blissful,' Victor purred. The door of the stateroom opened. 'And speaking of the finest women. Lucy, my dear, come in.'

Lucy Merriweather entered, carrying a guitar. She was wearing a plain red silk shift dress and a pair of silver sandals. In the photographs Harrison had seen, she had been a muscular girl, but her bare arms were pencil thin and her hipbones protruded through the silk. She wore red lipstick, thick black eyeliner and mascara, which didn't quite manage to hide the shadows around her eyes.

Her golden hair fell loose to her waist.

'Kostas!' she said.

Kostas stood, embraced her and kissed her hand. 'Lucy, I have missed you so much.'

'Where have you been?' Her voice broke.

He placed a finger over her lips. 'Hush, my love. Please, don't be upset. Look, there is someone here to see you. You remember my friend Alastair. He has come all the way from Scotland to see you again. I'm afraid you have made the poor man fall helplessly head over heels.'

Lucy looked blankly at Harrison, mouth half-open. 'I don't ...' She glanced back at Kostas, 'I'm sorry, I ...'

Harrison got up to greet her. Like Kostas, he took her hand and raised it to his lips. Squeezing it, he looked into her eyes, and the sordid details of her life came to him like reflections in shards of a broken mirror. She'd run away from a lot more than he'd realised. A lot more than even her mother realised. She smelled of alcohol and her mind was clouded. She was resigned and ready to accept whatever fate was going to deliver next.

He forced himself to speak. 'I can't tell you how good it is to see you again.' Please don't say you haven't seen me before, he thought as pointedly as he could. There was no way of knowing if it would reach her. 'I hope you'll do me the honour of singing for me.'

She slipped her hand out of his fingers and stepped back, radiating bewilderment. 'Okay. 'I'll do a Scottish song, if it's alright with Victor.'

'Lucy, everything you sing is alright with me,' Victor said.

‘I learned this a long time ago.’ She sang *The Dowie Dens o’ Yarrow.* The ballad unfolded tragically, telling the story of a girl whose father wanted to force her into an arranged marriage with a gentleman rather than allowing her to marry the boy she loved. Lucy sang it in broad Scots, in a voice sweet and clear as a blackbird’s. By their baffled expressions, Harrison suspected that Kostas and Victor understood few of the words. The song was her code, he realised. She was telling him a version of her own story, disguised in the verses of an ancient ballad.

When she finished, while Kostas and Victor were still applauding, Harrison kissed her on the cheek and made a show of lingering to nuzzle her hair. He whispered as clearly as he dared, ‘Don’t say anything. Grab your passport and hide it under your dress.’ She stiffened in his arms, but he knew immediately that she understood. Harrison let go of her, sat down beside Kostas and Victor again and said, ‘Lucy, I’m afraid you’ve broken my heart all over again. I wonder if you might wait in your cabin. I have something to discuss with Victor.’

She gave him a sideways look and said seductively, ‘I know what your game is. You get nothing for free here.’

‘Some things are worth paying for,’ he replied.

When she had gone, he turned to Victor and said, 'I want to marry her. Kostas and I would like to make you an offer for her. Kostas has agreed to pay whatever you require for your satisfaction, and in return he will receive a very favourable price for my estate.'

'You really do love this girl?'

'With all my heart. I will be forever in your debt.' They eyeballed each other across the table for a couple of seconds, and Harrison knew that Victor wasn't buying it. The old man knew a game when one was dealt out.

Even so, he liked to play. He closed his eyes and allowed a pained expression to cross his face. 'You must understand that Lucy is precious to me too. I couldn't let her go to just anyone. I think of her as a member of my little family here. Almost like a daughter.'

'But she's not your daughter. I believe you do business with Quentin Merriweather.'

Victor's eyes became meaner. 'We have worked together, on occasion. What do you know about that?'

'Please don't misunderstand me. I'm not in the habit of passing judgement on another man's business. But Quentin worries for Lucy. He would like her to be home in Scotland, and wouldn't like to think she was unhappy in any way.'

Kostas cleared his throat before this line of conversation could progress any further. 'Victor, I must confess. You know that I have also fallen under Lucy's spell and I care very deeply for her. Alas I am a married man and I still love Kaliope, so I must do the honourable thing and release her into the arms of my lonely friend.'

Victor made a show of considering their protestations, with an excess of huffing and sighing. He uncorked the Talisker and refilled all three glasses. He swilled his glass and stared down into it.

Then, at last, he nodded. 'If this is real love, then who am I to put a price on that? If she is willing to go with you, then you may take her freely.'

'Sir.' Harrison shook Victor's hand, once again detecting next to no emotion. 'Your generosity does you credit. I can't tell you how happy you've made me.'

Victor smiled. 'That is all the thanks I need. Let's bring Lucy back and see what she says.' He rose from his chair, pressed a button on an intercom, and issued an order to somebody at the other end. 'She's on her way.'

When Lucy returned, he asked her to sit with them at the table and, like a seasoned matchmaker, set out the proposal.

‘My dear, Mr McKenzie has professed his love for you in the strongest possible terms and I believe he is an honest and good man. I have agreed to let you go only on the condition that you do so happily.’

Harrison reached across the table and took her hand. ‘Will you marry me, Lucy? Come home with me?’

‘Marry you?’ she repeated.

He nodded, holding her gaze. ‘Will you come home to Scotland with me?’

‘Yes. She forced out a breath of giddy laughter as understanding dawned. ‘Oh my God, yes, I ... will.’

‘Ah, wonderful,’ Victor said. He placed his own swollen hands over theirs. ‘Then our business is concluded. Lucy, my dearest girl, I am so sorry to be losing you. You please wait here with your fiancé, and I will have your things packed and brought up. Excuse me for a moment.’ He disappeared out of the stateroom.

‘Have you got your passport?’ Harrison asked Lucy, who was sitting like a cat on a fencepost, ready to spring away.

‘Yeah. Who the fuck are you?’

‘Tell you later,’ he said. He got up and went to the door, listening intently for voices. It was strangely silent. Victor hadn’t alerted any of his staff to his suspicions; he wanted to take care of this business himself, without attracting attention. His intention wasn't to kill, just to threaten Harrison into leaving without a fuss. He couldn't afford to attract attention; the whole operation depended upon this island safe haven, where nobody saw or said a thing.

'He's not going to let me go,' Lucy said, her voice breaking with panic.

'Victor will keep his word,' Kostas lied.

'Quiet, both of you,' Harrison snapped. He closed his eyes and tried to follow Victor. The old man was in a smaller, windowless cabin with a desk and a safe concealed behind a panel. He opened the door, removed a gun and slipped it into the waistband of his trousers. It seemed that Amy's dream of a commando raid had not been as wide of the mark as they had hoped.

'He's coming back,' Harrison said, his heart banging. 'Kostas, take off your belt.'

'I beg your pardon?'

'Your belt.' Harrison did the same, and stood beside the door, holding the length of brown leather in his left hand. 'Stand behind me.'

'You can't…' Kostas floundered, realising Harrison's intentions.

'Yes, I can,' he said, realising that the whisky had probably made him over-confident. There didn't seem to be any other choice now. 'Do it.'

Shocked into submission, Kostas took off his belt. He and Lucy moved into place behind Harrison and pressed themselves against the wood-panelled wall.

Victor paused momentarily when he saw they were no longer in their seats. Harrison delivered a sweeping kick to his groin, dropping him to his knees, and followed it with one to the belly, winding him. As he lay shuddering on the ground, Harrison hauled his arms behind his back and looped the belt twice around his wrists. 'Get his ankles.'

Kostas did as he was ordered, securing Victor's feet. Harrison looped the two belts together so that Victor was bent back on himself in a way that no doubt caused his stiff, bulky body considerable pain. He writhed, still struggling to regain his breath. Harrison fished the gun out of the man's trousers and pointed it at his head.

'One telephone call from me, or my friend who is waiting for us just outside, and your whole sordid little trade will come crumbling down around you, Victor. You, Merriweather, and Mr Gianopoulos here. What do you say, Kostas? What do you think Victor should do?'

'He should keep his fucking mouth shut if he knows what's good for him,' Kostas said, very clearly, all pretence of friendship dropped.

‘And that’s what he’s going to do.’ Harrison stood up, still aiming the gun at Victor’s head. ‘Go, both of you.’

Kostas and Lucy scurried out of the stateroom, and Harrison backed out behind them, pulling the door shut behind him. None of Victor’s staff accosted them on the way out; Harrison suspected they were ordered to their cabins while Victor did business. He dropped Victor’s gun quietly into the water on the way out and caught hold of Lucy’s hand.

‘Let’s get you out of here.’

THIRTY-FIVE

Harrison walked hand in hand with Lucy off the Circe, with Kostas following behind. They walked straight past Amy, who was sitting in the sun at the end of the pier, writing in a notebook. She let them go by and, half a minute later, got to her feet and walked after them.

At a safe distance away from the Circe, she caught up with them. Up close, Lucy stank of old wine. She looked pale, ill and far too young. Under her makeup, her skin was waxy. Even the most striking beauty could ebb away under the wrong circumstances, and hers had been wrong for a very long time.

'The next hydrofoil is leaving in twenty minutes,' Amy said. 'We can make it.'

'Who are you?' Lucy asked, squinting into the bright sunlight. She looked like she'd been in a cave for several weeks. 'Does somebody want to explain to me what's going on?'

Harrison kept walking. 'You'll be glad to know you're not getting married.' He sounded shaken and a little bit drunk.

She shielded her eyes and tried to focus on him. 'You said your name was Alastair?'

'Oh ... no, sorry. My real name is Harrison Jones. This is my partner, Amy Bell.'

She wrenched her hand from his and stopped dead. 'Harrison Jones? Alastair McKenzie was more believable. Who are you, police or something?'

'No. Private investigators.'

'Private fucking investigators? Who sent you? Was it you?' She turned to Kostas.

'No, but they enlisted my help and I was only too glad to give it. Oh Lucy, I am so desperately sorry.'

'What are you sorry for?'

'For the things he made you do.'

'You bastard. How the fuck do you know what he made me do? How much money did you take for me?'

'None at all, I promise.'

'I suggest we have this conversation at another time,' Harrison said hurriedly. 'We need to get onto that bloody hydrofoil and away from here.'

'What's up?' Amy asked. 'How much did you have to pay him?'

'Nothing. He was persuaded to let her go.' He glanced at her. 'Just keep…' He waved his hand behind him. 'Watch our backs, will you?'

'Are you alright?'

'I'm fine.' But his voice was clipped, as if he was afraid of tempting fate.

They walked as quickly as they could toward the quay where people were already lining up to board. Amy's heart was racing as she glanced over her shoulder. The warning drone was louder now, and she had the same feeling she used to get on deployment, moments before something blew up. But scanning the harbour, she could see nothing untoward. 'I think we're clear.'

'Aren't you people even going to tell me where you're taking me?' Lucy demanded. 'You can't just put me on another boat.'

'We're all going together,' Kostas replied. 'We will go to Athens, and then the three of you will fly back to Scotland where you will see your mother.'

She rounded on him. 'Don't you speak to me about my mother. My mother doesn't care whether I live or die, and neither do you. If you loved me, you would have let me stay with you. You would have left Kaliope for me.'

'Lucy, your mother hired us to find you,' Harrison said.

'That's bollocks.'

'She didn't think you'd believe it either, but it's true. Look, you don't have to go back to her if you don't want to, but we need to get away from here.'

They joined the queue for the hydrofoil and moved toward the gangway. Lucy fidgeted and looked out towards the Circe, almost like she wanted to run back to it. She slid her hands up her bare forearms.

'It's going to be alright,' Amy said, trying to reassure herself as well as Lucy.

'I don't feel well. I'm so cold.'

'You can borrow a jumper once we're on board. Do you still have your passport?'

'I don't ...' her eyes darted between the three of them. Then she hitched up her dress and slipped it out of her underwear.

'I tried to escape, but ... '

'Let's talk once we've got somewhere more private,' Amy said, touching her arm. She withdrew their open-ended tickets back to Athens, including the one she'd optimistically bought for Lucy. The boat was busy and shapeless worries danced around on her chest, but the heavy metal gangway felt like a threshold into a safer place. She followed Kostas, Harrison and Lucy up the ramp, scanning in front and behind them, and wishing she had someone to watch her own back.

Kostas boarded and walked through the doors into the seating area. As Harrison offered his ticket to the collector at the door, a man in the dark blue uniform of the Hellenic Coast Guard stepped into view and blocked his way.

'I'm sorry sir, I cannot let you on board. You must come with me. And the ladies.'

'What's the problem here?' Harrison demanded in a voice that was not his own. 'Our friend has just boarded.'

'Mr Gianopoulos is free to go.' He grasped Harrison's arm and wrenched it harshly, forcing him to spin around.

'Are we under arrest? What crime have we committed?'

His tone was more argumentative than Amy thought wise at this stage.

The officer didn't answer. 'You must come with me. You women follow me, please.'

'Kostas!' Lucy shouted, pointlessly. Kostas had already disappeared, without a glance backwards.

The officer frogmarched Harrison down the gangway, through the crowd of staring people. When they had gained a little distance from the hydrofoil, he stopped, still gripping Harrison's arm. He nodded at Amy and Lucy.

'Walk in front of me. With him. Keep your hands where I can see them. Now move.'

‘Where are you taking us?’ Amy demanded, trying not to let her voice betray the fact that she had seen this coming. She should have said something. She should have warned Harrison.

‘To the police station.’

‘The police station’s the other way.’

‘You have been accused of the theft of property from the yacht, Circe. You will be taken for questioning.’ They were moving too quickly back in the direction of the Circe. Amy’s legs felt wooden, as if they had lost their connection with her brain, but the situation unfolded like a map in front of her.

The officer looked to be in his late fifties, with a paunch and a smoker’s wheeze: feathering his nest with Victor’s payoffs before slipping into a comfortable retirement. She was confident that she could take him down, if she had the guts to do what was necessary. She would have to be quick. Forcing herself to keep walking as calmly as possible, she allowed him to march them all the way along the stone quay toward the yacht. They needed to get around the other side of the boat, away from the village square and its unsuspecting citizens, so that the mob didn’t descend immediately and finish the job for him.

They came alongside the stern of the yacht. A voice burnt into her memory shouted ‘Now. Go now!' She squeezed her eyes shut, took a deep breath and stopped short.

As she expected, the officer raised his arm to prod her in the back. She stepped back against his hand, trapped his arm under her own and spun toward him as explosively as she could. With her free hand she grabbed his throat, while at the same time driving a knee into his groin. He wobbled and took a step back from her, wrenching his arm free and grasping for the pistol at his hip.

Harrison lunged forward. Amy screamed, 'Harri, the gun!' But momentum had already taken control of him. He seized the man by the collar and delivered a single, driving punch to his solar plexus.

The officer was stunned. He collapsed face forward onto the ground, the gun tumbling out of his hand. Amy snatched it and trained it at the back of his head until she was confident that he wasn't faking. Out of the corner of her eye, she saw motion on board the Circe.

She threw the gun into the water, snatched Lucy's hand and said, 'Run!'

THIRTY-SIX

They made it back to the hydrofoil just as the gangway was lifting, and were allowed to board without further challenge from the crew. The unspoken understanding of this place seemed to be holding; nobody had seen a thing. From his seat, Kostas observed them with a passive expression and an aura of hate. Lucy paused at his row and opened her mouth to speak.

'Walk past,' Harrison muttered. She said nothing and moved along. They slipped into seats, afraid to speak until the engines began to rumble beneath them. Sweat dampened his shirt. He cleaned his glasses and tried to regain control of his breath. His head spun and the back of his neck prickled. He glanced around, scanning the other passengers for signs of suspicion. There was nothing unusual, except the same restrained venom and fear coming from the direction of Kostas. Good, Harrison thought. Let the man stew in it for as long as possible. He deserved that, at the very least.

Amy peered out the window. ‘Harri, look.’

On the other side of the harbour, they could see the Coast Guard officer limping slowly along the quay, smoothing his hair. He didn’t appear to be in a hurry to catch the hydrofoil.

‘Glad I didn’t kill the bugger,’ he muttered.

‘That was a bloody perfect punch, by the way.’

‘Still think I can’t fight my way out of a paper bag?’ He massaged his knuckles.

‘I didn’t know about the black belt when I said that.’ Amy took his hand and examined it. ‘A bit bruised.’

‘It’s fine,’ he said, leaving his hand there longer than was necessary. Their eyes met for less than a second and he felt something like adoration for her. He might have kissed her now, if not for Lucy’s brittle presence. She was silent and dazed.

‘Lucy, you alright?’

She nodded almost imperceptibly, hugging herself. She was shivering. ‘I don’t know.’

Amy opened her rucksack and pulled out her spare jumper and leggings. ‘Here. Put these on.’

‘I’ll have to go to the toilet.’ She started to stand.

‘No.’ Harrison grasped her arm before she could escape. ‘Stay here. Just slip them on under your dress.’

She sat heavily again, staring at him. 'How did you find me?'

'Kostas brought us here.'

'How did you make him do that?'

'Let's just say we convinced him it would be in his best interests to help us.'

'You came all the way from Edinburgh for me?'

'Yes, we did.'

'Why?' Confusion leaked from her like pus. She was like a soft creature on the beach, dying inside its beautiful shell, and he wondered if she was beyond saving. There was more pain in her than he could take away.

He folded his hands under his armpits to avoid touching her again. 'Like I said, your mum hired us.'

'Does my dad know?'

'No.'

Her chest lifted and she began to cry silently, retreating inside and closing around herself. The hovercraft cruised away from the harbour, lifted itself and began to speed back in the direction of Athens.

Amy turned away from the window and leaned in. 'Victor's on the move.' She tapped the Perspex pane and Harrison glimpsed the Circe's sleek, white prow cutting south, away from the island. They watched it glide toward the silver-lit horizon. 'Into the wild blue yonder before anybody asks questions.'

'That cop was working for Victor,' Lucy said, swiping at her eyes and gathering herself back together.

'We gathered that,' Amy replied.

'He gave me back to them when I jumped overboard. I wish you'd shot him.'

'I was tempted, believe me.'

'There were other girls on that boat. Victor transports them around and sells them on. He knows I know it.'

'Lucy ...' Harrison paused. It was difficult to know how she might react, but she deserved the truth. 'They're all part of it. Victor, Kostas, and your dad. Some of the girls end up in Britain. I found some of them working at a property your father co-owns with Kostas in Leith.'

She leaned her head back against the seat cushion and smiled at the bitter knowledge. 'My dad. Fucking depraved bastard.'

'He may be that, but right now I think he's the one who's going to keep you safe. Victor doesn't want to hurt the daughter of his associate. It would be bad for business.'

'How do you know that? How did you even know they've met?'

'It's a long story. Just trust me.'

‘So why go through the whole *I want to marry her* routine?’

‘A face-saving exercise for Victor, to avoid bruising his ego. Unfortunately, that part didn’t quite go to plan.’

‘And he gets away with it as well? You’re going to let him go?’

‘I have contacts in the police. They’ll do their job. We’re here to get you back home, and that’s it.’

‘I don’t have a home,’ she said. ‘What about Tim? My boyfriend. Ex…’ She shook her head. ‘He probably never wants to see me again. Where is he, by the way? Do you know?’

Harrison and Amy glanced at each other. ‘I’m afraid we don’t,’ Harrison said.

It was nearly dark and growing colder by the time they disembarked at Piraeus. They huddled for safety among the crowd of passengers, moving as quickly as they could away from the quay and in the direction of the taxi rank. Kostas walked alone ahead of them, steadfastly refusing to look back at Lucy. Harrison could feel her silently cursing him and crying out for him at the same time, echoes of the same rage he had first sensed when he picked up the photograph of her in North Berwick. It was betrayal and poison: love turned inside out.

Kostas's Range Rover was waiting for him on the other side of the road. He climbed into the passenger seat, and it did a U-turn and barrelled toward them. They kept walking but the vehicle rolled alongside them and the door swung open.

'Get in,' Kostas said pleasantly. 'I will give you a lift to the airport.'

'Keep walking,' Harrison muttered, but his words had no impact on Lucy. He reached for the cloth of her jumper as she turned toward the door. 'Lucy, don't.'

She moved robotically, pulled away from his grasp and got in, leaving Harrison and Amy no choice except to go with her. Harrison heard Amy cursing inwardly.

'You are not safe on the streets,' Kostas said as they drove away from the port.

The air inside the car was heavy with threat. In the rear-view mirror, Harrison looked up and caught the eyes of the driver flicking back at him: it was the young man from the co-operative. Kostas and his man had no intention of taking them to the airport.

What now, he heard Amy thinking. He let his hand slip over hers. She was afraid, but still rational, trying to solve the problem.

I don't know, he thought back. Nobody spoke. Harrison closed his eyes and tried to listen to the internal traffic. Lucy, whose shoulder was squeezed against his, was entertaining delusional notions of going back to Kostas's country house to be pampered and worshipped. It was hard to tell whether she believed this would happen, or simply couldn't bear to consider any alternative. Kostas's mind was preoccupied with a dark, rocky cove at the edge of his estate, where the land crumbled away into the sea. There were men there, with a small boat. The driver was praying for the strength to do what he was going to have to do, now for the second time.

And then, very clearly, Harrison saw Tim, dressed in an anonymous grey tracksuit, his shaggy head shaved and his eyes open and staring blindly at the pricks of starlight in the half-clouded sky. He was lying at the bottom of a dinghy.

Harrison's eyes popped open. They had left the port and were winding their way through seedy backstreets. He remembered from this morning's drive that the motorway leading out of Athens was close by. If they got onto it, there would be no chance of getting out of this car.

Squeezing Amy's hand, he thought, *Knife*. Her fingers slid out of his, and very slowly moved around her back, under her coat. As she did, he took a deep breath and focused all of his concentration on Kostas. He gathered the pain and despair he had taken from Rima at the Western Harbour apartment, and Lucy's betrayal, and the terror of poor blundering Tim's final hours, and directed it all into the skull of the man sitting in front of him. Kostas fidgeted in his seat. He slipped a finger inside the collar of his shirt as if it was choking him, twisted his neck left and right. Harrison summoned the hungry blackness he had witnessed inside the Cerro Rico, and a winter sea fouled with rotting corpses, and the great circling condor that would come to clean the flesh from the bones. He prayed for Tomas to stay with him.

Kostas coughed and brought his hands to his chest.

The driver glanced at him and spoke in Greek. Kostas whispered something, his breath barely moving past his swollen lips.

'Kostas?' Lucy asked, leaning forward. 'Kostas, what's happening? Are you alright? Oh my God, stop! There's something wrong with him. He can't breathe.'

Amy raised the knife and pressed it into the side of the driver's neck. 'Pull in,' she growled. 'Keep both hands on the wheel.'

The driver's eyes flicked to Kostas, who was slumped against the door, barely conscious, before he pulled into a narrow lane between high-rise apartment blocks. The tip of Amy's knife just punctured the skin of his throat. A trickle of blood ran down to his collar.

'If you move, you die,' Harrison heard her say, and he knew that she meant it. She might be a lifesaver, but she had been trained to kill. He also knew this would cost her as much as it would cost him.

'Let me out,' he said to Lucy, shoving her out of the car. He slid out after her, and then dragged Kostas out onto the pavement. Lucy immediately squatted over him. 'Leave him,' Harrison barked, running around to the driver's door. 'Get back in the car.' To the driver, he said, 'Leave the keys and get out. Sit down there on the pavement with Kostas. Keep your hands away from your pockets.'

With his hands open in front of him, the driver did as he was told. Harrison took his place behind the wheel, slammed the door and put his foot down.

'Kostas is dying,' Lucy bellowed as they sped away. 'You can't just leave him! Turn around, for Christ's sake!'

The pain behind Harrison's eyes was threatening to blind him. It was hard enough to stay on the right side of these unknown streets without Lucy shouting in his ear, begging to return to her would-be killer. 'He's not dying, and they were planning to kill us,' he said, through clenched teeth.

'What did you do to him?'

‘Lucy,’ Amy snapped, ‘would you shut the fuck up and let him drive? We need to get away from here.’

Lucy ignored her demands. ‘Did you poison him?’

‘No, I didn’t poison him,’ Harrison muttered, ‘I hexed him, and he fucking deserves it.’

THIRTY-SEVEN

After a long wait in the airport, which Amy had spent watching for trouble in a state of twitchy hyper-alertness, they boarded a red-eye flight to Heathrow. The extra stop seemed preferable to waiting in Athens for the next day's flight to Edinburgh. Only after the plane strained up into the clear, starlit night did she dare herself to believe they were safe.

She knew from experience that it would take her a long time to come back from this, to learn to stop jumping at every little creak of the floorboards. The past year of work with her therapist might just have gone overboard and she'd have to start over again.

Or maybe the time had come to accept that she needed an altogether different kind of therapy. She had so much to learn about the capabilities of her mind. What she had seen Harrison do to Kostas was terrifying, but it also gave her the same perverse thrill as combat. She never imagined it was possible to have such power, at least not without a rifle in her hands.

Lucy huddled defensively against the window, staring out, just like a soldier looking back down at the hell from which she had escaped. Across the aisle, Harrison popped a couple of paracetamol tablets and leaned his head back.

Amy watched him pretending to sleep and wondered what would come next. They would both have to go back to their ordinary lives and make out that they were the same people they had been before this whirlwind hit. It was like coming home from Afghanistan, except you could talk about this even less.

What about us, she asked him silently. *Where do we go from here?* Their relationship had so quickly come to occupy every corner of her life that she couldn't imagine what it would be like without him.

'What's his deal?' Lucy asked, twisting the hem of her cardigan around a finger.

'Pardon?'

'Harrison.' She nodded in his direction.

'What about him?'

'He's a strange one. Going on about hexes. What's that about? He really just gave Kostas something to make him sick, right?'

'You'd have to ask him that. He's kind of into all that occult stuff.'

‘He’s one of a kind, that’s for sure.’

So are you, Bell.

‘Are you two, like ... together?’

‘Not exactly.’ Amy smiled and looked at him. ‘And he’s not sleeping, by the way.’

‘No, he’s not,’ Harrison sighed. He extracted himself from the seat. ‘Can I have a word, Amy?’

She followed him to the back of the plane, and they squeezed into the alcove in front of the lavatories.

‘I couldn’t tell you in front of her,’ he whispered. ‘I’m pretty sure Tim is dead. They dumped him out at sea early this morning. I saw it as soon as we got in the car with that guy. You were right. I’ll tell Colin Muir when we get back, and let him deal with the Greek police.’

Amy took a deep breath and waited for the shock to hit her. It came as confirmation rather than surprise. ‘I knew,’ she said. ‘I think I knew all along, even when he was with us in Athens. Maybe that’s why I let him have the room on his own. You can’t rewrite fate.’

‘Just ask Oedipus,’ Harrison replied.

‘I’m going to have to read that. God, his poor mum. They might not find him for months.’

Harrison didn't want to think about that. He slipped his hands around her and pulled her toward him. ‘I couldn’t have done this without you. Thank you.’

‘You’re welcome,’ she said into his chest, feeling small and cold and very close to tears. She waited until they passed before looking up, unsure why it should be embarrassing for him to see her cry. He would know, anyway.

Still, she was grateful that he didn’t say anything. ‘Should we tell Lucy?’

‘She’s close enough to the edge, and she won’t understand.’

‘I can’t say I really understand either. What *did* you do to Kostas back there?’

‘Like I said, I hexed him. You’ve heard of the evil eye, right? It’s a powerful belief, and apparently, it works.’

‘Have you done that before?’

‘No, never. I didn’t know if I could or not. I just…didn’t know what else to do.’

‘Indiana Jones, eat your heart out. What did it feel like?’

‘Awful.’ He paused. ‘And kind of good.’

‘Yeah?’ Amy snorted. ‘Well don’t make a habit of it, please, it’s fucking scary.’

‘Tell me about it. My head’s bloody killing me now.’

Back at the seat, Lucy was twisting her hair into a flaxen rope, letting it go and starting again, as though the feel of it gave her comfort. She was ghostly pale and her eyes were rimmed with red. She gave Amy a flickering smile. ‘You probably think I'm a stupid bitch for getting myself involved in all of that.'

'You didn't know, Lucy.'

'I did really think Kostas loved me. I wanted to believe he was different from the rest, you know?' Tears filled her eyes. 'Maybe the only one who ever loved me at all was Tim, not that I'm worthy of it.'

'You are,' Amy said, trying not to think about Tim. Lucy radiated the same self-loathing Amy saw in every abuse victim she encountered. Ricky had given her a big enough dose of it, and she knew its black lies and tricks.

'When we get back to Edinburgh, do you have somewhere to go that you'll feel safe?'

Lucy took a long, shaky breath and continued brushing and twisting. 'I have friends in Portobello, a house I used to live in. I could go there, I guess, until I figure out what to do.'

'You don't want to see your mum? You know, she's a victim in all this too.'

'No fucking way. If Victor wants to send someone after me, that's the first place he'll look.'

'The police will protect you. Both of you.'

'My mum did nothing to help me.' Lucy stared at her nails and bit at a cuticle. 'She's only ever thought about herself.'

'She was as scared as you were.'

'If I had a daughter, I'd give my life to protect her. That's what you're supposed to do, isn't it?'

'I wouldn't know.' Amy allowed herself to think about her mother for no more than a couple of seconds. 'I really wouldn't.'

The journey seemed to have taken days, but at last, they made a turbulent descent through the thick cloud that blanketed Edinburgh. Rain lashed the windows as they landed. Shuffling through the crowded terminal, Lucy veered suddenly toward a newspaper stand.

'Oh my God,' she said quietly, showing Amy and Harrison the tabloid, she had picked up. The front page featured a picture of Quentin, thick-necked and florid, beneath the headline, CAPITAL SEX SLAVERY RING BROKEN, PROPERTY MAGNATE DETAINED. They stood together and read the first few sentences of the article. Lucy took in the details without flinching and dropped the paper back onto the rack.

'Take me to my mother's,' she said.

THIRTY-EIGHT

'You look terrible,' said Elizabeth Merriweather, as Harrison stepped off the train and pulled up his collar against the North Sea wind. He'd been besieged for over a week by a particularly vindictive flu, shuffling between bed and sofa, swallowing paracetamol tablets like sweeties. The fever and aches had subsided now, but he'd lost his voice and still hadn't got back to teaching.

'I've been under the weather,' he croaked.

'And you sound terrible.' She was wrapped heavily in black wool, with dark sunglasses and a furry hat. 'I am so sorry for asking you to come all the way here. I should have come to Edinburgh.'

'I'm fine,' he said, although he didn't feel it. The curse he'd summoned for Kostas had sucked him dry. Psychic karma, he supposed; there was always some kind of fall-out. He hadn't felt up to driving and after the effort of a taxi and a train, he felt ragged and limp as an old sock. 'Better, at least.'

‘I’m glad to hear it.’ She offered her gloved hand. ‘I truly appreciate you coming today. I wanted so much to thank you personally, and I haven’t felt much like travelling anywhere. I’m avoiding town. The police have asked us to stay close to home, where they can keep an eye on us.’

He shook her hand and felt nothing through the leather. She did, however, smell distinctly boozy. He was glad it was only a short drive to her house. ‘How are you, Elizabeth?’

She filled her lungs with salty air and nodded. ‘I am ... starting over, if such a thing is possible. My car is just here.’ She had left her Merc in the disabled bay. Harrison opted not to berate her for this.

She got in and slammed her door. Before starting the engine, she said, ‘Quentin has been charged with human trafficking offences related to the apartments at Western Harbour. I expect you’ve heard.’

‘Yes. I’m sorry.’

‘Oh, please. I hope they lock him up forever. There were nine girls working there, all living in one apartment, not a single one of them over twenty. The poor things, I can’t fully understand why they didn’t simply walk away from there.’

‘Can’t you?’

Elizabeth chose not to answer his question, or perhaps not to hear it at all. ‘I think this must have all started way back when he and Kostas first met. This has been going on under my nose for years and I had no idea. I never picked up on things that should have been obvious. I am so disgusted with myself, with my complicity in all of this. It will haunt me for the rest of my days.' She shook her head abruptly, 'I honestly didn't know about the girls.'

Harrison wondered how far her ignorance stretched. She had known something, if not everything; she might have intervened earlier, if she had cared less about protecting her wealth.

'However, I did know about Lucy. I made her do it. I threatened her. I allowed him to use her.' She pushed up her sunglasses and wiped tears from her eyes. 'It was Quentin's idea, to put her on display like that. It wasn't just her voice. He made her tease and flirt like a prostitute, so he could make money. And I didn't stop it. She was a child.'

'You were frightened of him,' he said, without much compassion.

'I was, but it's no excuse.' She started the engine and sped down the hill toward the town.

Harrison held on and tried not to inhale her alcoholic breath or her cloying perfume. He wasn't in the mood to listen to her trying to off-load her guilt. 'How is Lucy, anyway?'

‘She’s letting me house her and feed her because she has nowhere else to go. Neither of us feel particularly safe in the house. We may have to sell it after all, because I’m not sure I can bear to live there anymore. I miss my dog more than I can say.’ Her eyes filled up again, and she ran her black-gloved fingers beneath them.

‘Is Lucy speaking to you?’

‘Essential exchanges only. Have you ever had a stray cat turn up in your garden? It doesn’t matter what you do, it will never allow you to touch it or love it. That’s how Lucy is. She’s a damaged girl. You know that, of course.’ The loss she felt was like cold, sucking sand. ‘I got some other news from Greece yesterday. I haven’t told Lucy yet, so please don’t say anything. Kostas is dead.’

‘Really?’ A shudder went through him. ‘How?’

‘He shot himself. I suppose he knew he was either going to prison or facing assassination by one of his former colleagues.’

Or he believed he still had a hex hanging over him, Harrison thought.

‘Kaliope rang me, actually. She’s in a terrible state, and she blames me, at least in part.’ Her voice caught and she gunned the car through a junction. ‘I actually find it hard to believe that he was involved in all of this. Quentin yes, but him?

He was so good. I know that sounds ridiculous now. I just really thought he was.'

Harrison studied her quietly. Her grief was real. 'It's alright to be sad.'

'Thank you for saying that.' Her eyes flickered toward him. 'You're the only person who hasn't immediately passed judgement against me. I'd like to thank you for that also.'

'You're my client,' he said coolly, grateful that his skull was a good deal less transparent than hers. 'What about Victor Mikos?'

'Lucy has given statements and apparently Quentin has also ratted him out. To my knowledge, he hasn't been charged yet. We can only hope that he will be, for everyone's sake. I'm not sure I'll rest until I know he's been locked up for a very long time.'

Harrison decided he wouldn't be taking a holiday in Greece anytime soon. 'It may be a good thing for Quentin that he's in jail at this point.'

'I hope the brutes in there punish him in the worst possible ways,' she replied, with dark delight. 'Anyway, thanks to you, neither of those monsters will be harming any other women.'

Thanks to Amy, Harrison thought. He felt alone and unexpectedly lost without her. They had made a good team and she had made a harrowing job almost bearable. Common sense told him this should be his last case, but he didn't know how to tell her. The university wasn't going to have endless patience with him. He had told an almighty pack of lies about his absence, and it might have been enough to fool Gordon Leigh-Davies on this occasion, but he couldn't afford to repeat it. Another one like this could get him sacked.

Never mind that. Another one like this could get him killed. They'd been lucky to get out of Greece alive.

The Merc shimmied too fast over the gravel drive and ground to a halt in front of the house. Before getting out, Elizabeth turned to him. 'I'm sorry for my cross words the last time you came here.'

'No apology needed.'

'I would value your friendship, Harrison. We could meet for tea, from time to time, when I'm in town.'

'I don't make a habit of staying in touch with clients, Elizabeth. I'm sorry.'

'Oh.' She was sniffy and disappointed. 'May I ask why?'

'It's ... cleaner. I'm taking your money for services provided, that's all. I'm as mercenary as anybody else. Don't take it personally.'

'I don't believe that. However, it's up to you.' She cleared her throat, opened her handbag and pulled out a plain brown envelope. 'I'd prefer to give you this now, to save questions from Lucy.

I've included your travel expenses and a little extra, as a token of my gratitude. Consider it compensation for all your troubles.'

'You don't have to ...'

'I do. Please, just take it and save an embarrassing argument.'

'Well. Thank you.' He could feel the stack of notes inside the envelope, but didn't open it to count them. He tucked it into his inner coat pocket.

A weak sun had penetrated the clouds. It provided no heat and did little to dispel the gloom that surrounded this house. It brought a feeling of frozen suffocation, like being buried in wet snow. One cup of her gut-melting coffee and he could add this house to a growing list of places he never had to come back to.

'Lucy wants to see you,' Elizabeth said, leading him into the study.

She was playing the piano. Harrison felt her presence before he saw her, the signature seductive tingle. Her voice was sweet and dangerous as a siren's. She stopped when she saw him.

'You look like shit.'

'But still alive, which is the most important thing. As are you.'

She smiled. 'I'm trying not to think about the alternative.'

'I'll let you talk,' Elizabeth said, and retreated hastily.

Lucy watched her go with cold, lupine blue eyes. The sunny, sweet girl Elizabeth had described for him was gone, maybe forever. 'I called Tim's mum. The Greek police are now searching for his body in the sea near Kostas's estate.'

Harrison sat down and felt slightly sick. There was still a very small possibility that he and Amy were both wrong about what they'd seen. 'I'm glad they're taking it more seriously now.'

'I was so awful to him. It's my fault if he's dead.'

'You're not the criminal here, Lucy.'

'No.' She danced her fingers over the high keys, making a soft, birdlike trill. 'No, I'm not. And I'm going to give evidence against my dad. Mum and I both are.'

'Will you stay here with her, do you think?'

'For a while, at least until I can get some work and find a place. Mum and I ...' she paused and changed course. 'It's a big house. We can avoid each other when we need to.' She looked at him with a strange expression. 'So how do you do it?'

'What?'

'The psychic thing. I thought you were kidding about hexing Kostas, but Mum told me about it. What's your trick?'

'There's no trick.'

She raised a single eyebrow and laughed. 'Right. My mother might be willing to believe anything, but I'm not.'

'You don't have to.'

'Prove it,' she demanded, staring at him.

'No. Like I said, nobody's forcing you to believe anything.'

'Prove it,' she repeated.

Harrison took a deep breath and fixed his eyes on her. More images of her life trooped one after the other into his mind. He knew what she wanted him to see. Her eyes met his, daring him to say it out loud. 'Are you sure?'

'Yes.'

'Tell the police, Lucy. Tell them everything that bastard did to you when you were little. Tell them how he used to come into your room at night. Tell them everything you've never uttered a word about to anyone in your life. Put him away and get your life back. Don't let him destroy you.'

Her eyes filled with tears. She stood, crossed to the window and stared out at the meagre mid-day light.

'For a long time, I didn't understand that it was wrong, until he said if I told anyone, he would kill me.'

Harrison nodded and sat with this knowledge, carrying its weight with her.

Eventually, she spoke again in a determined tone. 'I don't understand how you know about all that, but I will tell the police. I will tell them everything, I promise you.'

Harrison nodded, accepting her unspoken gratitude, and levered himself off the settee. It was the solstice, the turning point, and that always brought a little hope. He wanted to be out walking, somewhere remote and far from people. 'In that case, I think I'm done here. I'm going to beg a lift back to the station.'

'Mum's been drinking. I'll take you.' Lucy followed him out through the grand, frigid hall, pausing by the front door to pull on her coat and a pair of boots. Outside, she said, 'I owe you my life. If there is ever anything I can do for you, just tell me. I'll do whatever you like.'

He knew exactly what she was offering. He paused by the door and looked at her across the roof of the car. A lock of pale hair blew across her lips.

'Lucy, you don't owe any man anything.'

THIRTY-NINE

Amy finished her nightshift and walked home in the blue pre-dawn. She moved quickly, having learned to stretch her natural stride to keep up with Harrison, and the weariness of her long night fell away from her. The streets were empty and the city so quiet that birdsong was the dominant sound: sparrows in a hedge, starlings on an overhead cable, and a late squadron of geese high above. Her belly growled but she enjoyed the keen sharpness of hunger. It wakened all of her senses, especially the one that was only hers. She was still learning to recognise it, to be open to it and not to be frightened.

As she walked up South Clerk Street, she allowed a part of herself to sail, kite-like, up into the frosty morning. From a height, she could look down on the illuminated streets, spreading out like blood vessels from a heart. She could see Ricky, up early and restless for something to do, smoking in the kitchen.

She could see her sad, insomniac mother drinking tea and watching television at home in Belfast, and her brother Malcolm sleeping off his hangover. Later, her other brother Jeremy would come with his wife and their two little girls: the two nieces Amy had rarely seen, and who were being raised to believe that their auntie was mad and dangerous to know. Sometime between the overdone turkey and the store-bought pudding, they might all entertain their own thoughts of her. These would be more or less vindictive, tinted with a little miserly charity: they might allow themselves to feel sorry for her, or privately embarrassed by the way they had sometimes spoken to her. But they would not share these words with each other, and they would be relieved that she wasn't there.

She was also relieved. It was better to be alone on Christmas Day than in the company of toxic people, even if they were your family.

She stopped on North Bridge, on the exact spot where she had first met Harrison. Now she looked down over a melee of coloured lights and fairground rides in Princes Street Gardens, and thought back over everything that had happened since then.

'This isn't what you want to do,' Harrison had said. He was such an oddity, stepping out of the fog and reaching straight inside her, as if there was a door in her chest. He had taken hold of something in her, brought it out into the light and then given it back. It felt different now. She felt like a different person from the one he'd first met, five weeks ago. He had helped her see that a different life was possible to the one she'd felt so trapped in. With her new vision, she could see many roads laid out in front of her. All she had to do was choose.

'Anyone special in your life these days?' Aileen Jones asked her son, after dinner, pudding and too much wine. Her two single female friends had said their goodbyes and they were alone together for the first time that day. Harrison didn't look forward to being on his own with her; his mother's company was always easier when there were other people present. Her feelings about him were too painful and conflicted for him to carry for very long.

'Not as such.'

'I wish you'd find someone. I do worry about you, you know.'

It was her standard peace offering, but it never went anywhere. They were both afraid of allowing any more depth than that into their conversations. The list of things they couldn't say to each other was longer than he could tally. He stood up and began gathering the dirty plates. 'I'm fine on my own. You don't have to worry.'

'Don't I?'

'I give you permission not to worry about me,' he said, because it felt like what she needed to hear. Then he added, 'Anyway, you know it's pointless lying to me.'

'Stop that.' She rolled her eyes. 'I'm not lying, Harrison.'

'Okay,' he said, to avoid an argument. He carried a precarious load of dishes into the kitchen, leaving her sitting. After a couple of minutes, she followed, carrying the wreckage of the turkey. Her makeup had worn off and she looked tired and semi-drunk. The plates clanked together as she loaded them into the dishwasher.

'Good dinner,' he said.

'You can take some of the turkey home with you.' Aileen straightened up. 'You're too thin.'

'I didn't eat much while I was ill.'

'You're run down, obviously.'

'I've been working flat out.' She didn't know about Greece and he had no intention of telling her.

'And you should get the flu jab.'

'Remind me next year. Mum, do you still have those boxes of Dad's old notebooks and stuff?'

‘They’re in the cupboard under the stairs, I’m sure. I haven’t looked in them since I moved into this house, so I can’t guarantee they haven’t disintegrated or been eaten by mice.’

‘Do you mind if I dig them out?’

She stared up at the ceiling, trying not to show him her annoyance. ‘Why, Harrison? We’ve been through them so many times. You’re not going to find him in there.’

Harrison looked at her. ‘Have you finally given up on him?’

‘He’s dead,’ Aileen said, and she sounded more definite than she ever had. ‘It’s time.’

He pictured his dad, Alastair Jones, all six-foot-five of him, with his ginger beard and huge, resonant laugh. How could a man that big simply disappear? ‘We don’t know that.’

‘How come, with everything you…’ she flourished her hand in the direction of his head, ‘…everything you claim to know, you can’t accept it?’

‘Because I don’t actually believe he is dead. I think he’s out there somewhere, Mum, I really do.’

‘Well, he’s dead to me. Either he made a choice or it was made for him, and that’s that. But you can pull out the boxes if you want to. You can take them home. I have no interest in looking at them again.’

He'd never heard her so adamant. Maybe it was a positive step for her, after so many years, to finally close the door. For her, it was a door that could never be re-opened. For him, it could never be closed. 'Okay. Thank you.'

After she went to bed, he sat on the floor in the guest bedroom, opened the first of two dusty boxes and withdrew a black hardback notebook. These were his father's field notes, the observations and descriptions from his various expeditions, very like Harrison's own fieldnotes from Bolivia, except that they were concerned with plants, not people. The pages were yellowed and Alastair's tiny pencil script was faded, but the power was still there.

He held the notebook between his hands and felt the excitement and curiosity that his father had poured into the pages. He'd read the notes so many times, he practically had the words memorised. In his teens, he'd been through them over and over, compulsively looking for clues, convinced his father must have left a coded message hidden in those pages. He didn't want to look for anything now, or be reminded once again that the message he sought wasn't there; he just wanted to remember what his dad felt like.

But still, maybe if he looked with different eyes, he would see something new. From the top pocket of his rucksack, he took a small plastic bag containing a handful of dried Salvia leaves. He took one out and looked at it for a few seconds, wondering where it would take him. He never wanted to make another journey like that last one into the Cerro Rico, no matter how useful that had turned out to be. Maybe this time it would take him somewhere better.

He put the leaves into his mouth and waited, eyes closed, still holding his father's notebook against his chest. The city sounds outside were loud at first—tyres on wet tarmac and distant sirens—then they faded. In their place came the voices of birds and insects, crying, singing, droning, warning in their unintelligible languages. Something was out there: a ripple on the surface of the air, a little vibration under his feet, a voice from somewhere far distant. Somebody on the other side of that rope bridge was calling him, whispering answers into the breeze.

He was still too far away to hear them. He turned away from the bridge and Tomas was standing on the bank, waiting for him.

'Some day you'll get there,' Tomas said. 'But not yet.'

ACKNOWLEDGEMENTS

My most heartfelt thanks go to Stella Hervey Birrell, beta-reader and critical friend *par excellence*, and to Kelly Lacey, whose support and enthusiasm for this story was a lifeline when I needed it. Thank you also to Amanda Horan at letsgetbooked.com, for her excellent editing and design work. As ever, I owe an ongoing debt of gratitude to my family and friends for encouraging me to keep writing. All my love goes to Craig, Jamie and Susanna; I know it's not always easy to live with a writer. Susanna, you deserve special mention for showing me the magical proofreading power of Microsoft Word's Read Aloud tool. Thank you.

Printed in Great Britain
by Amazon

59769389R00246